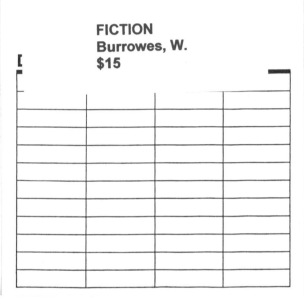

TRUSTED LIKE THE FOX

WESLEY BURROWES

Somerville Press

Somerville Press Ltd,
Dromore, Bantry,
Co. Cork, Ireland

First published 2017

Designed by Maurice Sweeney
Typeset in Adobe Garamond Pro
maurice.sweeney@gmail.com

ISBN: 978 0 9955239 75

LOTTERY FUNDED

For treason is but trusted like the fox,
Who, ne'er so tame, so cherish'd, and lock'd up,
Will have a wild trick of his ancestors.

Shakespeare, *King Henry IV, Part 1*

CHAPTER 1

Thursday, 29 June 1972

I hung up the phone and said a quiet dirty word, so quiet that the vowel disappeared. Then, remembering that I was alone in the house, I said it again, out loud. I had planned this weekend so carefully. Earlier that morning I had packed off my woman, Orla, to her loving and fruitful sister, and so skilfully had I organised the visit that I emerged as a kindly, solicitous man, anxious that she should not be left drearily at home while business called me away. It was almost too skilful, because she had come up with a last-minute proposal to come with me, though maybe that was just good manners. In the end, she had gone happily enough, asking if I was sure I would be all right. And I would certainly have been all right had it not been for that phone call.

My name is Bill Burgess. I had two Uncle Willies when I was growing up, so, to avoid confusion, I was called Billy, which, to be taken seriously, I changed to Bill. Originally from what is known down here as the Black North, I now live and work in Dublin, in TV Features. The business of television is asking questions, and since I have always had an inquiring nature, I am very good at it. In fact, to tell the truth, I am seen by my colleagues as an arrogant smartass with no strong beliefs, but a wide range of attitudes and a talent for stirring things up. I have no quarrel with any of that. I first learned in Sunday School, from St. Matthew, how foolish it was to hide one's light under a bushel. Even if the light is dim, it must be better to fan it into a flame than to blow it out.

The business trip, which I had described to Orla, with much

sighing and head-shaking, was an expedition to the West of Ireland, to find locations, I told her, for a television programme on hill sheep-farming in Connemara. I was to travel with the producer of the programme, Paul, a man of tastes similar to my own, and we were to be gone for three days. Our expenses would be paid; it was late June and the weather was set fair. We could look forward to a strenuous weekend, two nights' research on Galway's nightlife, and home on Sunday. For me, a mere writer, opportunities for this kind of thing came less often than for producers and directors, whose appetites could become jaded.

> *But when they seldom come, they wish'd-for come,*
> *And nothing pleaseth but rare accidents.*

Prince Hal said that. And I saw him as something of a role model.

But the trip was off now. Something had come up, an important commitment. Paul had not even had the courage to ring himself, or to give the job to his production assistant, the usual vehicle for producers' dirty work. I could have let off some steam at her; they expect it. The young woman's voice was unfamiliar. Tracy, she said. From Features. 'Paul asked me to call. Glad I caught you, something's come up, unavoidable, sorry for short notice, maybe next weekend, call back Monday.'

My guess was that she didn't work for the station at all; she was his important commitment, sitting with him at this moment in the MGB, on their way to the love-nest, giggling.

It was six o'clock. Automatically, I switched on the television news and sat blankly in an armchair. I have a slovenly disposition, and things like packing and shaving and taking a bath do not come easily to me. But I had done them all, slowly and thoroughly. My case was packed and lay in the boot of the car. I was not just clean – I glistened and smelled like an orchard. In a fit of affection for

Orla, of whom I'm actually quite fond, I had cleaned up the house, made beds, put out garbage, hoovered. There was no question of wasting all that effort. I would have this weekend if it killed me.

From the television set, a voice spoke of another murder in the North, a man shot in his bed. A Catholic. A revenge killing, they thought, for the previous week's pub bomb. One dead, four injured. I had learned not to listen to the details and wait for the pictures. And here they were. The remains of the pub, the shop next door, blinds drawn behind broken glass, tall policemen standing about, smaller soldiers with rifles cocked. Nothing new really. Another day, another murder.

I was reaching to switch channels when the close-up of the ruined pub turned into a wide shot of a town square, and I sat up, recognizing it instantly. It was Duncairn, the town where I had lived, briefly, thirty years before. I was ten years old when we moved there and we had stayed just a year. I had never gone back, rarely even thought of it. But, suddenly, here it was on the screen, small as life. The ruined pub was unfamiliar, but as the camera panned around the square, I began to search the picture for other features I might recognize, and there they were. Boyle's the Butchers, Furey's pub, the Gospel Hall. Then the picture was wiped away and the newsreader was back, talking with practised solemnity about the barricades in Belfast.

More pictures came on, great concourses of men in dark hoods and dark glasses, carrying wooden staves carved crudely in the shape of rifles. They wore a variety of shabby battledress, mottled green and brown and yellow. Where did they get them? I wondered. Army surplus? Fancy Dress shops? Did wives and mothers sit at their machines, sewing by candlelight?

Another picture now. A backstreet, garlanded with Union Jacks and lit by a bonfire, where more men in battledress, to show their

3

loyalty to the Queen, were raising barricades to keep out her enemies. At the end of the street, baffled young English soldiers with real rifles stood pressed against the gable wall, below the flaking mural of an earlier monarch, one with long black hair.

I switched off and went out, locking up carefully. This was Dublin, of course, a hundred miles from the war zone, but you never could tell. The original plan, before the phone call, had been to spend the evening on a pub crawl – to be described on the expense sheet as a planning meeting – which would take the two television executives twenty miles on the journey to the West, winding up at a hotel we had used before; check in for the night and set off for the West first thing in the morning. So whatever the morrow might bring, Phase A of the plan could remain in place.

First port of call was the local in Donnybrook, a pub used mainly by TV people winding down, something they did quite a lot of. It was crowded, with no one I really wanted to talk to. Little fast-talking knots. Technicians in artists' clothing. I moved downtown, Toner's, Tobin's, Sinnott's, meeting here and there some friend as aimless as I was.

'No I won't thanks, just came in for *one*.'

Forcing myself to move on, not to get involved. What was needed was a plan. And since, for me, to think was to act, the plan was ready by nine-thirty. It involved a change of direction. No longer West, but North. I drove to a small hotel near the airport, checked in and went to bed. I even had a glass of hot milk, to show I was serious. Next day, I would go to that small town on the shores of Lough Neagh, which I had not seen for thirty years.

Later, I could never say with any certainty what foolish whim had led to this decision. For a start, I told myself that after a week of planning and looking forward, it would be a kind of defeat to hang about Dublin for a long weekend. The West, on my own, would be a let-down. And, of course, a visit to '*A small town in Ulster,*' especially this one '*in the eye of the storm*' would qualify as research and I could claim expenses. But these notions, though attractive, were not the clinchers. Ever since that brief glimpse on television, and all evening as I toured the pubs, my mind had begun an exploration of its own into the wasteland of 1941, and the year I had spent there. It was like removing dust-covers in long-disused rooms. Or finding an old family album, smoothing the wrinkles on sepia-coloured snaps, protesting at the lies they told. I remembered the name of the town's only hotel, Hill's. 'Hill's Hellhole,' my granny had called it, believing it to be a den of sin. From my hotel room, I called the Belfast operator. It was still in business. Pleased at the feat of memory, I rang the number and reserved a single room in my name.

I started out before nine the next morning, a Friday. Friday, 30 June 1972, to be exact.

By early afternoon I was through Belfast and had begun the long climb north from the city, into County Antrim. I had not been on this road since I was a child, so perhaps I should not have been surprised to recognize so little. In Belfast there was much more that was familiar. I had lived there for fifteen years after my year in the little town by the lough shore. For another fifteen years, from the safe distance of Dublin, I had enjoyed the luxury of looking at events in the North with a mixture of understanding and impatience; and thanksgiving that I was no longer there. From this inventory, I had learned to choose carefully, according to the company, and generally managed to choose those attitudes that would set me off as an authority. A Northern Man.

But none of the newspaper reports and television pictures had prepared me for what Belfast had become. I thought I had become inured to the descriptions of news commentators, but now, seeing it all myself, the old words took on new meanings. I had prepared myself to be saddened, but not to be afraid. I had made the mistake, soon after leaving the motorway, of taking the short cut to the city through Roden Street, a narrow thoroughfare of red-brick terraced houses, a mile long. It was Protestant, but close enough to Catholic enclaves to make it a kind of No Man's Land.

I drove between kerbstones painted red, white and blue. Little ramps, six inches high, had been built across the street at intervals of twenty yards and it was not possible to drive above a crawl. Many of the houses had been abandoned, their windows and doors bricked up, and through the side streets I had glimpses of derelict open spaces strewn with rubble and the remains of bonfires. On the corner of each side street, under the gables with their fading pictures of King William crossing the Boyne, small groups of men stood watching. On the walls above their heads were printed, not words, but groups of initials: UVF ... UDA ... OVF ... UPV ... UWC. And one I could not identify at first ... FTP.

Reading these insignia produced a double tremor. First to have seen them in their real context, not on the smooth convex of a television screen, but on the scuffed façades of bricked-up houses. And a second shock when the mind translated them into words that carried real menace. Volunteers, Freedom Fighters. But FTP? There was something in my mind from far back, but though I tugged hard at the memory, nothing came. My eyes moved down to the men leaning on the walls, who seemed to stop talking as I edged over the ramps. They pushed themselves slowly off the walls to look carefully at the car, with its Dublin number-plates. At five miles an hour, powerless to move more quickly out of their range, I crawled between two walls of hostility, closing in on me, behind and before.

After Roden Street, I stayed on the main roads, not looking

right or left until I reached the Antrim Road. Despite the trickery of hindsight, Cave Hill was exactly as I remembered it. Then the Floral Hall, where twenty years earlier I had jived the nights away, then Bellevue, Glengormley, a sign for Ballymena. The rest was suburbia, anonymous, ringing no bells. Only the names were familiar: Templepatrick, Dunadry, Muckamore. I was looking for the first glimpse of my own time there, when suddenly, rounding a corner, I saw a long haybarn on the side of a hill, painted brick-red. Along the length of its side was a message in tall white letters, and even before I could focus on it, I found myself saying the words.

'FOR GOD SO LOVED THE WORLD that he gave his only begotten Son, that whosoever believeth in Him should not perish, but have everlasting life.' (John III. 16)

It was just as I had known it thirty years before, lovingly renewed who knows how often, but with one difference. Around and below the text, more crudely drawn, with strings of paint dangling from the letters, were the same harsh ciphers: UVF ... UVSC ... UCDC ... UDA ... DUP. And again the mysterious FTP....

The red shed disappeared from the driving mirror and, as I drove into the town and saw again the long downhill of Church Street, the memories came in a rush....

CHAPTER 2

Friday, 15 August 1941

It's nearly a year now since my brother Charlie and I have come to this wee town in Antrim to look after my mad granny in the house in Church Street, with the furniture shop in front. I am ten and a half. Charlie is twelve and a half. It's a big old house, with high pointy attics filled with trunks and boxes. It has two staircases which go their separate ways, meeting and parting without warning. There is a big drawing-room on the first-floor front, the width of the double-fronted shop and the length of the house. It has a piano and two harmoniums, thirty-four framed pictures and two commodes; these last are kind of lavatories in mahogany cases, but nobody ever uses them. They're just ornaments. The armchairs have leather straps draped over the sides, with brass ashtrays slotted into them, filled with Uncle Stevie's old Woodbine butts, stained with his spit. On either side of the big high brass fender are leather-covered stools. You can raise the seats and keep coal in them, but we have not seen a fire yet. The hearth itself is hidden by a tapestry screen showing two ladies who sit back to back winding wool into balls while two gentlemen with big beards stand holding the skeins. Off the drawing-room is the passage to the bedrooms, which are full of iron beds and marble-topped washstands. Behind, and on the floor above, are all the secret rooms, looking out on the yard and garden behind.

Uncle Stevie works in the shop and drives the lorry in which he collects and delivers furniture, but at this moment, four o'clock on a Friday afternoon, he is in bed. All day long, the granny has been banging his door and calling him a lazy clart and worse, but Stevie, who came in late last night and fell twice on the stairs, has locked his door and is not moving. Finally the granny, tormented by a raging headache and what she calls the gawks, has turned on Charlie and me and driven us out of the house into the back.

When we lived in Belfast, we had a small backyard and a patch of brown clay, with bits of yellow grass doing its best. But here we have a log cobbled yard with high three-level storehouses on each side, filled with springs and mattresses, and lit only by shafts of dusty light through small high windows. We leap like goats, bouncing on mattresses and finally dropping through a first-storey trapdoor to a hump of straw on the cobbles below. A narrow fast-flowing stream runs across the bottom of the yard and a little humpback stone bridge leads to the garden. The garden is fifty yards of high grass, wild oats, nettles, dock leaves, groundsel and dandelions, with a summerhouse at the bottom acting as ranch-house and control-tower.

A four-foot high stone wall separates our garden from the one next door, owned by the Fuscos, who have the ice-cream shop. Their garden is not like ours. They cut their grass once a week and all round the walls are fruit trees, plums and apples, and one peach tree which has never borne fruit. In fact, because of the war, I have never seen a real peach, just the sliced-up bits you used to get in tins. The plums and apples are almost ready for plucking, a fact that I keep pointing out to Charlie. But Charlie, who has brains to burn, says no. He has a plan of his own. He is standing up on the wall with a T-square. On the other side of the wall, at the spot where he is standing, a tree loaded with plums grows at a sharp angle towards our garden. As a result, more than half the branches of the tree overhang our garden. Charlie, top of his class in Geometry, has wedged his T-square between two bricks on a flat bit of the wall. A few yards down he has wedged a short plank between two more bricks and he is now tying a string between them.

'All the plums on our side of the string are our property,' he says, like a ruling from the Bench. It's my opinion that he is being pernickety, as he often is, but this is better than nothing, so I climb onto the wall beside him. As I am reaching for a plum, a roar comes from the top of Fuscos' garden. 'Hoor's Ghosts!'

Gianni Fusco is charging like a buffalo towards us. Gianni is thirteen, but already he is almost six feet and broad as a barn door. On his way he grabs a pole from the clothesline, bringing the row of vests and knickers to the ground. His young sister, Angelica, gets entangled with the clothes as she follows Gianni towards us. She is five years old and built like a small plum. Her name is Angelica, but it's not pronounced Anjellica, like the stuff my mother puts on cakes. It's Angeleeka. Charlie, who knows these things, says that's the Italian way.

'Hoor's Melts!' says Gianni, swiping the clothes pole in a wide arc in our direction. Foolishly, Charlie lunges forward and grabs the pole. He is swung off his feet and Gianni batters the back of his head. It's time to shout for help. 'Stevie....!'

'Go on, bring Stevie, you eggy wee shite,' says Gianni. 'Bring your granny as well. If either one of you touches our plums, they'll never walk again.'

As he tears away Charlie's apparatus, little Angelica climbs up into the tree. By now, Charlie is halfway up the garden shouting for Stevie. I move a few paces in that direction, holding the fort, but keeping an escape route open.

'Go on back to Rome,' I tell Gianni, keeping the fire fanned till Stevie gets back.

'I was never in Rome in my life,' says Gianni.

This is only the truth. But my granny is always telling Gianni's mother to go back to Rome where she came from, and it always seems to have a strong effect.

'Why are you wearing a necklace?' I ask Gianni.

'It's not a necklace.'

'It's a graven image.'

'Who told you that?'

'Doesn't matter who told me. It's a graven image.'

'It's a medal of St. Christopher.'

'Medal of me arse.'

There is no answer to that. I press home the advantage.

'And you have the Virgin Mary on the parlour wall.'

'We have not. It's a picture of St. Teresa.'

'Picture of me hole.'

Goaded by my greater debating skill, Gianni leaps over the wall, waving his pole. I head for the house screaming, and see Stevie and Charlie crossing the little stone bridge. Stevie is whirling a hockey stick, leaning forward as he runs fast and hen-toed. He meets Gianni with a smack of hockey stock and hard grey hands, bundles him to the wall and over.

'I'll show you who owns the fuckin' plums!'

Gianni has moved back, breathing hard, but there is not much he can do. He is big for his age, but Stevie is pushing thirty and built like a rhinoceros. He is stomping about now, honking to himself. My granny arrives in her wheelchair and sits grinning and thumping her stick. She enjoys a fight and joins in.

'Go on,' she shouts, in a voice like an old crow. 'Go on out to Abyssinia and fight the Fuzzy-Wuzzies. It's all you're fit for.'

This is maybe not quite fair. There is no conscription in Northern Ireland, but Gianni's father, who was born here, joined up in the Royal Ulster Rifles on the day war was declared and wasn't killed

11

in the rush of volunteers. And that bit about the Fuzzy-Wuzzies – I've heard my father talking about the hard time Mussolini's been giving the Fuzzy-Wuzzies in Abyssinia, but it's a bit much to blame the Fuscos. They couldn't possibly have been fighting the Fuzzy-Wuzzies; they've been here years and years. They have a granny even older than *our* granny, working the till.

But our granny hasn't finished. 'Popeheads,' she says.

Meanwhile, Stevie has taken the guy-rope from our garden tent and wound it round two pegs driven into the ground on our side. He is now up on the wall, fastening the other end of the rope around the thin trunk of the plum tree, more than halfway up. Little Angelica is beating at his head from above, but he seems not to notice. As Stevie begins to tighten up the guy-rope, bending the tree farther over on our side of the wall, Gianni turns and runs up the garden towards his house, followed by jeers from our granny about the brave Italian soldiers. By now, most of the tree is leaning over our wall and Stevie jumps down.

'Right, we'll show the bastards,' he says. 'We'll strip it.'

As we begin to do this, Gianni comes running down the garden with a long-handled slasher. Stevie is taken unawares as Gianni swings at the guy-rope. The blade slices cleanly through the rope and the tree rockets back to its rightful place in Fusco's garden.

There is a scream from above. We have forgotten Angelica. She has not been catapulted across the garden as Olive Oil might be in a Popeye cartoon, but she rises with the branch, clings to it in an attempt to stay on and finally falls through the knobbly boughs to the ground. Gianni drops the slasher and runs to where she is lying on the grass, bawling. He picks her up, lifts her high above his head to comfort her and she pees abruptly on his face and chest.

On our side of the wall we are all delighted. Among the cries and jeers I get my inspiration.

'Angeleekee's sprung a leakee!'

And I start to chant it out, to the tune of Na-na-ne-na-naa, the music of derision.

'Leaky Angeleekee…. Leaky Angeleekee….'

Charlie joins in the chant, and then my granny. She is the greatest in the world at abuse, so I take this as a true compliment. The chorus goes on. 'Leaky Angeleekee….Leaky Angeleekee….'

CHAPTER 3

Friday, 30 June 1972

The red shed disappeared from the driving mirror and, in a moment, I was driving slowly down Church Street, looking left and right, ticking off memories.

On the right, the Manse, with its cannons and stone elephants. It was from here that the antique side of the family business had been carried on. I used to wonder why it was called the Manse, for no clergyman, as far as I knew, had ever lived there. Just a half-remembered uncle, who ground his teeth and never smiled. He was the eldest of the family and was long dead, after a lifetime spent buying ancient furniture and paintings at house auctions around the country and storing it roof-high in the large dusty chambers of the Manse. Nothing ever seemed to be sold from the Manse, but it must have been, for if my uncle's name came up in conversation, people would nod slowly and wink a respectful eye. No flies on big Willie Burgess they would say.

Past the Manse, a row of little shops which I could not remember from my time. One of them, Doran's, rang a faint bell, but I couldn't think why. All the other shops were open, but Doran's had Venetian blinds on its windows and a black blind on its glass door.

Fifty yards on, I pulled up on the left and looked across at the shop, which had long since passed out of family hands, and the house above where we had lived for one eventful year. I saw that the shop still sold furniture, but the old painted sign was gone, replaced, in pale green letters on black vitrolite, by the words 'Ideal Furniture Emporium'. In the display windows was a single long settee in buff-coloured leatherette. Behind, but visible, were other pieces, traditional, reproduction, scattered thinly. In Stevie's day there was no display. It was not the customer's place to see what he wanted. They asked, and Stevie found.

Next door, Fusco's shop was gone, replaced by a chip shop called The Roma Grill. But there was a board advertising ice cream, so maybe the Fuscos were still there and had simply diversified into fish and chips.

The Presbyterian Church still stood on the corner of Riverside. On the pavement outside, the old horse trough was gone, but across the street, next to the bookie's, Furey's pub mocked the churchgoers from its double-fronted door. I remembered it as the place where old Jimmy Lamont had his stand, and I found myself looking at the pavement for the half-circle of spittle marks by which Jimmy punctuated his speech and kept his audience at bay. A few men leaned there now, holding newspapers open at the racing page. I drove on into the Square.

The woman at the desk in the hotel had a cylindrical body with surprisingly thin legs, like a two-pin electric plug. Her face, with lips pouting at the corners, as if on the brink of tears, had a set doleful expression. She looked up without speaking.

'Burgess,' I said. 'I have a reservation.'

'You have,' she said. Not a question.

She opened a book, apparently at random, made a slash with her biro and passed me a slip of paper.

'Fill it in, Billy.'

I looked at her, surprised, but her expression did not change. Later, I would find that it never changed. 'You know me?'

'How's your father?'

I was also to discover that she never answered a foolish question, simply passed to the next business.

'I'm afraid he died. Last year.'

She nodded, as if to say that you could trust nobody. I tried my warm smile.

'You remember us then?'

'You're like your father. I had a fair idea when I got your call and then, as soon as I saw you....' She handed me a key. 'Thirty-two. You'll have to leave your bag.'

'It's all right. I can carry it.'

'It's not who carried it, it's what's in it. Did wee Geordie not see you coming in?'

'No.'

'Wee bugger's always dukin' up to Furey's. Geordie's the security man.' She shook her chest briefly out of alignment, the nearest she would come to a laugh.

'If the Provos knew what they were up against,' she added.

'Couldn't I show it to yourself?' I asked.

'Do you always show it to strange women?'

I couldn't decide if she really meant it that way, but she went on in that deadpan cryptic fashion of the Northern people, a style I had almost forgotten.

'There's not many of your crowd left now,' she said. 'John and Tilly gone this years, Gordon and Sally in England, and you say now Harry's gone. He was the best of them.'

'He wasn't the worst,' I said, more and more conscious of having the inferior dialogue.

'There's only Stevie left now,' she said, shaking her head.

'I believe he's married—'

'And so he should be with ten or more childer. Poor oul Stevie.'

'Is he still the same?'

'Won't you be seeing him yourself?'

'Yeah I suppose....'

I hadn't thought about that. I walked to the window and looked out. Across the square was a high narrow hoarding around a badly scarred building. It was the pub I had seen the night before on television, the one with the bomb. One dead, four injured.

On this side of the square, two men in the uniform of the UDR stood by my car, while another walked around it, peering inside. I went quickly outside and opened it, allowing them to search it thoroughly and silently. When I went back into the hotel, the lady at the desk was biting into a cream bun. I smiled at her.

'If you know *me*,' I said, 'I must know *you*.'

She waited till her mouth was free before speaking.

'I was two years ahead of you at school,' she said. 'You wouldn't remember me.' She caught me calculating.

'I'm thirty-eight,' she said. 'I was smart for me age.'

'You must have been.' I tried a smile, but it was wasted on her.

'So what's your name?'

'Lily Blunt,' she said, with some defiance. 'One crack and I'll break your head.'

Lily Blunt.... I searched the memory and found nothing. A small ferrety man came in with the air of one who has overcome heavy odds to be present. Lily nodded towards the bag.

'Do you mind, Mister?' said Geordie.

'Carry on.'

Lily went back to her ledgers, but kept talking.

'Do you hear the porter slurpin' in him. Half the guests think it's the cisterns.'

Geordie straightened up, offended.

'I hadn't one drop this day,' he wheezed. 'True as God.'

He finished his search and went outside. I picked up the bag and leaned over to her.

'Tell me, Lily. Does anybody know I'm here? Besides yourself.'

'I told nobody.'

I thanked her and started towards the lift.

'But there's more than me here,' she went on. 'And your car's outside for five minutes. That means the whole town knows.'

I grinned at this. It didn't matter much, but I had been hoping to find the old gang and surprise them.

The door of the dining-room across the hall opened and a tall black-haired girl came over to the desk. She looked thirty, or a little more. Her hair was the deep black of boot polish, her mouth and nostrils a little too wide, and she was a few pounds too heavy, but for all that she was stunning. Her face and her figure were of an earlier age, like the picture of a lady in an oval-framed Victorian engraving called 'Hope', or 'Patience' or 'Resignation', demure and sensuous at the same time. Her walk too was old-fashioned, but no further back than, say, Joan Crawford. Or not Joan Crawford, someone else, I couldn't think who. Seductive was the old word. She took steps that were a little too long, so that one hip had to follow the other in gentle figures-of-eight, like the hind quarters of a departing horse.

Pressing the bell for the lift, I looked again, over my shoulder, and saw her passing back to Lily the slip of paper I had just filled in. She was picking up the phone as the lift arrived, and, as I stepped in, she looked again quickly in my direction. I held my finger a moment longer on the 'Open' button of the lift, then released it. Just before the doors slid closed, she spoke into the phone. Quietly, but I heard. 'He's here.'

I lay on green candlewick in my room, which looked out over the square. It seemed against all reason that she had been talking about me, but I was convinced of it. I had lost all contact with the town more than thirty years before. To find after such a gap that my visit might mean anything to anyone was crazy. Ties of childhood are loose enough to be broken without pain. I climbed off the bed, shaved and went down to the bar.

She was sitting at a corner table, writing. No one else was in the bar. She glanced up as I came in and went back to her writing. Too quickly. I sat for a moment at the bar and she looked across again, unwillingly.

'Can I get you something?'

'Yes please. I wasn't sure if—'

'I'm the manager. What would you like?'

'Whiskey please. Redbreast.'

I watched as she walked over to the bar. Ava Gardner, that's who it was. The Barefoot Contessa. I was determined now not to waste the opening.

'Will you join me?'

She shook her head, mumbled something.

'I used to live here, you know. Haven't been back for thirty years.'

'Yes,' she said. It could have meant anything.

'Burgess. The Antique Gallery. The furniture shop.'

She put the whiskey on the counter and looked at me, as if expecting me to say more, and not much caring if I didn't.

'It would have been before your time,' I said.

She said nothing so I pressed on. 'Have you been here long?'

'I was born here.'

I was surprised at that. She seemed too exotic for a home-town girl.

'Did you have older brothers? Maybe I knew them.'

'One,' she said. 'He knew you slightly.'

She stopped abruptly, as if she had said too much. I was almost ready to give up. Getting nowhere.

'It's more comfortable over here,' she said, and moved from behind the bar, leading the way to a bench seat in red leather. At first, I was inclined not to follow. It seemed, from her contributions so far, that I was boring her. So why didn't she just go away? Must excuse me, Mr Thing. Dinner Menus. Laundry List.

And yet that walk … so at odds with the frigid air of keep-your-distance in her eyes. Even her eyes were a contradiction. They were wide and almost black, and set against skin as pale and smooth as evaporated milk. They could have no hope of concealing anything. She must have been aware of this and it no doubt made her anxious. Later, I was to learn that this anxiety to hide her feelings led her to pretend that she felt nothing. I learned too that if I watched her as she spoke, I could know her feelings before she had time to cover them.

She had reached the bench now and sat demurely, knees tight together, touching with long fingers the thin gold chain on her neck, for want of something to do. I sat beside her and took a sip from the whiskey.

'You haven't told me your name.'

'Fusco.'

The answer, so plain and prompt, took me unawares. She was looking at me now, watching for my reactions.

'But you must have lived next door—'

She nodded.

'You mean you're Leaky?'

For the first time she smiled, raising her chin like a child.

'It's a long time since anybody called me that.'

'Sorry. It doesn't suit you any more.'

I had an afterthought. 'How's Gianni?'

'It's Johnny now.'

In the local accent, there was not much difference. 'How is he?'

'You didn't read about it?'

'No.'

'We sold the place and Johnny bought a pub. He's married now.'

I wondered what she meant, asking if I had read about it. It was hardly likely that Johnny Fusco buying a pub would make the *Irish Times*.

'That was it over yonder,' she said, pointing towards the window, in the direction of the hoardings on the ruined building across the square.

'You mean he was burnt out?'

'Bombed.'

I searched for something to say. 'When did it happen?' What a ridiculous question, I told myself, but she told me.

'Nine days ago. Nights rather. It was the Provos.'

Again, I had the feeling that I was being tested. That she was less interested in the story she was telling than in my reaction to it. I felt flustered.

'Was he hurt? I mean was anybody ... were there people in the pub?'

'Good few. It was a Wednesday evening, half-nine. There was no warning. One man killed, one lost an arm.'

I shook my head. 'What about Johnny?'

'Johnny was in the backyard; he got off light. But his wife and child were in the room above; they came through the floor.'

Again, I found nothing to say.

'It could have been worse,' she said. 'They were lucky.'

'Good,' I said. I was accustomed to general discussions on these matters, but at a safe distance. Nothing this close.

'Would you like another drink?' she said. 'On me this time.'

'Thanks, I would.'

She went to get it. That walk again....

'Did they find out who did it?'

I had called this out across the bar and she looked around

quickly. People did not ask this kind of question so loudly. She came back and sat with me.

'Yes,' she said.

'And the police have got them?'

She looked at me doubtfully, as if deciding how seriously I meant the question.

'Who said anything about the police?'

'But you said they—'

'Look, I don't want to talk about it – do you mind?'

'Of course.'

I sat back, trying to think of some way the conversation could be retrieved, unable to find any reason why she didn't simply go away.

'You're just here for the weekend?'

'Yes.'

'Business is it?'

'Something like that.'

I could tell she was not inquisitive by nature; she was too un-skilled. So why was she asking?

'Will you be looking up your old friends?'

'I reckon they'll be scattered by now, most of them.'

'There's your Uncle Stevie.'

'Yes, I'll look up Stevie. How is he?'

The question seemed to throw her.

'I don't know him that well,' she said eventually. She said it as though I had accused her. There was another silence that seemed endless. I fiddled with my glass.

'Is Tommy McGoldrick still here?' I asked suddenly, and again there was a flicker of hesitation.

'Yes. Why do you ask?'

'I knew him. He was in our gang.'

'Yes.' She smiled. 'I remember.'

22

'Has he changed?'

'Yes.'

It was a question that expected the answer 'No,' so the flat 'Yes' disconcerted me, but I was getting used to it.

'And then there was Ernie,' I went on. 'Ernie Swindle.' I watched her closely, but she nodded easily enough.

'He's in the bus station, in the office.'

'Maybe I'll go and surprise him.'

I finished my drink, looked at my watch and decided to take a chance.

'Could I take you out to dinner?'

'No.' The answer was quick, almost fearful. 'I'm sorry.'

'Well, too bad.'

I stood up, tired of her. Who did she think she was? I was already wondering why I'd come. I would look up a few old friends; courtesy call on Uncle Stevie, few drinks and home in the morning.

'Maybe we can have another drink some time,' I said politely.

'Yes, why not?'

She sat looking at me, leaving me with an awkward getaway.

'By the way,' I said, 'I can hardly call you Leaky.'

'No.' She smiled. 'I've dropped the Leaky bit. It's Angela.'

I left the hotel feeling half-relieved, half-disappointed. Passing the window of the lounge, I stopped to light a cigarette and glanced inside. Angela stood holding the phone, while Lily Blunt, looking huffy, gathered her papers together and left the desk.

As I moved on, I looked across the square at the hoarding around the shell of Johnny's pub. High up I could just make out a familiar hieroglyph, in new white paint. FTP.

And suddenly I remembered. Not just what it meant, but the first time I had said the words aloud, thirty years before, when other bombs were falling. The time of the Blitz....

CHAPTER 4

Saturday, 7 June 1941

There had been no bombing for a while now. Not that we've had much in the way of bombs. Davy Doak is in charge of the siren. He has never had a steady job before, so he takes it dead seriously. At the least sound of an enemy plane – once, so they say, it was a bee in the attic – he throws over his shoulder the wee square box holding his gas mask, squeezes the heavy old ARP tin helmet down as far as his eyebrows, runs to the gasworks and pulls on the handle that works the siren. It hardly ever comes to anything. We are fourteen miles from Belfast and there's nothing to bomb. Sometimes an off-course bomber, trying to find its way to the shipyards, or limping home half-lost, will drop a few incendiaries and set fire to a garden shed. The most they ever killed was four hens.

I remember one night last month there was a string of fires a mile long on fields of hay along the lough shore. Charlie and I, and every other boy in the town, made for the fields to roast spuds in the embers and look for souvenirs. For weeks after it, we were showing everybody old bits of tin and swearing to God that they were debris from the propellers of Heinkels, Fokkers and Messerschmitts. Any of us who find them come closer to the heroes of our day, Flash Gordon and Tailspin Tommy, Air Aces of the screen. And Rockfist Rogan, champion boxer and fighter pilot, in the pages of the *Champion*.

But for the last six weeks, there has been nothing. We have had to make do with standing on boxes in the attic, taking turns to peer out of the skylight towards Belfast, looking for the red cloud that tells us the city is on fire. But, from day to day, it has become harder to work up the old excitement at Davy's siren. The search for souvenirs and the weaving of stories round them has lost its magic. Charlie finds a tin number 2 and bravely claims that it comes from the shoulder of a Gestapo officer. But Ernie Swindle, whose father is a bus-conductor, spoils it by showing us an identical tin number from the shoulder of his father's uniform. Ernie doesn't often sit in the limelight, but he takes care to shield it from others.

A dozen boys from bombed homes in Belfast have arrived to sleep on palliasses in the Church Hall until homes can be found. They bring with them real souvenirs: polished metal bomb-cases, almost whole. They tell stories of thousand-pounder bombs whizzing down their chimneys. We listen in silence and go back to the old Gods, Rockfist Rogan and Tailspin Tommy.

For almost a year, my brother and I have been living here in the house over the furniture shop next door to Fusco's. Apart from Bessie, a cousin who does the cooking and the housework and never speaks, Uncle Stevie and my granny are the only other members of the family living here. My mother and father come as often as they can, but my father's job ended when the war came and he has gone with my mother to another town where he works in a factory making parts for aeroplanes. Charlie has put it about that he is making gun-turrets for Spitfires and I am supporting the story.

My granny is very old. Some of my uncles and aunties have children who have married and had children of their own, which I think makes her a great-grandmother. Everything about her is big. Hands, head, nose, ears. I have been told, quietly, that she was a Catholic when she met my grandfather, and turned her coat to marry him. I can hardly believe this because she seems to hate Catholics. All day she sits in her chair outside the shop, or just inside if it is raining, and sings to herself. When she is in a good mood, she teaches me her songs, but I don't often sing them since the day my father heard me and gave me a hiding. The song he heard was far from the worst I ever heard from her....

Slitter Slatter, Holy Water,
Sprinkle the Papishes ev-ery one!
If that doesn't do, we'll cut them in two
And give them a taste of the Orange and Blue....

Her name is Jane Burgess, but many people in the town call her by another name, behind her back. They call her 'Bell Dunty's granddaughter,' and this has always mystified me. No one can tell me who Bell Dunty was, but knowing how old my granny is, I have worked it out that this Bell Dunty was probably a Catholic, and must have lived about the time of Guy Fawkes. My granny takes very little interest in the war, probably because all her wars were fought a long time ago, at Derry, Enniskillen, Aughrim and the Boyne, Garvagh and Dolly's Brae.

She has songs for all of them, but it's funny to think that any of her ancestors who fought in them would have been on the wrong side. Because of this – at least I can't think of any other reason – she has never been let into the Orange Order. It is true that Uncle Stevie is a member, but we think this is for his exploits on the hockey field and his fame as a Lambeg drummer. For years now, Stevie has ridden the white horse as King William in the annual Mock Battle on 13 July, and manages to do more damage in fun than the real William of Orange ever did in earnest. Charlie, who is first in his class at History, has told us that King William was actually a small squinty man in league with the Pope, but Charlie likes to shock people in this way and no one believes him.

Stevie is my granny's youngest son. The shakings of the bag, they call it here. There is a strange bond between them. Both are hot-tempered and violent, and though there is more than forty years between them, they often come to blows. There are plenty of bedrooms in the house, but they sleep in the same room, a room I don't like going into because of the funny smell, like cabbage-water.

Stevie is a fearsome sight on the hockey pitch. Very often he is sent off the field by the umpire, though the same umpire never does it again. It is his fierceness which has made him a hero, for there are things about him which, in a more peaceful man, would leave him open to jeers and taking the mickey. He has a cleft palate and begins every word with a sound like 'ng'. Sometimes, for crack, we try to make him say things like 'Ballynahinch Junction', but even though he is not bright, we never push our luck too far. He is bandy-legged and hen-toed. His hair is black, long and oily, brushed straight back in the morning and falling apart for the rest of the day in flat strands like black tape worms. He has a permanent drip on the end of his nose which he never wipes away, and which leaves us holding our breath when he is drinking soup.

But alone of all our family, Stevie is well in with the Orangemen, and this feeling of being outcasts has made it hard for Charlie and me to make close friends in the town. Apart from Dan McGoldrick, Ernie Swindle and myself, all the other boys in my class are Junior Orangemen. They have not allowed us to join their gangs, so we have formed a gang of our own. With Charlie, and Dan McGoldrick's brother Tommy, we have five members. Of these, Ernie Swindle would most like to be an Orangeman, but his father is a shop steward in the Busmen's Union and does not believe in God, so he cannot swear allegiance to things. The McGoldrick brothers have parents who are so religious, they will not join *anything*, while Charlie and I are victims of Bell Dunty. And that is why we are a gang.

So, on this fine Saturday morning in June, the five of us are on the lough shore, poking for eels. Tommy McGoldrick and Charlie have left our school and so they travel during the week by bus to Ballymena, where they attend a grammar school and wear a uniform. Dan and Ernie and I are in First Class together. Saturday is pay day, so the talk is of how the money will be spent, though, since neither the cost of living nor the rate of pay have changed much lately, the talk is much the same as last week and the week before. About eight comics must be read, but only four need be bought, then swopped with Hughie Brown's gang for the other four.

Charlie is paid sixpence a week and Ernie and I fourpence each. The McGoldricks are paid nothing at all, on account of their parents' religion. They belong to the Brethren of the Elect of God and they are not allowed to go to the pictures or wear short trousers or talk to anybody except other Brethren. They believe that nobody but the Brethren can go to Heaven and that there is no point in wasting time now with people who will be going to Hell for all eternity. They read from Bibles with beautiful coloured pictures and with small illustrated text-cards stuck between the leaves. They are not allowed to read comics. Just thin books called *Will Your Anchor Hold?* and *The Sower and the Seed* and *Fanny Crosby, the Blind Poetess*.

They are not allowed to have a wireless or a gramophone in the house, nor a telephone, in case someone who is going to Hell might ring them up. They may not spit, curse, or attend the Irish Dancing Class. They are allowed to speak to girls if it is necessary, but not to touch them. Every weekday evening they have a Meeting in the Gospel Hall and sing songs about joy and gladness. On Sundays they are not allowed to do anything at all, not even cook, so their mother cooks on Saturday night, and all day Sunday they spend in the Gospel Hall with breaks for cold meals between the giving of testimony and the singing of songs.

Jesus bids us shine with a clear pure light,
Like a little candle burning in the night.
In this world of darkness, we must shine,
You in your small corner, and I in mine.

Tommy and Dan do not care for this at all and have joined our gang, even if it means going to Hell. I have noticed Dan worry about this sometimes, but Tommy is probably the wildest in our gang and steals cigarettes and sweets from McCullough's shop. The other boys at school are fond of calling the McGoldricks names, like Holy Willy, but Tommy is very good at fighting, so only Dan suffers from cat-calling now, and never when Tommy is in earshot. Tommy's reputation has risen ever higher since he was found to be the best farter in town, maybe even in the county. Riding the butcher's bike, he will greet a friend by raising himself from the saddle and farting the first phrase of 'Colonel Bogey'. This we know only by the words of the song about the balls of Hitler and Himmler and poor old Goebbels. Once, and in our presence only, Tommy succeeded in farting the first two lines of 'God Save the King'.

And yet, despite these accomplishments, the sad truth is that the McGoldricks are given no pay by their parents. Tommy earns a little money by doing deliveries on the bike for Mr Boyle the butcher, but he will not buy comics. First, because he uses all his money to buy sixpenny savings stamps. His plan is to save enough before he is eighteen to emigrate to Canada and join the Mounties. And second, because the shop that sells the comics is right across the street from the Gospel Hall and he dare not be seen going into it. Mr McQuade, the shopkeeper, is a Methodist, and the Brethren shop only from other Brethren.

So we sit, on a very still day, tired of poking for eels, tired of pelting one another with the sticky burrs of Robin-Run-the-Hedge, and talk of how our pay is to be spent. Dan sits cross-legged, hanging his head, surly. He knows he will be allowed to share the sweets and that he will have his turn to read the comics. If there is a windfall, he may even join us at the pictures, but he has not been for weeks and he'll be lost in the plots of the serials. So he looks off into the distance, taking no part, pretending he doesn't care. Charlie, having the most money, buys two comics, the *Magnet* and the *Wizard*. I am to buy the *Champion*, whose greatest asset is Rockfist Rogan, and Charlie is trying to force Ernie to buy the *Adventure*. Ernie wants to buy the *Hotspur*. So there's a row.

'You're not buying the *Hotspur*.'

'I am so buying the *Hotspur*.'

'You're buying the *Adventure* and that's all's about it.'

'Who'll make me?'

'I'll make you.'

'You and whose army?'

Charlie is taking off his coat. 'Come on.' He is standing over Ernie.

'Couldn't be bothered.'

'You're eggy.'

'Who's eggy?'

'*You're* eggy.'

'I'm buying the *Hotspur* and nobody's stopping me.'

'Sure Hughie Brown's gang buys the *Hotspur*. Who's going to buy the *Adventure*?'

No answer.

'All right,' says Charlie. 'Buy your *Hotspur*. But if you want to read my *Magnet*, it'll cost you an extra ha'penny.'

Charlie has very strong principles. He is able, without any suffering, to do without reading a comic altogether if he feels a point needs to be made. Ernie will refuse to pay at first, but later, about Wednesday, he will weaken and find the ha'penny somewhere. In this way, little by little, Charlie is able to build a cache of extra money, and once a month he buys envelopes of foreign stamps which he sticks in his album, with the values written below them in Indian Ink, taken from the three-year-old Stanley Gibbons Stamp Catalogue in the Carnegie Library.

Ernie jeers at the very idea of paying a ha'penny to read the *Magnet*, but Charlie ignores him and goes on talking, setting out the budget.

'That leaves me fourpence and thruppence each for you two. Tuppence each for the pictures, so I have tuppence left and you two have a penny each, that's fourpence. Thruppence for a big bottle of Cream Soda and a penny for gobstoppers.'

'Hang on a minute,' says Ernie. 'Gobstoppers is six a penny.' We all look at him.

'So,' he goes on, 'if we have only a penny, we'll only get six.'

'Brilliant,' says Charlie. 'What about it?'

'There's five of us,' says Ernie. 'Who gets the extra one?'

'I do,' says Charlie.

He makes no bones about this. We know he has tuppence more in the kitty than we have. But, still, we feel cheated.

We are paid after lunch on Saturday and there is just time to reach the picture-house after a call in McClure's on the way, to buy the *Champion*. But on this Saturday I get delayed, caught up in a row between Stevie and the granny. I have just found out that she drinks. In fact, that she is drunk every night. I am surprised at

31

this because she is always saying what an evil thing drink is. She is frightened that Stevie will get a fondness for it and indeed she is right to fear it, because I know that Stevie drinks too.

This Saturday, Stevie and his team, Dunadry, have a hockey match with their bitterest enemies, Randalstown, and the granny is trying to make me go to the match with him, thinking that, with a child by his side, he will stay sober. But Stevie will not have me with him and the argument becomes so fierce that I can slip unseen from the upstairs parlour, minutes before the pictures open. The last thing I hear, as I run on the balls of my feet, keeping close to the wall, is the strong complaining voice of my granny, rising and falling above and below the honking of Stevie, talking through his nose.

When I reach McClure's, I find it full and noisy. If I stay, there will be no hope of being in time for the pictures. And, anyway, the shop will still be open when the pictures finish. I slip out and across the street, where an untidy queue of boys is trickling into the Adelphi like water into a plug-hole. I start across towards them and this big Alsatian dog appears in my path. Although no one knows this, I am dead scared of all dogs, especially Alsatians. I have been told that they can smell fear and will attack it. If this is true, I must smell very strong indeed, so I turn and walk quickly into a shop, moving blindly to the counter.

'What can I get you, son?'

Looking up, I see a woman with a long face and black hair tied up behind. Her fingernails are long and shiny red. She blows on them and flicks them about like propeller blades in sunlight. Drying the varnish. 'Come on, son. If you're going to the pictures, you'd better get on with it.'

I look around me and find that I have never been in the shop before, though it is full of glass bottles of sweets in rows that reach the ceiling, and a white tub of ice cream in the corner, with wooden clappers for making sliders.

'How much are the gobstoppers?'

'Ten a penny.'

I have asked the question just for something to say, but the answer pulls me up short. The lady and the shop and the bottles of sweets suddenly come into focus.

'How much did you say?'

'Ten a penny. It's the cheapest you'll get. How many'll I give you?'

I must think now. What would Charlie do? Before I even have the question out, I know the answer. He would plunge. He would sell gobstoppers all week at seven a penny and buy packets of stamps. But hold on now. Do I spend the whole fourpence? Should I not keep tuppence for the pictures?

'Come on now, son, I haven't all day.' Still flicking her fingers, but smiling. A nice woman.

Deep breath. 'Give us forty, please.'

'Forty?'

'I said forty.' James Cagney.

As she takes down the jar of gobstoppers and screws off the lid, a young lad my own age comes out from the door behind her. He checks to see she's not looking, slips his hand into a big ice-cream freezer and lifts out two ices on sticks, one lemon, one chocolate. But he drops one and she whips round and sees him.

'Well, you cheeky wee article. Put those back where you got them.'

I've seen this lad round the town, but I don't know him. He's not at our school.

'Ah, Mam,' he pleads.

'I'll "Ah Mam" you,' she tells him, whatever that means. 'Put them back!'

33

He puts the two lollies deep in the box, but I can see that he has slipped one of them, the chocolate one, up the sleeve of his jersey, so when he takes his hands out and shows them, they seem empty.

'You'd want eyes in the back of your head,' she says to me, but she is smiling. 'Go on,' she says, and as he goes out the front door of the shop, his head down, he winks at me. She starts counting out the gobstoppers.

'Mind you don't eat all these at the one go.'

I am checking the count. No time to listen to her.

'No use eating them just to sick them up. You might as well get the good of them.'

36 ... 37 ... 38 ... 39 ... 40.

To my surprise she puts in three more. Should I tell her? I decide not to.

'There you are.' She hands over the bulging bag and takes the money. 'I threw in a few extra, for the big sale.'

She smiles again and I run from the shop. What a discovery! What a shop! And lovely tiles on the floor and their own special sweety-bags with the name of the shop on them. No one, outside the gang, is to hear about this shop, though it seems strange that none of the rest have discovered it.

I'm hoping that one of the gang will still be outside the picture-house. Forty-three gobstoppers should be enough for a loan of tuppence. But there is no-one. They have all gone in. I turn away, not too unhappy.

And I have work to do. The gobstoppers must be taken home and hidden in some cool place before they grow hot and start to stick together. Already the neck of the bag is dark with sweat.

To reach the stairs to my bedroom, I have to pass through the shop, a narrow passage with beds and chests and wardrobes piled high on either side, leading to the kitchen where the stairs begin.

Beside the range, half in shadow, my granny sits singing to herself. It's a lively song, but her moaning voice turns it into a dirge.

And when we were assembled, sure it was a glorious sight,
To see so many Orangemen, all ready for a fight,
To march around the oul demesne and hear the pipers play,
And the tune they played was 'Kick the Pope' right over Dolly's Brae –
And the tune they played was 'Kick the Pope' right over Dolly's Brae.

I have reached the foot of the stairs when the song breaks off.

'What's in the bag?'

'Sweeties.'

'Are you not going to offer your oul granny a sweetie?'

'They're gobstoppers; you wouldn't be able.' My granny has no teeth.

'I can suck them,' she says. 'Don't they change colour when you suck them?'

Ah well, what's one? I'll have forty-two left. I reach the bag to her without moving closer. I have never liked the smell of old people and she is very old, with layer on layer of flannelette. She opens her mouth, pink and black like a young bird's, and a gobstopper disappears.

'Give us a look at the bag,' she says, and I hand it to her. Looks like I'll be down to forty-one. Suddenly her large hand clutches my hair and pulls my head cruelly down on her lap where the other hand rests, still holding the bag. Another painful jerk as she twists around to spit her gobstopper out onto the hot plate of the range. A trail of pink spittle sizzles and begins to dry.

'What's the matter? What did I do? Stop it, will you. Stop!'

She is pulling my hair first one way and then the other, pushing my face against the bag, strong as an old horse.

'Where did you get them?'

35

'I don't know – a shop.'

'And do you know what shop? Do you see the name?'

She pushes the bag in my face and I see nothing but a blur of blue letters, a hand with big brown mottles, fingernails all thick yellow at the sides, and spilling gobstoppers.

'Cassie Doran's!' Her voice cracks as she spits the words and her dark juice is on my neck. 'A black Fenian!'

'I didn't know.'

Another twist turns me round and now her stick comes up in her other hand and begins to flail at my back and legs.

'You gave your good money to her and do you know where it'll go? The half of it to the Free State for guns for the Sinn Feiners and the rest into the plate in the Chapel to buy us all into bondage!'

She flings me across the room. 'There'll be no Catholic sweets in this house!'

And she hooks the plate from the range with the crook of her stick, and throws the bag of gobstoppers into the red fire.

'No, Granny, no –' I reach for the range and her stick comes down, pinning my hand to the hot surface. I hardly notice the pain.

'They'll burn in the flames,' she shouts. 'Like the Fenian hoor that sold them.'

I stumble out of the room, half-run, half-walk through the shop and down the street, holding my damaged hand at the wrist and shaking it, for all the good it does. Past the Adelphi, where I should be now, laughing at the Three Stooges, suffering with Pearl White or Flash Gordon, passing along the bottle of Cream Soda. Turning down Riverside, I see Tommy McGoldrick on Mr Boyle's delivery bike. As he passes, he raises his bum from the saddle and farts the first bit of the Hallelujah Chorus, but it does nothing to cheer me up. I reach the path along the Sixmilewater and run along it to the lough shore and fall on the prickly grass.

'Forty-three of them.' Thumping the grass, not caring if it hurts.

'No sweets, no comics, no pictures, nothing for a week....'

I sit up and look at the black water. I think about the shining shop and the dark woman, flicking her fingers.

'Wait till I grow up.... By Jesus I'll get them. I'll clear the place of Papishes.'

Into my mind come the words of my granny's song.

Just then two priests came up til us and to Mr Stokes did say,
Go down by any other road but never by Dolly's Brae....
Begone begone, yez Papish dogs, you've scarcely time to pray,
Before we fling your carcasses right over Dolly's Brae –
Before we fling your carcasses right over Dolly's Brae.

'Wait till I get them ... them and their Chapels and their Virgin Mary and their Holy Water and their Pope.'

I look quickly round to make sure I am alone.

'Fuck the Pope,' I whisper.

CHAPTER 5

Friday, 30 June 1972

I stood for a moment, looking across the Square. Was that really me? I thought.

Since that day, so clear in my memory, I had neither said it nor heard it said. But here, it had never gone away. There it was, the famous Protestant prayer – reduced to 'FTP' – scratched on a hoarding.

I crossed the Square to the bus station, diagonally opposite the hotel. It was a plain high building, painted dark grey. Built originally as a garage for the buses, it now had two glass-fronted offices on either side of the high entrance. As I walked to the door, two soldiers appeared, guns cocked, startling me. The search was brief and silent.

'What's your business?' It was the Sergeant who spoke, in a local accent.

'No business. I'm an old friend of Ernie's.'

'Ernie who?'

'Swindle.'

Funny name, I thought, as I said it. Never struck me before. The Sergeant nodded towards the larger of the glass boxes.

'He's on the phone,' he said.

This was a bit unnecessary, since Ernie was plainly visible. Then I realized that I was being told not to go in until the call was completed. I watched Ernie through the grimy glass. I wondered if I would have recognized him, passing on the street. In fact, if

I had been asked for a description of how Ernie looked thirty years ago, I would have been hard-pressed. Unlike the others, the McGoldricks, Johnny Fusco and Hughie Brown, Ernie had left almost no impression. He was sitting now with his back to the window as he spoke into the phone, his free hand cupped to his ear. He swivelled his chair to face the window and I gave a nod and a smile. Ernie held up his hand.

It was a 'Don't disturb' sign rather than a greeting, but I decided to misinterpret, wrenched open the door and went in. For a moment Ernie was disconcerted, then shouted into the phone.

'Right y'are, Frankie, I'll do that. Yeah…. Somebody just walked in…. Yeah right … right….' His eyes flickered towards me. 'I'll see you to'morra all right? And bring a few pound.'

He laughed inordinately, put the phone down and looked up at me, giving an impression of a public servant, anxious to be of help.

'Now what can I do for you?'

I knew straight away that the question was as false as the scrap of conversation I had just overheard. And I knew who had made the phone call. I just didn't know why.

Ernie was my own age, but his hair was white and, since it grew nowhere else, he had allowed it to curl thickly round his ears. His eyebrows were still black and spiky, but these apart, his features, under a patchy pink skin, closely shaved, were like an Identikit drawing. To make up for his facial anonymity, he wore a blazer with silver buttons, one missing. On the pocket was a badge displaying what appeared to be two pale goats embracing in a hedge. A scroll below said 'Quis Separabit' and below that the initials MBC. I began to wonder if there was a word for this obsession that Northern men had with initials. Monogrammania? Cipherophilia? Was it a liking for mystery, for symbols, for keeping things hidden? An expression of their sense of displacement?

I should have know, for I was one myself, but I was a long time gone. I had forgotten.

Ernie's tie was black, with thin yellow and red diagonal stripes, another badge of identity. The knot had been tied once, on the day he'd first worn it, and every night since simply loosened and taken off like a halter, until the knot had become dark and wrinkled, small as a raisin. He wore tan trousers, stained round the fly, and open-toed sandals over brown check socks. His fingers tapered oddly to small pink nails. He had a habit of stretching his lips quickly in a grimace before speaking, as if tasting in his mouth a sudden sourness. It was as though he was cultivating the appearance of a man faced with a thousand problems, solving them one by one through a swift and painful application of the mind. I gave him my friendly smile.

'You don't know me, Ernie?'

I wanted to see how long Ernie could keep up the pretence, how convincing would be his gasp of recognition.

'There's something familiar,' he said.

'Didn't Angela tell you?'

'Angela?'

'Angela Fusco. She just phoned you.'

Ernie stretched his lips again. His way of saying 'to be perfectly honest,' a signal of the lie to follow.

'I know Angela all right,' he said. 'But I don't know all her friends. And it wasn't her that rung me.'

'Well, no matter. I'm Billy Burgess.'

'Billy…? You mean *wee* Billy?' It was a good performance. 'God's truth, it's not wee Billy is it?'

He was around the table with his hand out. 'How long is it now?'

'Thirty years. Thirty-one actually.'

'God is it that much? And how long are you staying?'

'Just the weekend. And don't ask me why I came – it was just a notion.'

He seemed to consider this for a moment, then went quickly on.

'And you went and saw Angela? Well begod you were right. She's the only one of the old crowd who improved with age.'

'She turned out well,' I conceded.

'She was only a child when you left, but she wasn't long fillin' out. By the time she'd finished school, she'd have taken the sight from your eyes. The Pride of Petravore.'

He gave a lecherous smile and I smiled back.

'You never got hooked yourself, Ernie?'

'Never did. What about yourself?'

'Twice, I'm afraid.'

'Glutton for punishment, wha'?' Again the inordinate laugh. 'You'll take a cup of coffee?' He pressed a button on the tiny intercom and a voice crackled.

'Two coffees.'

He waited for an acknowledgement, but the crackle simply stopped and he released the button, a little put out. Ernie was not one to take his authority lightly.

'How's the rest of the gang, Ernie?'

'Well I suppose they have more sense and less hair. Who's this they all were?'

'The McGoldricks, Tommy and Dan. Hughie Brown. Johnny Fusco.'

I watched him closely. He stretched his lips again.

'All still here – except Dan, as you know.'

He shook his head reverently before going on. 'Tommy's runnin' the father's business now of course. Has the big shop in Ballymena, as well as here and Randalstown. Hughie went into the contractin', heavy machinery. He made a pile and drank it all away. Now he's back drivin' a bulldozer for the man that took him over.' He paused.

'Duffy,' he added.

'From Toome?'

'You've a good memory, Billy. Of course Hughie's easy-goin'; nothin' bothers him.'

He seemed to blame Hughie for lying down under an indignity. The Duffys were Catholics.

'What about Johnny?' I asked it casually. I knew what had happened to Johnny, but I wanted to hear it from Ernie.

'Johnny Fusco?' said Ernie, giving himself time, watching me closely. 'You heard he bought Fulton's pub?'

'Yeah I heard. I believe he had a bit of trouble.'

'Where'd you hear?'

'Angela.'

'And that's the first place you heard it?'

I could quite easily have said that I saw it on television, and that would have been an end to it. But with that perversity that had got me into trouble so often in the past, I decided to keep it going.

'Let's just say I got word of it,' I said.

If I had known where all this play-acting was leading me, I would have walked out of the office there and then and driven far away from a place that I still wanted to see as a backdrop for some sepia-tinted scenes of childhood. Many of those scenes were ugly enough, but none as terrible as the things that had happened since. But I stayed. I had got Ernie going, and I was enjoying that. Ernie stabbed again at the intercom switch.

'Hurry up with them coffees.'

He looked up now and smiled, as if happy to be reunited with his boyhood chum.

'Of course,' he said, 'you'd hear these things, Billy. Aren't you in the TV news below in Dublin?'

'Ah no, Ernie, that's not my side at all. I'm just a writer. Documentaries, the odd feature. I was never inside the Newsroom.'

'Well, sure no matter,' he said, stretching the lips. 'It was hard on Johnny. Harder again on the ones that ended in the hospital. Or the morgue.'

'Terrible,' I said, shaking my head. But I had lost interest. This was not the journey I had come on, the road back into the past. It seemed I would find no one to go back with.

'Any idea who did it?'

I threw out the question without thinking, without caring even. But it seemed to catch Ernie on the raw.

'You're askin' a lot of questions, Billy.'

'Sorry if you think that. I knew Johnny. He lived next door.'

'That was a long time ago.'

He stretched the lips and leaned forward. Cards on the table, he seemed to say.

'What are you doin' here, Billy? What are you after?'

'Not a thing. For God's sake, Ernie—'

'You asked Angela the same thing—'

'So it *was* Angela on the phone—'

'I never said that—'

A girl came into the room with a tray, two cups and a plate of biscuits. Custard Creams.

'You took your time,' said Ernie.

The girl appeared not to hear him. She put the tray on the table. Dark red varnish had flaked from her fingernails. She wiped her hands on her smeared white overall and left, banging the door. Ernie watched her go, making a mental note to pay her back one day. When he spoke again, his irritation was plain.

'Who are to tryin' to cod, Billy?'

'I don't know what you mean.'

'What did you come here for? You're out of it thirty years and then you show up out of nowhere, this week of all weeks.'

'I didn't pick it, Ernie…. And what's so special about this week?'

'All right, we'll play it your way.' The old B-Movie cliché came strangely from him. 'We'll let on you know nothin'.'

He came around the desk and perched on the edge, looking down. I thought of that scene in 'The Great Dictator', with Mussolini looking down at Hitler, and smiled. I could see how Ernie was enjoying it all, drawing importance, down to the lighting of the cigarette and the long first exhalation.

'A week ago last Wednesday,' he said, 'a bomb went off in Johnny's bar. There was no warnin'. No reason. Some of them thought it was because he was born a Catholic and turned, but that was a long time ago.'

I remembered. Ernie sucked on his cigarette.

'He was in with our crowd of course, but he wasn't too deep in.'

I had an inkling of what he meant, enough to make me uneasy, but I said nothing. Ernie went on, watching me.

'It was a Protestant house, so there wasn't any doubt it was the Provos. They claimed it anyway. And the night before last, one of them was executed.'

It was said so flatly that I took a moment to grasp it.

'Shot in his bed,' said Ernie. 'Never woke.'

'Did I know him?'

'You might have. Mikey Doran.'

The name meant nothing to me, but I was not thinking of that. I was trying to remember the story on television, a Catholic shot in his bed, revenge killing…. I should have listened more carefully.

Ernie still sat looking down, watching me.

'You remember Mikey?'

I shook my head. 'How did you know he never woke?' I asked.

It seemed not to worry him. 'That's what they said.'

He spoke dismissively and moved back to his chair. He said nothing for a moment, then put his head on one side and spoke confidingly, as between old friends.

'You know somethin', Billy? I've an idea I'm not tellin' you anything you don't know already. Maybe you know more than I do.'

'I know what you've told me. Nothing else.'

But I was annoyed. Ernie had got to me. 'I'll tell you something else, Ernie. I'm not even interested. I mean, when people get killed or injured it's tragic. I hate it, just as every… everybody else hates it –'

I had just stopped myself from saying 'every right-thinking person'.

'– but it doesn't affect me personally,' I went on. 'Johnny was somebody I knew for a few months when I was the kid next door. We weren't great mates either. Mikey Doran I never heard of. You're telling me the whole thing is none of my business, and I agree with you.'

But even as I said the name Doran, something came back to me. Ernie was talking now, telling me how wise I was to take this attitude and how much better off I'd be to stay clear of it all. It was a speech that would have annoyed me even more if I had really listened, but there was something else in my mind. A picture of a dark-haired woman in a sweetshop, smiling, flicking her red fingernails….

'Cassie Doran,' I said, half to myself.

Ernie broke off and I looked at him.

'Is she still alive?' I asked.

He nodded.

'It was Cassie Doran's son?'

He nodded again. 'Came back to you very sudden, didn't it?'

'I met her only once. Never even knew she had a son.'

'She hasn't. Not any more.'

He smiled as he said this. He had never been a very pleasant person.

'Who would want to kill him?' I asked.

He came round the desk to me, his head on one side.

'I thought you were goin' to be sensible, Billy. Didn't I hear you sayin' it was none of your business? And that you weren't goin' to ask any more questions?'

'I'm not asking who killed him. I'm asking why he had to be killed. I'm asking what anybody gained by killing him.'

Ernie leaned over, held me by the collar and hissed in my face.

'Listen, Billy' – I couldn't decide which annoyed me more, the bad breath or the bad acting – 'I'm givin' you a bit of friendly advice. Because you and me's old mates—'

'No we're not, Ernie. We were never mates. Dan McGoldrick was my mate, or maybe you've forgotten Dan.'

It was a cruel thing to say, and I meant it to be.

'Fair enough, Billy,' he said. 'But that was a long time ago. We're not a gang of kids any more.'

'Aren't you? I don't see a lot of difference, except you're using real guns now.'

'All right, now shut up and listen.' He was angry now, red-faced. 'I've been tryin' to give you good advice, but you don't want it, so this is the last time I'll tell you. If you know what's good for you, you'll get out of here. Back to Dublin.'

'There's a stage leaving at noon,' I said. 'Be on it.'

'You still think it's a game, Billy, but it's not. This is in earnest.

I could give a few orders and you'd be out of here like shit from a goose. But I don't want it that way....'

It was the Ernie of old, boasting that his father could stop all the buses running if he felt like it. The rest of the gang would make fun of him and he would fly into rages. I remembered how dangerous those rages could be and so I stopped mocking him.

'All right, Ernie, I've listened to you. I don't know why you're so anxious for me to leave and I'm not even curious. I wish I could say it was nice to see you again.'

'Times change, Billy.'

He stood to show his old mate the door. 'You'll be leavin' then?'

'I'll leave when I'm ready. But don't worry, I think I'm just about ready. It was a mistake coming here.'

'That's the truest thing you've said.' He stuck out his hand. 'No hard feelin's, Billy?'

It was such a ridiculous thing to say that I smiled. Ernie took it for conciliation and pumped my hand. As I was leaving, he spoke again.

'If you're stayin' the night, Billy, don't get too pally with Angela.'

'Why not?'

'You're a divil for questions. Just stay clear of her, and that's good advice.'

Leaving the office and walking across the Square, I was annoyed with myself for letting Ernie get to me. For allowing him to think that I could be frightened that easily. I was angry, I told myself, not afraid. And yet, as I walked, I had the feeling of being watched. Where did that feeling come from, if not from Ernie? I had decided to go and see my Uncle Stevie, but I would not ask for directions, not here. It would be reported back, as all my movements so far had been. Or was I becoming infected by the air of the place?

I knew Stevie lived on the Randalstown Road, so I would drive there and look for him. Approaching the car, I was making a conscious effort not to hurry, to keep my pace even, feeling as I had felt earlier in the day driving through Roden Street.

As I approached the narrow exit from the Square to the Randalstown Road, I slowed to allow a man to cross before me. He was a huge man, with thick hair. He wore no jacket and his right arm was in plaster. As I slowed, the man turned his head towards me and nodded to say 'thank you' for letting him cross. Then he moved on and walked into the bus station.

The last time I had seen him was in a back garden, shaking a plum tree.

CHAPTER 6

The Randalstown Road ran out past the railway station, at right angles to the long straight slope of Church Street and the Square. The station had once marked the beginning of open country, and it had been possible to look out from a passing train and see the hill striped by long narrow back gardens, from the brown junkyards of the shops in the Square to the greener strips behind the houses of Church Street: Fusco's orchard, our own wilderness, and, fifty yards above, the neat paths and borders of the Manse. Reaching the station, I looked right and saw, not sheep and cows, but a vast terraced hillside of houses, where almost everyone had someone to look down on. On the left were still more houses, where woods had been before, the woods of Masereene with the lough shore beyond.

Finding Stevie's house would be harder than I'd imagined. In the village of thirty years before he had been a folk hero, but the myth could hardly have survived in the new town of today. I stopped twice, but the people I asked hurried on, shaking their heads. In the current climate, it was not just children who were warned against talking to strange men in cars, especially a car with a Southern registration. Then I saw a man sitting on a doorstep, just looking. He seemed out of place, as if accustomed to another kind of doorway, in a city maybe, with no garden to separate him from the street, or from his neighbour. A street like Roden Street.

'Would you happen to know where Stevie Burgess lives?'

I found myself emphasizing my faded Northern accent, to reassure him. The man looked warily at the car.

'I see him now and again,' he said. 'I could give him a message.'
It was an odd offer. Maybe he took me for a debt-collector.

'I'm his nephew,' I explained. 'I used to live here.'

The man widened his eyes slightly, but went no further. Feeling a little foolish, I pulled out a banker's card and showed it to him. The man examined it closely and seemed for a moment to assume the importance of someone used to checking credentials.

'I wouldn't know the exact number,' he said eventually. 'But it's about a hundred yards up on this side.' Then he had an inspiration. 'There's a name on the gate,' he said. 'Stevannie. That's after their two names you see. Stevie and Annie.'

This surprised me. I would never have taken Stevie for a sentimental man.

'I never knew he had a nephew,' the man said.

He had dozens, but I didn't trouble to say so. There was a time when the family was important in the town, when the funeral or the marriage of a Burgess would pack the church. But it seemed that time was gone. Still, the information was useful. I knew that Stevie had a wife, but now I knew her name. Annie. It would have been embarrassing to have to ask.

I found 'Stevannie' easily and was a little disappointed. I had expected an older house, or one that was different. A house that people passing would point to and say 'That's Stevie Burgess's house....' and grin and talk of the hard man he was, the rough diamond. But it was identical to all the other houses, and better kept than most.

I knocked the door and stood looking at the plastic swan posing by the lupins; and the cardboard clock-face on the step, pointing to the unusual figure of ten pints. A sudden noise from inside caused me to step back. It was like standing under a railway bridge when a train suddenly passes overhead. The door was pulled open and four children jerked to a halt and stood staring up. They had obviously been expecting a familiar face and looked disappointed. They ranged in age from about seven to ten, but it was impossible to tell their sex, since all four wore jeans and had identical hairstyles, like little Roundheads. They continued to glare.

'Is your mother in?'

They stared again, briefly; then, with startling suddenness, they all shouted 'Mammy!' and ran inside, adding that there was a man wanted her.

'Will y'all shut your gobs, or I'll shut them for you!' said a woman's voice from inside. Then the children reappeared and she came behind them, wiping her hands on a teacloth. She stopped a moment to look from the kitchen doorway, then came towards me. Three more children, a little older, appeared behind her and she stood surrounded, like Snow White.

'Yes?'

There was suspicion in her eyes, and unease.

'You must be Annie,' I said, smiling. 'I'm Billy. Harry's son.'

She still looked blank.

'Billy Burgess,' I said, and almost reached for the banker's card.

'Och you're not!'

Her face wrinkled into a smile that transformed the thin pointy face, making it almost pretty. I found myself calculating her age. To judge by the kids, she could not be far into her fifties, but she looked more. She was tall, but, as she would have said herself, skinny as a rake. Her hair was long and pinned back. As she smiled, she stretched up and loosened it, like a comedian about to do an impression. It was thick-brown and young, but the face was old, with webs of lines spraying outward and upward from pale lips. She had been fitted with false teeth, but too late. The words of a song came to me – 'No matter how young a prune may be' – and

I felt ashamed, as if she might have read my mind. But she went on smiling and the children followed her lead and showed me their teeth, small and gappy.

'Come on in, for dear sake, and don't be standin' there on the doorstep.'

I followed her into the kitchen and was pressed into the good chair, while the children stood in a line grinning at me.

'Would you credit that now?' said Annie.

'Credit what?' I asked.

'Wee Billy a grown man and losin' his hair.'

I had been composing myself to brush aside compliments, but I took it bravely. 'It comes to all of us,' I said.

'Indeed it doesn't. Stevie has his hair yet and he's sixty.'

'He's not!'

There was no reason to disbelieve it. I could have worked it out for myself.

'Not sixty surely.'

'Sixty-one at Christmas,' said Annie.

She had spread a linen damask cloth on the table, brilliant white. A wedding present, I guessed. And now she was working at the door of the walnut china cabinet, unlocking the bone china tea-set. She went on talking.

'You see, the way Stevie talks about you, I always picture you as a child.'

She stumbled over one of her own on her way to the table.

'Will you get out from under me feet! Why don't you go and play in the yard?'

They all told her that it was raining.

'Well go upstairs then. And don't be tossin' the beds.'

They began to file out, still grinning, and she cuffed the ear of the last to leave.

'Standin' there runnin' about,' she added obscurely. 'I declare to God they'd put years on you.'

She said it without any particular emphasis, just something she always said.

'Tell us now, what happened to wee Charlie?'

'He's in Geneva.'

She looked blank.

'At the university,' I explained. 'Professor of Linguistics and Philology.'

'What in the name of God's that?'

'Nobody knows. Except Charlie.'

'Isn't that a wonder to the world now?' she said, 'Wee Charlie a Professor.'

She shook her head and sat at the table. 'The tea'll be infused in a minute,' she said.

It was the genteel way to put it. I remembered my own mother saying it when the Rector called.

'You've a big family,' I said.

'Didn't do too bad for a late starter.'

'Seven is it?'

'Twelve. Nine at school and three working.'

She got up and went into the scullery before I could decide on the right reaction. I looked around the little kitchen, cluttered but clean, without any of the smell of damp newspapers that I remembered from the kitchen behind the shop in Church Street. The pattern on the linoleum had been polished into a blur, and a few rugs, home-knotted, worn flat and waxy, were laid in odd positions, probably to cover the parts where corky fibres showed through the lino. There were pictures on the wall: children in various permutations, enlargements of Polyfoto photographs taken in Robinson and Cleaver's during visits to Belfast. Among them hung a little framed scroll. I stood to get a closer look. It was a copy of a famous document, one I had heard of from my father and others, but never before seen. The Red Hand of Ulster was in the top corner and it was dated sixty years earlier, the year after Stevie was born.

ULSTER'S
Solemn League and Covenant

Being convinced in our consciences that Home Rule would be disastrous to the material well-being of Ulster as well as the whole of Ireland, subversive of our civil and religious freedom, destructive of our citizenship, and perilous to the unity of the Empire, we, whose names are underwritten, men of Ulster, loyal subjects of His Gracious Majesty King George V, humbly relying on God in whom our fathers in days of stress and trial confidently trusted, do hereby pledge ourselves in solemn Covenant throughout this our time of threatened calamity to stand by one another in defending for ourselves and our children our cherished position of equal citizenship in the United Kingdom and in using all means which may be found necessary to defeat the present conspiracy to set up a Home Rule Parliament in Ireland. And in the event of such a Parliament being forced upon us we further solemnly and mutually pledge ourselves to refuse to recognize its authority.

In sure confidence that God will defend the right we hereto subscribe our names. And further, we individually declare that we have not already signed this Covenant.

--------God Save the King--------

It was signed, in a beautiful copperplate script, by William Burgess, and dated 'Ulster Day,' Saturday, 28 September 1912.

As I finished reading it, Annie came back with the teapot.

'That was your grandfather's,' she said. 'All that's left of him. I used to keep Stevie's Pledge beside it.'

I stared. 'You got Stevie to take the Pledge?'

'Oh I did. But I never got him to keep it. So I stuck it up on the bathroom wall opposite the lav, so as he'd be lookin' up at it when he was on the throne.'

She laughed, to take the harm out of it.

'How is he?'

'He hasn't been too grand lately. There's not a lot of work for him, with the Manse closed.'

I was still standing by the framed Covenant. I touched it, to set it straight, and a folded piece of thick paper fell from behind. As Annie went back to the scullery, I unfolded and read it.

Being convinced that the enemies of the Faith and Freedom are determined to destroy the State of Northern Ireland and thereby enslave the People of God, we call on all members of our loyalist institutions, and other responsible citizens to organize themselves immediately into platoons of twenty under the command of someone capable of acting as Sergeant. Every effort must be made to arm these platoons, with whatever weapons are available. The first duty of each platoon will be to formulate a plan for the defence of its own street or road in co-operation with platoons in adjoining areas. A structure of command is already in existence and the various platoons will eventually be linked in a co-ordinated effort.

Instructions: Under no circumstances must Platoons come into conflict with Her Majesty's Forces or the Police. If through wrong political direction Her Majesty's Forces are directed against Loyalist people, members of Platoons must do everything possible to avoid a confrontation.

We are Loyalists, we are Queen's Men! Our enemies are the forces of Romanism and Communism which must be destroyed. Members of Platoons must act with the highest sense of responsibility and urgency in preparing our people for the full assault of the enemies within our Province and the forces of the Eire Government which will eventually be thrown against us. We must prepare now! This is total war!'

It was dated August 1971, less than a year before. How little had changed in sixty years, I thought. Looking up, I saw Annie watching me. I held up the paper.

'Stevie's?'

She nodded. I folded it carefully and replaced it behind the framed Covenant. 'Did he join them?'

'He was one of the first…. But it's a young man's fight.'

'I remember he was always very strong for it.'

'He's a Queen's man, like the rest of us,' she said proudly. 'Sit down to your tea.'

I sat, grateful that, for once since I'd come home, someone seemed to trust me.

'Mind you,' she went on. 'He was very upset about five or six years ago, when Gusty Spence got life. He said Gusty was right and there wasn't many sayin' it then. Though there's plenty sayin' it now.'

'Hard to know,' I said safely.

'They were warned and they let it happen. O'Neill. And Chichester Clark. They're the ones I blame, encouragin' the Catholics, givin' in to one thing after another.' She spoke without rancour, in the calm confidence of knowing what was right.

'They took Stormont off us and now they're goin' to sit down and talk to the IRA. Who's left to fight only ourselves?'

'You must be tired of the fighting all the same—'

'Of course we're tired. But we're not *that* tired. Take a bit of bannock there.'

I spread butter on the warm bannock. The first in all those years.

'I suppose everybody here feels the same,' I said.

'Everybody *I* know.'

'I was hoping to find some of the old gang. Only found one so far. Ernie Swindle.'

'Oh that skitter.'

I grinned. 'You don't fancy him?'

'He'd see the grass growin'. Sittin' there in his glass box with his eyes out on stilts. I hope you told him nothin'.'

'Nothing to tell.'

'Because he'd land you in trouble, the same Ernie.'

'Does Stevie still see him?'

'Aye, but he doesn't see Stevie. Too grand all of a sudden.'

'I gathered he was mixed up with this crowd.'

I nodded at the paper I had just read.

'He is, but he's not liked. They only use him as a messenger boy.'

'I suppose all my old mates are in it.'

'It depends who you mean. Hughie Brown's in it – wasn't he a friend of yours?'

'He was.'

'He's the only one still comes to see us. Nice wee lad, easy-goin'. Fond of the drink.'

She drank from her cup, her finger extended, then withdrew the cup and left her head where it was.

'You knew Tommy McGoldrick?' she asked.

'I did of course. I'm hoping to see Tommy.'

'You'll find he's changed.'

'Haven't we all?' I laughed a little. 'It's funny to think of it, the old gang, the different ways we've gone.'

'It's still a gang, Billy, only bigger. And Tommy's the chief buck cat.'

'Really?'

'The Colonel.'

'Tommy?'

She nodded firmly. 'He's harder than he was. The best of them.'

I was nodding foolishly, trying to sort it all out in my head. It seemed to me that Ernie, acting on his own, would never have had the nerve to threaten me. And I thought I knew now where the orders had come from, though I was no closer to knowing why. But was I pushing Annie too far? Maybe I should lighten things.

'You should be more careful, Annie,' I said.

'Why?'

'Giving all these secrets to a Free Stater like me. How do you know I'm not spying for the other crowd?'

She laughed. A rare thing, I thought, to find someone so open.

'I'd be sorry for you if you were,' she said. 'If Ernie knows you're here, you can be sure the rest of them know it. You'll be watched.'

I wanted to ask why, but she was off, to warm up the tea, and I went on turning things over in my mind. Maybe Angela had phoned Tommy. And Tommy had phoned Ernie. And with all the warning noises around me, why did I want to know?

But there was something in Annie's openness that lulled me, and something in my own nature that prompted me to go on digging.

'I heard about Mikey Doran,' I said.

That was good, I thought. No opinion. Just 'I heard....'

She had just come back from the scullery and put the teapot quickly on the cork mat. 'That oul handle would scald you,' she said.

I could hardly say it again. Twice running would sound anxious. But she had heard.

'Och anee,' she said, and paused. 'Poor wee Mikey.'

'They say he was a Provo.'

'Not at all!' She said it vehemently. 'He was a wee Fenian and his mother spoiled him rotten, but he wouldn't have hurt a fly.'

She smiled as a thought came to her and she said it out.

'Mind you, he was brave and handy with his *own* fly.'

I didn't follow at first.

'I hope you're not a prude, Billy – I know you were a bad-minded wee bugger as a child…. But Mikey was a terrible wee man for his nuts.' She laughed and shook her head. 'He'd get up on a cracked plate so he would.'

I was surprised, even a little shocked. I was well enough used to dirty talk from young women – in fact I liked it – but from this middle-aged matron, my auntie, mother of twelve….

Still, she laughed as she said it; no harm was meant. So Mikey was fond of his nuts? Which of us wasn't?

'They'd hardly have shot him for that,' I said.

'No. He was a wee Fenian. I suppose that was enough.' She paused. 'Enough for Johnny anyway.'

'Johnny Fusco?'

She nodded. 'Johnny's terrible bitter. And he'll be worse now. You heard they bombed his pub?'

'Yes.'

'Coulda killed him. And of course you know what they say. There's nobody as bitter as a Taig that turns.'

I had to remind myself that in this part of the world to 'turn' has a single and serious meaning – to change your faith. No greater sin.

Annie was still talking. 'Did you see Johnny since you came?'

'No….' I hesitated. 'Not badly hurt was he?'

'Broke his arm. Could've been worse.'

I agreed. And of course I *had* seen Johnny. We just hadn't spoken yet. 'I met his sister,' I said.

'Oh aye, Angela. You'd have met her at the hotel. Fine wee girl.'

For Annie, anyone younger than herself was wee.

'As a matter of fact,' I went on, 'I asked her out this evening. But she turned me down.'

'Just as well.'

'Why do you say so?'

'I know somebody wouldn't like it.'

'Who do you—'

As I started to ask the question, the front door opened and feet were pummelling down the stairs. Then Stevie came into the room, children hanging from his coat, scuffling in his pockets. 'What did you bring us, Daddy?'

I was glad the children had distracted him. It gave me time to recover from the shock. My last memory of Stevie was of an athlete, all muscle and sinew. This was a humpy-backed old man. His skin was pale and bluish, except where the veins were broken on his cheeks. As Annie had said, he still had his hair, but it framed an old face, as Annie's did. His eyes, sagging red like a gundog's, had a constant look of faint surprise, the only disguise he knew for the vacancy behind them. His lips were shaped in a smile, fixed, a kind of pretext, a defence against anyone who might call on him for more than he could offer. His clothes were old, almost threadbare, and they looked a size too large, as if he had grown too small for them. But there was a neatness there, maybe a lesson, remembered from childhood, that it was important to look decent.

The children had their sweets by now. Annie shunted them from the room and pointed to me.

'Do you know who this is?'

There was no pretence in the emptiness of his stare. The grape-vine, however far-flung, had not reached Stevie.

'It's wee Billy.'

He said something, a question maybe. As a child, I had made out what he said easily enough, but whether I had simply grown accustomed to it then, or it had become a great deal worse, it was now just a jumble of nasal sounds, produced with much effort. Annie spoke to him good-humouredly and he seemed to understand, offering me a limp handshake that reached only the ends of my fingers. He had been drinking, just enough to know he ought to disguise it. He removed his coat in a deliberate, preoccupied way and hung it on a hook behind the door. Then he sat carefully on a kitchen chair, pulling up the knees of his trousers as he had been taught.

Annie went on talking, telling him all the things we had been saying and he nodded and smiled, repeating often the phrases she used, like an echo. I made an effort to take part, asking if he had any interest still in the hockey and the cricket, but he just smiled and said he was too old now, he needed none of them and he would go his own way. There was a hint of pride as he said it and I told him he was right. The gap between an independent and a derelict was narrow enough to allow him that much.

Annie's way with him was oddly gentle. It was plain that he was hardly a good provider, but she seemed not to expect that and made grumbling jokes about the pubs and the bookies in the way she would tell one of the children not to pick his nose.

I watched and listened. I had never been close to Stevie, but I had once been in awe of him. Now that this was gone, there was nothing left except a wish to escape from a feeling of decay so strong you could almost smell it. And as soon as I decently could, I took my leave. The children, who up to now had not spoken to me, were prompted into Bye Byes, hands on mouths to keep from laughing, checking with each other if the money I had slipped them was divided equally.

'Ah now, Billy, you shouldn't, that's too much, say thanks to your cousin Billy....' But it was cheap enough.

I took a detour going back, by way of the Carnegie Library, a place for which I had good memories. It was on the way home from school and I used to go in almost every day. The William books were my favourites then, and Biggles. And when I had changed my books I would go into the Reading Room and study the latest edition of *Picture Post* while the old men of the town, saving tuppence, read the *News Letter* or the *Northern Whig*. I walked in now and found little had changed except that, as with everything revisited, it was smaller than I remembered.

In the Reading Room, the newspapers still lay in their binders on the sloping shelves where you could stand and read them at leisure. I headed for the *Belfast Telegraph* and turned back the pages until I reached the edition of the particular Thursday.

There it was, on the bottom of page 4. 'SWEETSHOP MURDER' was the headline. I read it quickly, as I had learned to do, registering the essentials.... Michael Doran (40), Teacher of English and History in St. Cronan's College.... Death instantaneous, said State Pathologist ... all the hallmarks of a sectarian murder....

I looked again at the name. Michael Doran (40). I thought back the thirty years to the day I had bought the gobstoppers from the woman with the long fingernails. Cassie Doran. And the boy who nicked the choc-ice and winked at me as he left.

She hadn't said his name, but that was Mikey. And he would have been forty now.

Would have been.

CHAPTER 7

It was near seven when I walked into the hotel and realized that, apart from Annie's bannock, I had eaten nothing since breakfast. There were two unhappy-looking diners in the dining room, no drinkers in the bar. It was the beginning of a fine weekend in summer, but the hotel, with its potted plants and terrazzo, was like a crematorium. It seemed proper to ask for my key in a whisper. Lily Blunt found it by touch and handed it over.

'Are you going out on the tear?' she asked.

'I might be. Will you join me?'

'You wouldn't be able for me. If you're late, Geordie'll let you in. That's if you can wake him.'

I turned to see Geordie crouched in the window-seat, giving a slow nod that denoted reliability, rising above his martyrdom.

Lying on the bed in my room, I went over in my mind the strange dislocated nature of the last few hours. First there was Ernie Swindle. Only a messenger boy, Annie had said, and I found that easy to believe. So it seemed certain that Tommy McGoldrick, my friend of schooldays and now commander of the town's Defence Forces, had heard I was here and wanted rid of me. And Johnny Fusco, with a score to settle – what part would he play? All the cloak and dagger warnings could be put down to the phobias of people under siege, people who for the past three years, or three hundred, had lived their lives among the columns of secret armies. And now their eyes had grown accustomed to the dark. Now they had learned to suspect everyone, especially perhaps an ex-townsman turning up after years of exile in the enemy camp, the classic fifth-columnist. Then, recognizing that even to think in those terms was to join in the mad melodrama of it all, I grinned, shook my head and rolled off the bed, my mind made up.

I would go home immediately. It was annoying to leave Ernie with the impression that I had heeded his warning, but I was already thinking of Dublin on a Friday night, of noisy pubs and gamey women.

If I left now, I could make it before closing time, maybe move on to one of those impromptu Dublin post-pub parties in a basement flat where you came with a brown bag under each arm, pressed the bell with your elbow, and everyone knew everyone, but nobody knew the host. A modest enough prospect, but seen from here, heaven. Telling myself that it was boredom, not fear, that persuaded me, I packed in seconds. I had not slept in the room, but there would be a bill of sorts, which I would be only too happy to pay. Thinking that I would ring Lily to have it ready, I reached for the phone. It rang as I touched it.

If only I had phoned Lily *before* packing, and told her I was leaving, maybe it wouldn't have happened, but doesn't every down-and-out in the world have his own boring story of the short head that cost him a life of ease? It was Angela. She hoped she was not disturbing me. Still distantly polite.

'You asked if I could join you for dinner?'

'Yes.'

'I can make it after all, if you're still free.'

It sounded mechanical, rehearsed.

'Actually I was thinking....' I hesitated.

'Yes?'

I had been in two minds, but Angela's 'Yes?,' spoken close to the phone, swayed me.

'I was thinking I hadn't eaten all day. Will we eat in the hotel?'

'No. I know a place.'

'Are you in the hotel now?' There was a pause, barely noticeable.

'Yes.'

'I'll come straight down.'

'No, better not. Pick me up at the bus station. In ten minutes.'

'Right. And thank you.'

But she had hung up. Her talent for small talk had not improved. As I shaved, the suspicion came to me that the change of
mind might not have been her own idea, but I pushed it aside.
She would of course have checked with Lily that I was booked in
for the night. And if she had come to decision not to let me out
of her sight for the evening, it was an arrangement that suited me
well enough. I began to wonder if it went further than that ... if
she could be acting on orders....

Or was I growing as paranoid as everybody else up here?

And, there was no doubt, the prospects for the evening had
improved. I could leave just as easily in the morning, and if Angela
wanted to maintain surveillance till then, I would have no objec-
tion. To turn down such a prospect would be foreign to my nature.

The Venetian blinds were closed on Ernie's office, but I was still
nervous waiting there, in the car with the Dublin plates. I turned
sharply once or twice, hoping to catch an eye quickly withdrawn
from its peephole. I found myself whistling, a trick I used to have
for seeming not to mind when a dog sniffed my leg. I was watching the hotel, but she came from behind, surprising me.

'You look marvellous,' I said.

It was true, though I would have said it anyway. Unexpectedly,
she blushed, something not many grown women did these days.
Someone once told me that blushing was not a sign of maidenly
modesty, but of sexual hunger; that you can't raise a blush with
cold blood. True or not, I took it as a good sign.

65

She seemed distant at first, holding her chin high. But once in the car, giving me directions, she became less tense and sat leaning on her right shoulder, looking at me. I thought at first she was watching me, but she was just looking. We were two people driving out for the evening, and if there were hidden potholes, she seemed as anxious as I was to avoid them.

I drove, at her direction, well outside the town and stopped at what seemed to be a very large double barn, squatting like a pair of children's building bricks in two or three acres of asphalt car park. I never discovered its name, but a huge neon sign near the road said 'ROADHOUSE', with the first 'o' missing. It was barely half past seven, but already the car park was more than half-full. We went into a large entrance lobby with embossed wallpaper and a deep red carpet with yellow explosions. There was a long counter where men's coats were taken and, behind it, a large framed print of the Queen, looking nervous, between two glass cases, each displaying a sash, one orange, one a sort of lilac. Above the picture, and dwarfing it, was an enormous flag of Ulster. At the end of the lobby were two doors, one displaying a top-hatted Gent, the other a crinolined Lady. I would not have been surprised to see the two doors labelled William's and Mary's.

When Angela emerged, surprisingly quickly by ordinary powder-room standards, she was wearing a dress of some metallic fabric that would have made any other woman look like a magician's assistant. On Angela it looked wonderful, though she seemed unaware of it. She walked into the big bar-like dining room as if she was crossing a road, and as we walked to our table, it was I, the great sophisticate, who felt gauche and self-conscious. Men sitting with their wives watched her pass by with an exaggerated nonchalance that fooled nobody. Again, she seemed not to notice.

66

As she sat at the table, there was no glance around the room to check who was there. She looked only at me. The intimacy felt real. And I consider myself a fair judge of these things.

We had Mouclade Islandmagee to start, following by Saumon Grillé Lough MacNean. The menu was all like that, with every corner of Ulster packed into the freezer. The dishes differed in texture, but hardly at all in taste. Still, Angela ate everything and went on about how lovely it all was. She told me about the chef, who was from Scotland; a genius, she said. She wished she had him at the hotel. I pushed the bits of broccoli around my plate, making little patterns. She was watching me and smiling.

'Eat up,' she said. 'You're in your granny's.'

I took it literally at first and thought she was talking about my own long-dead granny, whom she would barely have remembered. Then I recalled that it was what everybody said in the North and smiled back, feeling silly. It reminded me that I was a stranger now, an outsider. But I pushed the thought away.

'Do you come here often?'

She laughed, as if I had said something witty. I was puzzled.

'What did I say?'

'Nothing….'

Then I remembered, and smiled. It was what you said at dances, in the old days, the conversation-starter.

'It's just so long since I heard anybody saying it,' she said. 'There's so many normal things you can't say any more. People have got so cynical.'

'Well *do* you?' I asked.

'Do I what?'

'Come here often?'

'I come when I'm asked,' she said coyly.

'And how often are you asked? Often enough I'd say.'

'Questions, always questions.' Her head was on one side and she was smiling. 'They'll be the death of you.'

For a moment I wondered if it was another warning, but it was only a moment. You have to stop this, I told myself. Stop the questions ... lighten up.

'You're dead right,' I said. 'I just needed to know that you've been saving yourself for me.'

'Of course I have. All these years, wondering would I ever see you again.'

'I was ten and you were—'

'Five. Beneath your notice. I've kept a lock of your hair ever since.'

'Yeah…. I remember the day you pulled it out.'

'Maybe I should give it back, now that you need it.'

It was all like that, trivial, silly, but it was warm too. We went well together.

Three bald men, in evening clothes too young for them, arrived on a small rostrum and began to play gently on piano, bass and drums. The music they played, *Pal Joey*, *Carousel*, *Showboat*, suited our mood and we sang little snatches to each other in a parody of Sinatra and Hayworth, forgetting the words and tailing off. But we were a bit past that kind of thing, and when the first selection ended and everyone clapped, there was a silence, a kind of back-to-earth before Angela spoke again.

'You saw your Uncle Stevie?'

'Yes. I couldn't believe how failed he was.'

She said nothing for a moment, seemed about to speak, then just shook her head. 'Poor Stevie,' she said.

'I saw Ernie too. He didn't seem too happy to see me. But maybe you'd know more about that than I would.'

She looked at me blankly. For a moment the wall was up again; then she took up the tune the band was playing.

Others find
Peace of mind
In pretending....
Couldn't I, couldn't you,
Couldn't we....

I could just have joined in, stayed in the mood. But the question had come back into my mind and refused to leave.

'Did you ring him?'

'Who?'

'Ernie.'

'Why on earth would I—'

'Somebody did. He was expecting me.'

'That's not so surprising. Things like that get around quickly. Stranger in town.' She spoke easily, taking it in her stride.

'He pretended to be surprised to see me,' I said. 'But I could see he was expecting me. He kept tripping himself up.'

She shrugged. 'That's Ernie. He couldn't lie straight in the bed.'

'And he knew I'd been talking to you, so naturally I assumed you'd—'

She put a finger to my mouth.

'I never rang him! I've better things to do.' She smiled. 'Better things to talk about, for that matter.'

'But you rang *someone*.'

I was beginning to bore myself.

'Billy, will you forget about it? You're as bad as Ernie is.'

'He threatened me. That's not so easy to forget.'

'He shouldn't have done that.'

'You mean, he went beyond his orders?'

She was nodding and shaking her head at the same time.

'Don't, Billy, please. There's nothing I can tell you.'

Her self-assurance had left her and the intimacy had gone with it. I told her I was sorry, partly because it was true and partly because I wanted back into the cocoon. Her hands lay on the table and I thought they looked like wax, but when I touched them they were dry and cool. She did not respond to the touch, but I began to press her fingers with my thumbs, like pressing a bell, and she raised her head again and half-smiled. Again, she was offering a truce and again I blew it.

'He told me about Mikey Doran,' I said.

I felt her fingers tighten, but I went on. 'You knew Mikey—'

'Of course.'

'How did you feel when he was killed?'

Her eyes flared. 'How do you think I felt? You're on the TV, Billy. You have all the words at your fingertips – take a pick.'

She was right. All the words. Disgust, despair, abhorrence, devastation, revulsion, horror, nausea. Leaders of Church and State, All Right-Thinking People, Men of Goodwill, all of them had long since run out of words. But that was not what I had meant.

'I mean, how do you feel now, knowing your friends killed him?'

Her shock seemed real. '*My* friends?'

'The UDA. Or the UVF. Or Tara, or the Red Hand Commando – whatever banner they were carrying the night they shot him.'

'You're going too far now, Billy—'

'Not as far as your friends went with Mikey.'

'Why do you keep saying *my* friends? You're just guessing—'

'It seems like common knowledge. I thought they were proud of operations like this. Haven't they taken credit yet? Used it as a warning to Republican elements?'

'There's nothing I can tell you, Billy. Don't ask me.'

It was plain that she knew more than she would say about how Mikey had died. And yet I was sure that she was genuinely surprised, upset even, to hear that I had been threatened. If there was a link between the two things, bullying Angela would not help me to discover it, or so I told myself. Maybe I was a little ashamed.

'Sorry, Angela. Ernie got under my skin, that's all. No need to take to out on *you*.'

She nodded, but she had her guard up still, suspecting that the third degree wasn't really over, that I was manoeuvring, looking for a fresh angle. And, in a way, she was wrong. It was not in my nature to follow a plan of action, so I rarely made one. If I made a decision to say something, I could easily find myself saying something quite different. At this moment I had decided not to mention Ernie again. The musicians were playing 'Bewitched' and, to show my erudition, I began to sing the rarely sung verse about the ants....

Romance, finis....
Your chance, finis....
Those ants that invaded my pants, finis....
Bewitched, bothered and bewildered no more

'Never heard that one,' she said, smiling.

'You don't like Ernie either, do you?' I said.

'Ernie?' She considered an evasion, then shook her head. 'He makes my skin crawl.'

She looked around quickly, a little guiltily, and lowered her voice.

'Did he tell you to leave?'

'Yes.'

'Then maybe you should.'

'Because Ernie says so?'

'No. He wouldn't have the guts to do anything himself. But

71

there's others, they wouldn't think twice – don't ask me, please!'

She looked frightened, and not just on my account.

'Do *you* want me to leave?'

'Yes!' It was almost a whisper, but there was no mistaking the strength of it. I had thought things were going well, and this brought me up short. Then she leaned across the table.

'But not yet,' she said. 'Tomorrow morning.'

I recovered quickly. 'And how will I pass the time till then?'

'I can't think.' She laughed, like a schoolgirl.

The whole evening was like that, doors opening and slamming shut. I thought of a children's puzzle I got one Christmas, a little glass-topped box in which you tilted the painted rabbit this way and that, trying to make the ball-bearings settle in the sockets of his eyes.

Suddenly, a sort of strangled cry fell on the room and Angela held my arm, leaving it there and drawing her chair closer when the source of the noise was identified and applauded by the diners. It was the cabaret. The lights were dimmed and a broad spotlight fell on the very active lady who had joined us. The spotlight had to be broad, in order to contain the lady. She moved energetically in a short ellipse before the piano, throwing lefts and rights and grinning fiercely.

Everything, she sang, was coming up roses. She had long black hair which she tossed about like a frightened horse; a large hooked nose, a wide crescent of thick lips and a surprisingly white and shapely neck that corrugated into chins only on the very lowest notes. Her large moon breasts jostled about, half-in, half-out of the shining low-cut bodice, and from her waist the full floor-length skirt billowed out like a crinoline, giving her the overall appearance of a cottage loaf. She wore elbow-length black gloves, and her upper arms, bare to the shoulder, were curiously white and firm and shaped like cantaloupes. Pumping her arms, as she did to set the beat, and moving with an agility that sometimes took the moving spotlight by surprise, she gave the impression of having four breasts.

'What's her name?' I whispered. We were sitting side by side now.

Angela's shoulder leaned against my chest and her mouth brushed my cheek as she turned to answer. It was like a moment from a far-off tennis-club dance.

'Ruby,' she said.

'She's got four tits.'

She hit me with her elbow and told me to be quiet. It was like asking someone to stop whistling during a rocket launch.

The roses had all come up and Ruby was thanking her audience and introducing a very special request. It was 'Amazing Grace', which she sang very solemnly, like a large nun. She stayed very still for this one, her hands clasped in the shelter of her bosom, but she used a great variety of vocal tricks and ornaments. The pianist, who had switched to an electric organ, for greater piety, had the task of guessing when exactly she had finished with one note and was going on to the next, but on the whole he kept up very well. Then she sang another special request, this time in French, a song that had a quiet intense verse followed by a wild emotional chorus that made us all jump. She went on and on, one moment sad, Giving her Wedding Dress Away, the next happy, saying Good Morning to the Starshine, and the audience loved her and shouted for more. Now and then, a voice would call on her to sing her 'Ulster Song'. After each number, the shouts for this grew louder but, like a true trouper, she ignored them until it turned into a chant. Then, with a word to the musicians, she raised a podgy hand for silence, a set of look of dedication on her

73

face, and stepped down from the rostrum, pulling the hand-held microphone with her like a bull-whip.

The organ played a few bars of the tune and the audience roared its approval. I was puzzled, for it was the tune of a satirical republican song called 'The Patriot Game', much beloved of ballad groups south of the border. I wondered for a moment if they had learned in the North to sing southern songs in the way that late drinkers in a Dublin pub will sometimes sing an Orange song, to show the world how broad-minded they are. The notion soon faded when I heard the words. Some of the diners sang along with Ruby; others just punctuated the lines with cheers. A number raised their glasses and smiled at one other. It was the solidarity of people with a cause, a mood described on casualty lists as 'valour'. The words were ordinary enough. But in the belief that their right to utter them was under threat, they sang like pilgrims.

Come all Loyal Protestants and list while I sing,
For the love of old Ulster is a wonderful thing.
We'll fight to defend it with tooth and with nail,
And we will make certain that truth will prevail....

Around sixteen-ninety, at a placed called the Boyne,
Our forefathers gathered with William to join,
God's blessing was on them, as they entered the fray,
And thanks to those heroes, we're free men today....

Angela sat quite still, taking no part. I squeezed her arm. 'You awake?'

'Yes. You want to go?'

'I thought you were enjoying Ruby.'

'No.'

She stood up and I followed, a little too conspicuous for comfort. Ruby was moving among the tables now as she sang. People looked around as I fumbled with money, whispering with the waiter, feeling as if I were leaving Church during the sermon. Ruby sang straight at me.

When world war was raging, in nineteen sixteen,
Those treacherous rebels from Dublin did scheme
To take our six counties they thought they'd the nerve,
But the Black and Tans gave them just what they deserved.

Our loyal Scotch Brethren have given their word
That if danger threatens, they'll take up the sword,
Then all over Scotland, you'll soon hear the cry,
For God and for Ulster we'll fight and we'll die....

I smiled warmly at Ruby and edged from the room with the smile still fixed, hoping to dispel any notion that I might be leaving in protest. Angela seemed not at all concerned and walked like a duchess past the disapproving head waiter.

'A bit warm,' I said to him foolishly, but he appeared not to hear. The door closed behind us, but we still talked in whispers, as Ruby's voice followed us across the lobby.

... so one final warning to rebels I'll say,
Don't try to take Ulster or you'll rue the day,
For we'll cut you down and you'll fall like the rain,
We did it before and we'll do it again....

CHAPTER 8

I had thought we were leaving the building, but Angela led me across the lobby through another door and into a covered windowless passage.

'You don't want to go home yet?'

It depended, I thought, on what she meant by home.

'No,' I said. 'But where are we going?'

'The Lounge. It's good on Fridays.'

It was a long passage and at the end was a thick door, covered in dark red felt. I pushed it open and saw what she meant.

It was a very large room, less a Lounge Bar than a Banqueting Hall. There were about two hundred people there, but it was less than half-full. It was a miracle of sound insulation, for although we had heard nothing from the restaurant, the noise here was much greater. One wall was filled with portraits, one of Queen Victoria, and on either side of her a line of stern-faced men in morning-coats, who, I felt sure, would not have approved of what was going on. On the opposite wall were framed photographs of men's and ladies' hockey teams in full colour, and a notice which said 'No Spitting'.

Maroon-coated waiters strode aggressively among the tables, taking orders in the style of roll-call at a military college and bugling them back to the bar. On the platform was yet another musical group, but this one was all-electric, with guitars, drums and a keyboard, before a bank of electronic equipment which would not have seemed out of place at Cape Canaveral. Two of the band stood farther forward than the others and it turned out that although the group was at the moment singing ensemble, these two generally sang the songs, or as they called them, the vocals. They were contrasting figures. One was tall and morose. He sang country vocals, very dismal accounts of personal suffering, some telling of his remorse for his selfish treatment of his parents, now dead, others describing his depression over his wife's infidelity or recent death. His announcements were made in the tones of his native Ballymena, but his vocals were sung in the accents of a runaway slave.

The other soloist (rock vocals) used the same accent, but he had nothing of the brave resignation of the country vocals man. Whatever the words of the song, his face as he sang it would be contorted with pain. Neither technique seemed well suited to the words they were singing as we came in.

And we play, all the way, for Leeds United,
Elland Road is the only place for us....

And though I imagined few of those present had ever been to Elland Road, they all appeared to enjoy singing along. At home I would have run a mile from such goings-on, so I was surprised to find that I enjoyed it too. Maybe it was the wine I had drunk, or the Black Bush whiskey I was drinking now, or the closeness of Angela, but although I felt no kinship with the people around me, I had begun to feel carefree and at home, like a stranger at a wake. I looked around at the pictures on the wall and began to laugh, but I quickly changed it to a cough. Angela followed my eyes, looking for the joke.

'It's herself,' I said, pointing to Queen Victoria.

'You don't think she'd be amused?'

'She'd be frightened to death. Tell me something. What would happen if a Catholic got in here?'

'If he was from round here, he wouldn't try. And if he was a stranger, he'd soon get the message.'

'I'd forgotten all this....' I shook my head. 'It's so strange to me now. In the south, a pub is a pub. Up here it's a church hall.'

She smiled.

'Do you ever come to Dublin?' I asked.

'My mother took me when I was seven. It was wartime here, and the blackout. All I remember of Dublin were the coloured lights, the neon signs.'

'Why don't you pay us another visit?'

'Why? To see the lights?'

I shrugged. 'Fun.'

'Sure there's fun here.'

'But it's all so ... I don't know ... determined. Like a holiday camp. Dublin people don't seem to work so hard at being happy.'

'I'm sure they don't.' She paused, measuring her words. 'You see, they got what they wanted. Their Free State....'

It was hardly accurate, but I let it pass. She talked on. 'So why can't they settle for that and stop wanting to take us over?'

'But we don't, unless you want to join us. That's the deal.'

I had meant to say 'they', not 'we'. To act as a neutral. But it was too late. She was already accusing me.

'I know what you say, but look what you *do*.'

'Tell me.'

'Look at your government. They started the Provos, ran guns to them. You give them a place to hide, a place to attack us from. You let them recruit and raise money on O'Connell Street. They drill in the open and you look the other way. They even have an office in Dublin. They come up here and bomb and murder and then run back across the border and you won't even send them back for trial. Half the ordinary people in the Free State support them.'

They were the standard Orange beliefs and she believed them utterly. I had all the standard answers. And I would have begun to give them air, but stopped myself, realizing that, though I would believe in what I would say, there would be no point. Views like these were destined to run endlessly on parallel lines, like the port and starboard wheels of tramcars. When both sides had been put, neither I nor Angela would have shifted in our views. Not an inch.

In one way, I thought, she was at least half-right. It was when she said that the South had got what it wanted. The thinking on both sides was changing, slowly, but in the South the change was voluntary. In the North, the changes in the last three years had been forced on them, by the men they had looked to for protection and support. The Mother of Parliaments, having given them power, now blamed them for using it. And so they felt deserted. The old certainties of Loyalism were in tatters. What did it mean if the people to whom they were traditionally loyal showed no loyalty to *them*?

Time to put a stop to this, I thought. Lighten up.

'When I had an argument with my father,' I said, 'he used to close it with a remark that always drove me mad. I think I'll use it on you.'

'Go on.'

'He used to say – "You're wrong, Billy, but no matter".'

I had hoped for a smile, but it was very faint one. She was looking intently at me.

'How do *you* feel?' she said.

'About what?'

'The IRA.'

I searched for an answer.

'Killers,' I said, eventually. 'Killers with a cause, like all the others. No worse, no better.'

She kept watching me. Then, without looking away, lifted her glass. 'More please.'

She put her glass in my hand, leaned forward and kissed me, leaving me pleasantly confused. I was glad that the discussion was over, not just because it was damaging my prospects for the evening, but because it had been conducted in loud tones, in competition with the music. I was a little worried that someone might read my lips, or that the music might stop suddenly and leave me bawling out sentiments that might not be too well received. It never occurred to me at the time that the conversation could have any other importance. Angela's questions seemed to be no more than curiosity. The old debate. And if she had any other reason for putting them, if she was under orders to report what I had said, I was not greatly worried. Either way, I felt I had passed the test.

The rock vocals man was not, like his country friend, restricted to the two archetypes of faithful mother and faithless wife, and he was performing a song about a faithless mother. It seemed that he woke up one mornin' and his momma was gone.

When he had finished, his lugubrious partner stepped forward to announce that his next vocal would be dedicated to a good friend of us all, and that we would all know who it was when we heard it.

A spotlight, from a stanchion onstage, was switched on and trained on a table in the farthest corner. The music began and applause broke out from the adjoining tables. Everyone looked that way, and Angela stood up, smiling proudly as she joined in the applause. There were chants of 'Up! Up!' as the song began.

Six foot six, he stood on the ground,
He weighed two hundred and thirty-five pound,

But I saw that giant of a man brought down
To his knees by love....

The shouts of 'Up' were almost drowning the song, when a man wearing an embarrassed smile stood up from the table in the corner. The cheers went up and he tried to acknowledge them by clasping his hands together above his head like a prizefighter. But one arm, in plaster, would not rise higher than his shoulder. As the song promised, he was a giant of a man.

He was the kind of a man who would gamble on luck,
Look you in the eye and never back up,
But I saw his cryin' like a little whipped pup
Because of love....

Angela told me what I already knew.

'It's Johnny.' She was smiling, proud of her brother in the spotlight.

'He seems popular.'

'He is. And wee Amy. Look, he could carry her in his pocket.'

Amy stood briefly, covering her face with her hands.

'She's his wife?'

'Yes. They were going together for years, had a little baby girl. Then last month they got married. The night they came back from their honeymoon, the bomb was waiting for them.'

I shook my head. 'I suppose they were lucky,' I said. And wished I hadn't. I tried to explain what I really meant, but she talked me down.

'They've always made fun of Johnny, I don't know why. I suppose because he's good-natured. A big softie.'

'He had a temper once I remember.'

'Still has, but not with his friends.'

Looking around the room, I could see that he had many friends, and wondered about his enemies. I was remembering what Annie had said about him: 'Johnny's terrible bitter…. There's nobody as bitter as a Taig that turns….'

Johnny was half-pushed, half-pulled on stage and stood among the musicians, trying to smile. The Rock Vocals man stood on a chair beside him, clowning and sparring, topping him by no more than an inch or two. Johnny looked in the direction of Angela and she waved. He appeared not to notice us, but when he climbed down, to more applause, he looked quickly in our direction before returning, relieved, to his own table.

Angela went on talking about him in the same protective, sentimental way, but I was only half-listening. I was wondering if there might not be a far simpler reason for the suspicions that seemed to surround me since my arrival.

Suppose it was Johnny who had killed Mikey Doran? Suppose then that Angela knew that, and that her only concern was to protect a brother who was in danger, who had turned in blind rage against an imagined enemy and shot him. From all that I remembered of Johnny, and from all I had heard since, from Annie and Angela, he was a man of no great intellect, but strong emotions. He had seen the life of his new young wife endangered by people he had grown to hate. So could it simply have been Angela, rather than some unknown go-between, who had asked Ernie to persuade me to leave? And now, worried at the thought of further violence, reluctant to use threats against me, was she doing the only thing she could think of, staying close to me, distracting me from the truth? It was more plausible than anything I had imagined so far. And more frightening.

I heard her saying my name. 'Billy?'

'Yes?'

'Don't fall asleep on me.'

'I'd love to.'

The place was filling up and the noise was building. I was being pulled along by the current, drinking too much, too quickly. I made two plans. One, to drink no more. The other, to drink more, but to do it more slowly. Hoping in some way to combine the two, I went out to the cloakroom, filled a basin with cold water and dipped my face in it. A man stood over an enamel stall, peeing in a gush.

'This is where all the big nobs hang out,' he said.

I was always confused by this. No matter how often I had heard it said, I never knew how to reply and used to wonder if I was expected to look.

I came back into the bar, walking with all the careful balance of the almost-drunk, so intent on carrying it off that I had almost reached the table before realizing that Johnny was there. Not sitting, but leaning far over to reach his sister's eye-level, talking hard. With his arms planted tautly on the table and his back running straight to the broad rump and stiff thick legs, he looked like the head ape, laying down the law to the family, comic and dangerous. Angela's hand was held up like a policeman's, behind his back. It may not have been meant as a warning, but that was how I chose to take it, feeling that this was not the moment for a reunion. So I changed course and began pushing my way past other tables in a wide detour, trying to look as if I knew where I was going. Which of course carried me into the path of Johnny as he broke abruptly away from our table and towards his own.

For a moment, he stood scowling as we faced each other in the narrow space between the tables. Almost involuntarily, I pushed out a hand. 'How are you, Johnny?'

Johnny pushed his own hand forward, then thought better of

it and pulled it back, but he made no attempt to move past.

'I saw you earlier,' I said. 'I don't think you knew me.'

Still Johnny never spoke. I went on talking rubbish. 'It's been a long time,' I said. 'Not long enough' would have been the response to maintain the intellectual level, but Johnny stayed quiet.

'Well maybe I'll see you later in the weekend,' I said.

Johnny spoke at last. 'You'll be sorry if you do,' he said.

He moved his good arm to brush me aside. It looked gentle, but maybe because I had been fearing the worse, I stumbled into a chair and knocked it over. Johnny walked on and back to his table. As I picked up the chair, Angela appeared and took my arm.

'You shouldn't have egged him on,' she said.

'Sorry if it looked that way.'

She seemed not to consider apologizing for her brother, but she offered an explanation.

'I don't think Johnny likes you.'

'But he hasn't seen me for thirty years.'

'He never liked you.' She smiled, with something like family pride. 'You remember the fight about the plums?'

I remembered vividly. But I could not believe that a schoolboy squabble could ferment over thirty years into the kind of bitterness I had seen on Johnny's face. Still, I let it go. Whatever Angela might let slip about her friends, she would never say anything to incriminate her brother. If Johnny had done something criminal, she would do anything to protect him, especially if, as I now believed, her whole purpose in being with me tonight was to stop him from doing it again. There was still the most of a glass of whiskey on the table, but I left it there.

'It isn't that I don't like your friends,' I told her. 'Not to mention your relations. But couldn't we go some place where there's a few less of them about?'

She was standing close, so that our bodies touched. 'How few?'

'None at all, for preference.'

'I know just the place.'

She swayed away and I swayed after her, muzzy with noise and whiskey. Afterwards, I was never quite able to piece together the journey we took in the car. I could only assume that, having left the Roadhouse, we drove back to town, but that this time we drove through the Square and turned down Riverside to the lough shore. In a rare fit of prudence, I must have given Angela the keys, because I was in the passenger seat when I was shaken awake by someone, and found myself looking out on a view I had last seen thirty-one years earlier. It was that part of the lough shore where the boats went out fishing for eels and pollock. But now we were on a narrow surfaced road which had then been no more than a path of trodden-down grass. On the right, where I remembered hayfields, was flat hard earth with dusty tufts of grass, and beyond, running out of view, hedges of veronica enclosing the boxy back gardens of bungalows, two by two. But on the left the shapes were still the same, the rows of fishermen's huts, the narrow slipways and the long reeds which seemed to sway from habit, since there was no breeze.

I must have seen all this in the headlights of the car, which kept flicking on and off for a while after we had stopped. I remember thinking it was like sitting in a lighthouse. At the time, it hardly seemed worth wondering why I was there, looking out at brief, half-remembered tableaux. Then suddenly the lights went out and a stronger beam, from somewhere else, threw a shaft of light out over the reeds to the waters of the lough. I shook the sleep from my eyes and turned towards Angela. I reached up, trying to turn her face towards me, but she stiffened and leaned forward in the seat.

'No.'

It could have been a rejection, but it wasn't. She was not even looking at me. I followed her eyes to the hut from whose open doors the light was streaming. Three men came out and approached the car. I shook my head again, searching for my wits, and pulled down the window, a sign of friendship. The snout of a gun was pushed through and rammed against the side of my neck. I wondered if it was an Armalite, as if it mattered. Angela leaned urgently across me.

'No, Dessie!'

The appeal, I thought, seemed to put her on my side. Yet she had brought me here. Even in my fuzzy state, that much was plain. And she knew them. They were expecting her. I could see no more of Dessie than arm and midriff and I had no inclination to move my head for a better view. Two other men stood a little way off, a tall and a short silhouette against the stream of light from the hut. The tall man spoke.

'Easy, Dessie.'

The man came forward, moved Dessie's gun barrel to one side and leaned his head to the window. He smiled. An expression I remembered well, the lips compressed, the eyes narrowing upwards, the short black sidelocks, the skin stretched tightly on bony temples.

'He could be armed,' said Dessie.

Without taking his eyes off me, the man at the window motioned Dessie away. In this light, at least, his face did not appear to have changed at all in thirty years, though from his nostrils to the corners of his mouth there were deep lines that had not been there before. He had the complexion of a man who shaved several times a day without ever quite stemming the growth and, though he looked as if he smiled less often now, I could not have mistaken him. But there was nothing of the relief I should have felt on finding an old friend in such frightening terrain. To tell the truth, I felt more chilled now. When eventually I spoke, I tried to show relief, some faint hope that all the misunderstandings would now be cleared up.

'Glad to see you, Tommy,' I said.

The chief buck cat, Annie had called him. The Colonel. Tommy McGoldrick. I remembered the McGoldricks so well. Tommy the strong one, and his brother Dan. Whoever else was here, Dan would not be among them. That much I knew.

I remembered the last day I had met Dan here. Perhaps on this very spot....

CHAPTER 9

Saturday, 7 June 1941

The prickly grass of the lough shore has softened under the warmth of my body. My grief at the loss of the gobstoppers has been soaked up by the Pope and Cassie Doran, but my hand still stings. It never occurs to me to curse my granny. It would be like cursing God. My eyes are half-closed and I am staying that way, with some idea that if I can lie here and not move till next pay-day comes round, I will have lost nothing. I keep wishing that Uncle Stevie had been there. He would not have allowed it to happen, not for any love he has for *me*, but because he always takes sides against my granny.

'Are you not at the pictures?'

Opening my eyes, I see Dan McGoldrick standing over me. Dan is skinny and wears glasses. He has a habit of asking you things and looking away as if he doesn't care whether you answer or not. But if you don't answer, he asks you again.

'Why are you not at the pictures?'

I know I will have to tell him, no matter how long and boring the telling will be. So I go over the whole story of my granny and Cassie Doran's shop, leaving out the part about the dog. At the end he says nothing, but I know he feels sorry for me because that's the way he is. Soft. His brother Tommy is different. Tommy will laugh at the story, if he bothers to listen at all.

But the others in the gang are sorry for both the McGoldricks, because their parents are very religious and believe that the best way to prepare for heaven is to get in as much suffering as they can here on earth. Tommy has his own mind and he has learnt to go through the motions of the Brethren of the Elect of God without believing anything. But Dan is no good at pretending. I know he is religious, but not in the same way as the other Brethren. He worries about things that never worry the rest of us. Famine. And cruelty to horses. He has even shamed us by crying at the pictures, at parts the rest of us find boring. Tommy is very smart at seeming to obey all the rules of the Brethren when other Brethren are looking, but Dan has no such skill. He is always being punished for looking out through the tall windows of the Gospel Hall when his head should be bent in prayer, a slip that Tommy would never make. And still, if their religion was to be judged by the standards of the Ten Commandments, Dan would come out far ahead, because he breaks none of them.

Tommy, on the other hand, takes the name of the Lord his God in vain. And covets his neighbour's goods. And if our Sunday School teacher is right about False Gods, Tommy may be breaking that one as well. She says that any excessive pride in your accomplishments is a False God. And Tommy takes excessive pride in farting. I'm not sure if farting can be called a False God, but there is no sure way of finding out. You can't go around asking your Sunday School teacher about farting. Tommy says there is no Commandment saying 'Thou shalt not fart', and you can't argue with that.

'She took them all away?' Dan and his questions. 'Forty-three of them?'

'Yeah. Oul bitch.'

'You shouldn't say that.'

'Why not? She *is* an oul bitch.'

'It's against the Fifth Commandment,' says Dan.

'No it's not. The Fifth Commandment says you're to honour

89

your father and your mother. It doesn't say anything about your granny.'

'It's the same.'

Dan looks away. He has this habit of saying things and then not bothering to defend them. He knows he's right and that's enough. It makes him a hard person to argue with, but I do my best.

'If you *think* your granny's an oul bitch, you might as well say so.'

He says nothing, so I take the argument a step further.

'Your mother's an oul bitch if it comes to that.'

Dan says nothing. He just goes on looking out over the lough. If I said this to Tommy, he would do one of two things. He would agree with me, or throw me in the lough. You knew where you stood with Tommy.

'What are you lookin' out there for?'

'Just looking,' says Dan. 'Do you know what's out there?'

'A lot of water. And Sammy Laird's boat.'

'Do you know where the lough came from?'

'Yeah, my da told me. Finn McCool the giant was annoyed with somebody in England and he picked up a handful of muck to throw at him and the hole he made was Lough Neagh and the muck landed in the sea and made the Isle of Man.'

Dan shakes his head. 'Na...' he says softly. 'That's only a yarn.'

'You're not going to start readin' me out of the Bible are you?'

'Na... Will I tell you?'

'You might as well.'

I turn over on my stomach, so that he won't see me not listening.

'There was this King—,' he begins, and I stop him in his tracks.

'There was no King in Ireland.'

'Indeed there was. There was plenty of them, one for each Province and a High King over them all. This was the King of Munster—'

'You mean he was in the Free State?'

'Yeah, Munster—'

'That's all right then if it's the Free State. There was never a King in Ulster.'

'Well, there was,' he says, 'but it doesn't matter. This was the King of Munster.'

And he goes on and on. I give up trying to annoy him with interruptions because it never works. I have heard it all before, the story of the ancient city on the lough floor, a city that was drowned in the water when some stupid woman left the cover off the well. My mind is on real things like money and gobstoppers when he stops and I realize that he has come to the end. I wait a moment to see if he will go on, but he just sits there. I feel I ought to make some comment.

'Load of shite,' I say. But it's no good. You can't have a fight with Dan. 'You don't really believe all that?'

He turns to stare at me. 'I've seen it,' he says.

'You must be mental.'

'I swear I've seen it. The houses and the barns. As clear as I see *you*. You see it better at night, especially if there's a moon.'

He says nothing for a minute, then – 'There's a moon tonight.'

'Do you mean you go out on the lough at night?'

'Plenty of times. I could show you if you like.'

He turns to me, really steamed up about it. 'Will you come and I'll show you?'

'Your bum's out the window,' I tell him. This is my honest opinion, but I'm curious. 'Has anybody else seen it?'

'Plenty of people.'

'Who?'

For the first time, Dan looks uneasy.

'Name one that's seen it,' I say.

91

'Jimmy,' he whispers.

'Jimmy who?'

'Jimmy Lamont.'

I roll about the grass repeating the name and laughing. To have Jimmy Lamont for his only witness should tell him that he's just lost the argument, but he seems not to see it that way. He just waits for me to finish my performance to speak again, in the same quiet voice.

'Will you come? Tonight?'

'Maybe.' I stand up now, feeling much better.

'Come on, the pictures are out.'

I start running over the hummocky grass and Dan follows.

It is about a mile from where we have been lying on the lough shore to the point where the Sixmilewater River enters the lough. The broad grassy verge of the river narrows here to a path running along the backs of the houses on Riverside. The houses are so close to the river that the path hugs the back walls on one side and drops sheer to the river on the other. The upper stories of the houses jut out over the river and I sometimes wonder what stops them from breaking off and falling in. Dan and I are walking along this path when a voice calls to us from above.

'Hey Specky!'

We look up and see Hughie Brown's face framed in a small round hole cut into the underside of one of the overhanging gables, looking down at us. Hughie is the leader of a rival gang at school, but there is no reason why we can't be polite, so I reply. 'What are you doing, Turdface?'

'Fishing,' says Hughie, and, moving his head slightly, he drops a line with a lead sinker into the water a few feet from where we are standing. He is actually fishing through his lavatory seat. Most of the houses on Riverside have this sort of lavatory, a hole in a kind of wooden bench over the river. The boys who live in these houses try a little fishing from time to time, but they never catch anything, which is not really surprising. When fish have a whole river to swim in, they can't be expected to hang around under Hughie Brown's bog-hole.

'Why are you not at the pictures?'

It is Dan who asks this and I begin to wonder if it is the only question he knows.

'Band practice,' says Hughie. 'Where are ye for?'

'Up the town.'

'I'll see ye round the front.'

His head disappears and we go on walking, glancing carefully upwards as we go, in case of treachery. Hughie is an important figure at school and it will do us no harm at all to be seen with him. His father is a top Orangeman, who carries the banner in front of the largest Lodge in the district. Hughie carries the pennon that flies from the side-staff and he has learned to imitate the lilting zig-zag movement of the banner-carriers. He also plays the flute and is already a member of the Reverend Hugh Hanna Memorial Flute Band. To be strictly accurate, he does not really *play* the flute. He is what is known as a *dummy* flute, which means that he goes through all the motions of puffing his cheeks, fingering and even knocking out dummy spittle, without ever actually blowing. All bands have dummy flutes, to make up the numbers, and it is not easy to pick out the real players.

Hughie has always suffered because of this awful poem we're taught in first class. I think every child in Ulster has to learn it.

He's gone to school, wee Hughie,
And him not four.
Sure I saw the fright was in him

As he left the door....
He took a hand of Denny
And a hand of John,
With Joe's oul coat upon him,
Och the poor wee man....

And it goes on and on like that. So since First Class, Hughie has had to put up with being called Wee Hughie. He is actually not very big, but he gets away with a lot by claiming to have a knowledge of jujitsu, which he has learned by close study of his screen hero, Mr Moto, the Japanese detective. He tries to alarm people by going about with hooded eyes, another of Mr Moto's tactics.

He is waiting for us at his front gate and together we walk up Riverside till we reach the Square. At the corner, outside Furey's pub, we stop and join a group of men standing in a semi-circle, grinning, as they watch Jimmy Lamont going through his routine. Jimmy is a looney who lives with his mother in Ballymena, and, like all looneys, his age is hard to tell, forty or fifty. He is tall and skinny and wears wellington boots stuffed with newspapers all year round. Every morning he walks the six miles from Ballymena to Duncairn and spends the day going round the shops collecting empty cardboard boxes. Then he walks back to Ballymena in the evening, wreathed in boxes. He says he gives them to his mother, but what she does with them no one has ever found out.

They say Jimmy knows the lough better than any of the fishermen. Sometimes, instead of walking home to Ballymena, he goes down to the lough shore at night and sits with the fishermen. Few of the fishermen bother to learn to swim, but Jimmy often jumps in and swims about, without removing a stitch of clothing or even a boot. They enjoy watching him, and Jimmy loves to please.

For an hour or so every day, he takes up his position outside Furey's pub and talks to anyone who will listen. Although the things he says are always the same, there is usually a fair audience and Jimmy enjoys the limelight.

'Too far to walk to Ballymena,' says Jimmy.

'It is, Jimmy, it is.' The audience grins encouragingly.

'Six mile there and six mile back. Too far.'

'How many miles is that, Jimmy?' someone asks.

'What's six and six?' says somebody else. But Jimmy knows his lines and won't be side-tracked.

'They should shift Ballymena nearer Duncairn,' he says.

'They should, Jimmy, they surely should.'

He has reached his punch line. 'Or shift Duncairn nearer Ballymena.'

He looks eagerly for his laugh and gets it. And the success goes to his head. He becomes excited and starts saying his patter in the wrong order. Everything he says he punctuates with spitting. His head darts about like a sparrow's, but the range is always the same, so that after a short time there is a perfect half-circle of spits on the footpath and no one crosses the line for fear of being spat on. Charlie has estimated Jimmy's spit at six feet and goes on from that to say that the area of the semi-circle is therefore 56.7 square feet, which is typical of Charlie. He'd put years on you.

As Dan and Hughie and I arrive, Jimmy's performance is nearing its end and the audience is breaking up. He is gathering up his boxes and preparing to move on when I tap his arm.

'Hey, Jimmy.'

'Too far to walk to Ballymena,' he tells me.

'Dan says you've seen the city under the lough.'

'Cut it out, Billy,' says Dan, embarrassed.

Jimmy looks bewildered.

'Tell us about it, Jimmy. What's it like?'

'Go on, Jimmy,' says Dan, miserable. 'Tell him.'

'I seen the....' Jimmy hesitates, searching for the words. He starts over.

'I seen the....'

'The round towers' – Dan prompts him.

'I seen the roundy towers and the pointy spires,' says Jimmy, getting into his stride. 'And the wee houses with the weeds growin' out of the chimleys. True as God.'

He looks at Dan for approval and Dan nods. 'I know you did, Jimmy.'

Jimmy gets excited as he remembers something new. 'And there was one night in the full of the moon I was out in Sammy Laird's boat and didn't his line get caught and didn't I go in after it, a mile or two down I had to go, and do you know where I found the hook?'

We all shake our heads. 'It was stickin' through the winda of a jewellers' shop.'

Hughie bursts out laughing and Jimmy is delighted and laughs back. He wonders for a moment why Dan is not laughing, so Dan gives him a kind of smile and walks away. Hughie and I follow and I go on tormenting Dan about his crazy stories and his crazy friends all the way down the Square to the picture-house. The pictures are out and among the crowd we see Tommy and Charlie and Ernie. Ernie is re-enacting a scene from one of the films, in case the others missed it, but when we come up to them, he stops, hand on holster, and looks at Hughie.

'What are you doing with *him*?'

Hughie is hooding his eyes like mad, but it is not having much effect. The rest of us are not sure what to do. We probably prefer

Hughie to Ernie, but we have to be loyal to the gang. Loyalty is a big thing round here.

'He's all right,' says Tommy, and it is accepted as the final ruling. Tommy doesn't say much, but what he says goes. So with Hughie's crisis over, they start asking why I wasn't at the pictures and my own crisis begins. I know that if I tell what really happened, I will get no sympathy, especially from Ernie, and I haven't had time to invent a story.

'Couldn't be bothered,' I say, trying to suggest that I've gone off the pictures.

'Where's your money then?'

They are after me like bloodhounds, but then Dan does this really strange thing, something that goes to show how peculiar he really is.

'He spent it on us,' he says.

'On who?' asks Ernie.

Charlie comes in to point out what Ernie means is 'On whom?' This is Charlie all over, always correcting people.

'He spent it on Hughie and me,' says Dan. 'Isn't that right, Hughie?'

'That's right,' says Hughie. He knows it isn't right at all, but takes the chance of bringing Ernie down a peg.

'We spent it on cider.'

This is the best thing Hughie could have said, for Ernie is always demanding cider for the gang and Charlie always vetoes it.

'Well,' says Ernie, 'you're not reading my *Hotspur*.'

He is doing his best, but he knows he is beaten. Dan has got me out of a tight spot and I don't know why, after the jeering I gave him earlier. Anyway, they all start telling us what we missed in the pictures, how Tailspin Tommy has been left unconscious in the cockpit with blood coming out of his nose and his plane diving vertically into a volcano, what Hopalong Cassidy said to Windy and what Windy said to Smiley, how Hughie Louis beat Buddy Baer in the Newsreel. I give a good show of no interest in any of these events and they grow tired of it.

It is not quite four o'clock and we have to decide how to spend the rest of the afternoon. The drums will start at six and there's a fair chance that both Hughie's father and our Uncle Stevie will take part. It will go on into the small hours of the morning and it will sound as if the town is under bombardment by heavy cannon. No one will be able to sleep, so we'll be allowed to stay up, but for now we are left with two hours to fill.

'We have a Meeting,' says Dan.

This is greeted with groans and jeers. The Brethren of the Elect of God spend most of their time having Meetings, in their Meeting Hall, meeting one other. Almost every other human activity is sinful and the Meetings help to put in the time while they wait for the joy of the life to come. Strangely, although they are careful to steer clear of sinners in their daily lives, they welcome non-Brethren, especially children, to the Meetings.

You pay a price for this, since you are expected to sit through a lot of praying and singing and maybe even to give your testimony, in which you tell them all that you have accepted Christ into your life. They don't take your word for this easily, so your story must be backed up with accounts of the sinful depths you had reached before the Lord raised you up. I have tried it myself, telling the congregation that until quite recently I had been a drunkard, an idolater and a fornicator, but no one seemed too impressed. All in all, a Meeting is poor entertainment for a summer's day, but the Brethren, despite their other faults, are very generous with the tea and buns after the Meeting, so Dan's announcement deserves some thought.

'What sort of Meeting?' I ask, when the jeers have died down.

'A special one,' says Dan. 'Conversions.'

'Will there be buns?' I ask, getting down to essentials.

'Suppose so,' says Dan.

While we are all standing, trying to decide, Tommy tells Dan to come on and they walk away. They have to go, of course, and the rest of us simply follow Tommy, as we usually do.

CHAPTER 10

Friday, 30 June 1972

Now, half a lifetime on, I was seeing Tommy again, still leading, others following. As I stared at him, the stock of Dessie's rifle was again pushed through the open window, catching me below the ear. I felt blood first, pain later.

'Easy, Dessie,' said Tommy. It could have been a military command, but he spoke the words quietly, like a man training his dog.

'You're back, Billy,' he said.

I thought of replying to that. Something about the welcome home I'd had. But I decided against it.

'What has you here?'

'Pleasure.'

'We'd like to believe that,' said Tommy. 'We'd all like to believe it.'

'I hear you're a commander now,' I said. 'Colonel McGoldrick.'

Tommy said nothing. I turned to Angela, who was looking straight ahead.

'I think Corporal Fusco here should get a citation. She was terrific.'

If I was hoping for a reaction from Tommy, I was disappointed. Just the same calm look, almost regretful.

'Billy,' he said. 'For a man that's here on pleasure, you've been asking a lot of questions.'

'I always did, Tommy. Maybe you don't remember.'

'Oh I remember it well. In fact, if I hadn't taken that into account, you'd be at the bottom of the lough by now. You should think yourself lucky.'

'Oh I do. It's a nice feeling, to know you're among friends.'

Tommy straightened and opened the car door. I made no move and a hard hand gripped my neck and jerked me out of the car, leaving me face down on the grass. I looked up at the car to see Angela still staring rigidly ahead, her knuckles white on the steering-wheel. As the car door was pushed shut, a heavy old-fashioned boot caught me on the side of the neck.

'Get up,' said Dessie.

The faint hope that Tommy McGoldrick, my old friend, would never harm me, had faded into panic. Tommy seemed not to notice Dessie's actions. It was as if he saw Dessie as he would see a dog trained to catch rats, who could be controlled only by allowing him small regular doses of aggression.

I got to my feet and faced Dessie, too frightened to show fear. A hard moist hand stretched over my face, two black-rimmed fingers probing into my eyes. As I tried to sway back, the heel of another hand caught me on the underside of the nose, striking upwards. I lost balance and sprawled against the side of the car, where Tommy still stood.

'That'll do you, Dessie,' said Tommy quietly. 'Wait in the hut.'

'Shout out if you want me,' said Dessie, and spat.

It wasn't a gesture. He just needed to spit. Tommy walked away towards the lough and spoke over his shoulder.

'We'll take a walk, Billy.'

He seemed to take it for granted that he would be obeyed, as if rank had gone to his head. And then I remembered that he had always been that way. I stood for a moment, weighing the odds between a show of spirit and another belt of Dessie's Armalite.

'You'd better go with him, Billy.'

It was the voice of the shorter man, speaking for the first time. I walked towards him and the face emerged from shadow. A grey

101

face, one or two days of stubble merging with thick hair, white-grey like ashes. He was chewing gum and showing a faint smile in which I thought I could see warmth, though I couldn't be sure of anything.

'It's Hughie Brown,' he said.

For a moment, I forgot my surroundings and took his hand. 'Hughie, I'd never have known you.'

'You've changed a bit yourself, Billy.'

'Do you still play cricket?'

'I do surely. We've a match tomorrow.'

'I'll come and watch.'

'You won't, Billy.' He spoke sadly. 'One way or another, you'll see no match.'

I stared at him, trying to understand. 'You'd better go on,' he said.

Tommy stood waiting for me, a dark shape in the light from the hut behind. I went to join him and we walked together into the darkness where the lough shore came out of its ellipse and ran straight to the west. Tommy walked a little ahead, not looking back. For whatever pig-headed reason, I was determined not to speak first.

'All right, Billy, you've got questions.'

'Sure. Who made you a Colonel?'

God knows from where I dredged up such a stupid question, but Tommy seemed to take it seriously.

'We're fighting a war here, Billy. Every army has its chain of command.' He paused. 'But that's not what you wanted to know, is it?'

'No.'

'You're a Republican now?'

'I live in a Republic. I don't make a career of it.'

'But you have your loyalties....'

And as he began to talk, it occurred to me that it was not really directed at me. It was more like a prepared statement. One he had delivered before.

'We've lived on loyalty up here for near a hundred year. Some would say three hundred. And now there's nobody left to be loyal to. We've lived in fear of murder and rebellion as long as we've been here and we've stuck to our tradition. We've been loyal to the Crown, but the Crown has never been loyal to *us*. We have enemies to the south and more enemies to the east and the only place left is the sea. We're not English and we're not Irish, but we're here and we'll stay here. And what we have we hold, though God knows we haven't much.'

He was silent again, but I held my tongue, knowing there was no point; he just wouldn't be interested. The mantra resumed.

'So when Bill Craig says that we'll fight and kill to keep our way of life, he's talking our language. We have nothing more to lose. They took away our democratic rights when they abolished Stormont. Any day now they'll call a truce and start to trade with the IRA. When that happens, there'll be nobody to fight for us only ourselves. And we're ready to fight. We have to be.'

He seemed to remember my presence and turned to me.

'I hear what you're saying,' I said, searching for an answer which I knew wouldn't matter anyway. I considered using the old man's line again – 'You're wrong, Tommy, but no matter' – but I thought that might be pushing my luck, and didn't.

'It's just … not my fight,' I said finally.

'You're right. It isn't.'

'So why drag me into it? Why beat me up? Force of habit is it?'

'I never laid a hand on you—'

'Oh for Christ's sake, Tommy—'

'No need to swear.'

It was such a weird thing to say, I might have laughed, if something in his expression had not checked me.

'You didn't do much to stop Dessie,' I said.

'Dessie's a good man. His best mate lost a leg in the Abercorn.'

I searched my memory. I had seen it on the news, three, four months ago. Abercorn Restaurant and Bar. I remembered it well, great pub on Castle Street, a no-warning bomb, three killed, scores mutilated.

Tommy went on talking, but he seemed now, for the first time, to be talking just to me, rather than a public meeting.

'You see, Billy, we're on our own now. And in a war situation you haven't the time to sit down and make considered judgements. If you're not for us, you're against us, simple as that. That's the way I want my men to think and it's the way Dessie thinks. I won't change him.'

For a moment, the moon emerged from behind a cloud and went back in. There was a glimpse of Tommy's face and it had no expression.

'We should turn back,' he said.

I knew that if I was to have any answers, it must be now. As we turned to go back, I spoke quickly.

'I came here for no reason, Tommy. Except maybe to see old friends....' I did a quick re-think – 'Well, they're not friends any more, I understand that; they have more important things, at least more important to *them*....'

I cursed the whiskey as I floundered about, trying to keep to the point.

'But that doesn't explain why I've been watched and threatened ever since I got here. And dragged down here and beaten. Why?'

He took time to reply, as if he considered the question futile, but that courtesy required him to answer.

'We're serious, Billy. The things we're fighting for are more important than any one man's feelings ... or that he might call his rights.' He spat out the last word as if it was a curse. When he went on, he was back in his old detached way of talking.

'It's sometimes hard to make people see how serious we are. Sometimes we have to do things we don't like doing, just to make it clear.'

I had an idea that this was as close as he would come to any expression of regret, but it was not an apology I needed. I had to know the answer to my first question: Why me? But I didn't ask it again. What was the point?

'The funny part of it is, Billy, I'm inclined to believe you.'

'Believe what?'

'That you didn't come here to spy on us. Actually I never thought that, though the lads did.'

'Which lads?'

'Johnny, Ernie. Even wee Hughie. Big shot on the Southern TV, turning up out of the blue.'

I smiled at that, shaking my head modestly.

'You can search me for cameras, Tommy....'

'I told them that. But they worry you see. And then when you started to ask questions—'

'Wouldn't *you* have asked questions?'

'Ah well I'm not *you*. The fact is, you came here at a very inconvenient time for us. There's things happening that we'd prefer to keep to ourselves. You're a danger to us, whether you intended it or not. We want rid of you, Billy, and we'll do it one way or another.'

'But why? Is it because of Mikey Doran?'

Again no answer. I was learning that Tommy never answered.

'I never even *knew* Mikey Doran,' I told him.

'You know *us*.'

105

We had reached a low wall running alongside a slipway. Twenty yards away, chinks of light appeared in the window of the hut where Dessie, Hughie, and presumably Angela, were waiting. Tommy stopped and sat on the wall, allowing his last words to hang on the air.

'I knew you once,' I said.

He went on as if he had not heard.

'You were always a contrary wee bugger, Billy. Once you got hold of a thing you wouldn't let go…. And I liked you for that. It was a good thing in a wee lad, but it's a foolish way to be these times.'

He looked out to the lough.

'I could order you killed, but I don't want to.'

He went on before I had time to react, express my appreciation.

'So no more questions. I'll tell you as much as I can. If you try to find out any more … well, we haven't the time to waste on diversions the like of yourself. You understand me?'

I nodded. A gentlemen's agreement. No need for anything in writing.

'You heard they bombed Johnny's bar?'

'I heard.'

He produced a pipe and began to knock it out on the stone wall, like an old man in a chimney corner starting to tell a tale.

'Maybe Mikey was shot in reprisal,' he said.

'Well I guessed that much,' I said. 'But why Mikey Doran? He wasn't a Provo.'

'Who says?'

'What does it matter? You know it's true.'

He puffed his pipe a moment before replying. 'He probably wasn't.'

I waited for him to go on, but he simply looked off again towards the lough, as if he had lost interest.

'So why in God's name was he shot?'

There was a long silence before he answered.

'He was a legitimate target.'

'You mean – he was a Catholic?'

'He wasn't with us.'

I remembered the words and said them out. 'He that is not with me is against me....'

Tommy nodded. 'Matthew Twelve, Verse Thirty,' he said, and smiled faintly. 'It wasn't all wasted you see.'

I opened my mouth to reply, but he turned sharply on me.

'No more, Billy. I said I'd tell you what I can. Don't interrupt me again.'

I felt I was back at school, and I'd been called up to the blackboard. I was not to swear, I was not to interrupt. If I did, I would be shot, expelled from the world. The quiet hard voice went on.

'In a war situation, the fight must be carried on, not only against the enemy, but against their passive sympathizers. The IRA draws its sympathy and support from the Catholic population. Every member of the Catholic Community is therefore a legitimate target.'

It was coming out like a litany. The ritual phrases: passive sympathizers, legitimate target.

'We have to avenge the spilling of innocent blood.'

I wondered if he realized he was using Cromwell's phrase.

'All right, Tommy,' I said. 'I've listened to you. Just one thing I don't understand. Mikey's gone now; you've evened the score. Isn't it over now? How can I harm you?'

'But it's not over.'

There was a new note, almost of regret.

'The man who shot Mikey Doran must be punished.'

CHAPTER 11

I thought at first that I had misheard. I started to speak, but Tommy held up a hand. He hadn't finished.

'I don't know if I can make you understand this, Billy. As a matter of fact, I don't know why I'm trying. Maybe if I *could* make you understand....'

He shook his head, as if he had caught himself indulging a weakness.

'You see, if a cause is worth fighting for, it's worth living up to. We're fighting for the Protestant tradition, and we'll fight it by Protestant standards.'

'Like murder?'

It had come out without my intending it. I braced myself, but he just shook his head.

'No murders. Acts of war. The one thing we can't do is tarnish the cause. There must be no personal gain, no motive that damages our ideals. We're not in existence to gratify the appetites of criminals.'

I could tell that they were words quoted, words he had seen written down or that he had written once himself.

'The man who shot Mikey Doran was a criminal. He brought shame on us. And he'll be punished.'

'But he was one of your own. Carrying out orders.'

Tommy was shaking his head. 'I thought you'd know more than that, Billy. You and your TV lectures about the paramilitaries. Operations are carried out by individual volunteers or by small groups. They report back only on completion of a mission.'

'So he was on a mission – why do you call it a crime?'

Tommy shook his head. 'He was on a mission of his own. A mission to rob – and that's a crime. It was in the course of that crime that Mikey Doran was killed.'

I stared at him, and again my mind went back.

'Tommy,' I said, '*you* used to steal, remember? From Russell's shop and Woolworths. You were the best in town. Sweets, jigsaw puzzles, a bottle of ciderette. Once you stole a wheelbarrow—'

'Those were games!' His voice was angry now. 'This is a war, and in a war you have to have rules!'

In time, I supposed, I would grow accustomed to these strange rules: that murder could be a deed of honour and theft a capital crime. There were men who carried such principles into battle like a sword or a shield, a banner or a cross. In Tommy's case there was nothing so fanciful. He held his tablet of stone close and tight, like a welder's mask.

'We don't want thieves,' he went on. 'Men that'll use the cause as a cover for crime. Robbery, extortion, drugs … rape. It's started in Belfast, but I'm going to see it doesn't happen here.'

He said the words in a harsh whisper, willing himself to utter them. It seemed for a moment that it was not Tommy I was hearing, but his father.

'There was a man in Belfast,' he said; 'his name doesn't matter. He spoke out against the thieves and the murderers, the men who were letting us down. He was murdered for speaking out. But the two that did it were beaten senseless when they went to prison. We look after our own, you see.' It seemed a strange way to put it, but there was no hint of irony.

He sucked at his failing pipe. 'Then there was the crowd that shot the informer on the Crumlin Road. They did it in our name and they were right – he was under sentence. Before they did it, they made him watch while they raped his mother. They're in jail now, but when they come out....'

He was using his absent yarn-spinning manner, which seemed to make the things he was saying all the more terrible. But I was still no nearer to knowing what new acts of savagery they were planning in the name of the cause, and why my presence should interfere with their plans. He seemed to guess what I was thinking and turned to face me. He was the Colonel again, reading the orders of the day.

'Tomorrow night there'll be an inquiry into the circumstances of Mikey Doran's death. If there's any evidence of crime, the volunteer responsible will face a court-martial. Any sentence of the court-martial will be carried out immediately. No one outside the court can be privy to the proceedings. Any person attempting to interfere will be dealt with summarily.'

He stood still for a moment, and I thought he was going to say 'Dismiss!', like in the Scouts. But he just turned abruptly away.

'Wait, Tommy.'

He stopped, without turning round. I could see, from the muscles on his neck, that I was pushing my luck again.

'You didn't answer my first question, Tommy. Why *me*?' He stayed motionless and I waited for an answer, but none came.

'Who did it, Tommy?'

Still no answer.

'It was one of your own men. Do you know which?'

I knew now that he would tell me nothing, but I persisted.

'Does he know *himself* about tomorrow? Does he know he has only one day to live?'

'Stay,' he said, as if talking to his dog, and started walking back to the hut. He pushed open the door and from behind him I saw Dessie and Hughie come quickly to their feet.

'Colonel,' said Dessie, and saluted.

I thought of other Colonels. Blimp, Gaddafi, Papadopoulos. And Colonel Sanders, with his chickens. Tommy didn't seem to fit any of these, but Gaddafi came closest. He spoke briefly to Hughie and Dessie, then turned, without a glance in my direction, and walked towards the car, where I saw that Angela was sitting. Hughie spoke, from inside the hut.

'Come on in, Billy, out of the cold.' He spoke softly, as if a cup of tea was on the way, and a long leisurely chat about old times. And he began to talk in that way, almost reassuring me.

'Do you remember Miss MacMurray, and old Sailsey?'

He spoke as he always had, hardly opening his lips, so that all his 'o's and 'a's came out the same, rhyming with 'lawn'.

'He was a hawrd mawn old Sailsey.'

He was inviting me to reminisce with him about our teachers in the old days, but Dessie, twenty years younger, had no time for nostalgia. He was busy with two short lengths of thin rope, the kind you use for clotheslines, joining the two of them into a figure of eight.

'Give us,' he said and, grabbing my arm, slipped one of the loops over my wrist and pulled it tight, leaving the other loop dangling. He did the same with my other wrist and told me to get up. Hughie went on talking.

'Do you remember the dawncin' clawss?'

'For Christ's sake, Hughie, what's he doing?'

'Just do what he tells you, Billy; it'll be far easier.'

I was being pushed into the middle of the floor and my left arm stretched upwards towards two metal hooks in the beam two feet above my head. Dessie threw the loose loop over one hook and tightened it. It was an uncomfortable stretch, and when he took my right wrist and fastened it to the second hook, I felt my ribs contracting and my lungs straining.

'Hop and back and one-two-three-four.'

Hughie was remembering the dancing lessons.

'You remember oul McConnell, the dawncin' mawster. Such a dirty oul mawn that was. The way he stood you in front of him to folly the steps and run your hawnd up against his willy john. You remember?'

To gain some relief, I had brought my legs together and stood on my toes, exhaling as the strain on my chest eased.

'Hop and back and one-two-three-four, you remember, Billy?'

'I remember.'

'Open your legs,' Dessie said, standing close behind me, an iron bar in his hand.

'Open them, Billy,' said Hughie.

I shook my head, but in the same moment a heavy blow from the iron bar crashed against my kidneys. I kicked out, catching Dessie on the shin. He swore and the bar came down again, in the same place. I would have cried out again, but I didn't have the breath. As I sucked in the air, the pain increased and I knew that drowning must feel like this. There was a kick at my ankle.

'Open them.'

I shuffled my feet until they were a few inches apart, closed my eyes and allowed my head to fall forward. I heard the sound of the door opening and twisted my head to look.

'Stay, Hughie. Don't—'

But the door closed quietly behind him, just as Dessie's club whistled up between my knees and into the crotch. My body tried to double up, but it stayed stretched like a bowstring, unable to obey the need to shrink and roll up like a hedgehog. My crotch seemed to melt in the scalding pain, but there was no breath to scream with. Then there was nausea, but I could not have retched, dangling there from my hooks like mutton, shivering and convulsed, alone with Dessie.

My head was jerked back by the hair and something was slipped over my head. It felt like a coal sack of the old kind, tough close-woven hessian, heavy with damp, as if it had lain for a winter on an earth floor. He was gathering its mouth loosely round my neck and tying a drawstring. The darkness was total.

'Where would you like it now?' Dessie's voice, close by. 'Another wee dose in the kidneys maybe?'

There was some reassurance in that. He would hardly propose shooting me in the kidneys. So it was just a beating.

'Or the balls.'

The voice still came from somewhere close, but from behind. I listened for some sign of movement, but there was none. He was talking again.

'Maybe you'd like a wee message carved on your back. You could get your friends to read it for you.'

My back stiffened involuntarily and the bar crashed on the backs of my knees. The pain of the blows was bad enough. Worse still was not to know where the next would fall. It was a struggle to make my legs support me, to shift the burden from my arms and chest. I could make out small movements behind me, as if Dessie was positioning himself for another blow with the bar, but where would it come? My back, I was sure of it, flexed the muscles and waited, but no. I tried to relax the muscles, but they refused to obey. Still nothing. Maybe the stomach, the throat, the balls again. One by one, every muscle knotted with cramp and fear, until I was ready to beg him to hit me again, anywhere he wanted, anything to ease the waiting. But no blow came and I knew it was crueller that way. I don't know how long I stayed there, stretched, half-standing, half-hanging, knowing what it was to be literally rigid with fear.

He was doing something with his rifle, the breech, the thing, whatever you called it. The only feeling that came to me was that the pain would be immediate and blinding, blowing away the other pains and scattering them into the dark.

'That'll do you.' It was Hughie's voice. He said it like a barber.

Quickly and gently, Hughie removed the hood and untied the cords on my hand. I blinked at the light and saw that Dessie had left. So he wasn't a complete sadist. He hadn't hung around to gloat; the job was done. My knees were still weak and I tried to sit on one of the benches that ran around the walls. It was lower than I had judged and I fell over and lay panting on the floor. Hughie stretched his hand out to help me up, but I knocked it away. It didn't seem to offend him.

'You let him do it,' I said. 'You stood and watched.'

'He had to. Somebody had to.'

'Why? What was it for?'

'You know the oul yarn, Billy. Fella gets married, takes the new wee wife home and beats the lard out of her.'

I knew it, but I hadn't the energy to stop him.

'"What was that for?" says she. "For nothin," says he. "Now God help you if you do anything."'

He seemed disappointed not to get a laugh. So he repeated the punch line and laughed himself, in the way of country people.

'It was only a wee taste, Billy,' he said. 'You'll go back now where you came from.'

I said nothing because I knew it wasn't a question. He got to his feet. 'You'll have to go now, Billy. We're lockin' up.'

I felt like the last customer at closing time. Painfully, I stood and allowed Hughie to guide me to the door. As I emerged, the car lights came on and I saw Tommy and Johnny Fusco standing by the driver's door. Angela was at the wheel. The men were quiet in the way of people who have just been arguing, looking at Hughie and me to avoid looking at each other. I looked at Angela with all the venom I could call up, knowing that venom would have no effect on the others. She looked past me at Tommy.

'Take him home,' he told her.

I told him I would drive myself.

'You wouldn't be able.'

He opened the passenger door and I got in, too tired to argue.

'I'll go with them,' said Johnny.

'No,' said Tommy. He slammed the door shut and leaned in.

'Get sense, Billy. Go back to Dublin.'

'Is there a deadline?'

'No. I don't think you'll annoy us any more. We'll be watching you. What's the use?'

Angela started the car and drove away. No one said good-night.

CHAPTER 12

Saturday, 7 June 1941

The Gospel Hall is fuller than we expect for a hot Saturday afternoon and, as we go in, many of the regular Brethren look round at us, dead suspicious. Mrs Goldrick, a sharp-nosed lady in a mauve twin-set, is seated at the organ playing 'The Old Rugged Cross' on the Dulciana. As she finishes, Mr McGoldrick comes in, raises his arms above his head and calls 'Let us Praise God!'

We all scuffle to our knees and Mr McGoldrick shouts up to God for about a quarter of an hour. He is a small man with wavy silver hair and he smiles a lot in a heavenly kind of way, though he can change suddenly to a scowl when he stops buttering up God and starts to tell Him what a rotten pack of miserable sinners we all are.

Eventually he winds down and we all scramble up, grab the hymn books and start singing 'There were ninety and nine that safely lay in the shelter of the fold'. There appears to be a verse for each of the ninety and nine, but when it is all over, Ernie's watch says only a quarter past four and the tea and buns seem a long way off. From other meetings I've attended, I know that the giving of Testimony should come next and this is usually the highlight of the Meeting, but today, instead of calling on Brother Mahaffy or Sister Todd, Mr McGoldrick himself steps to the edge of the rostrum and looks gravely around the hall.

'Brethren,' he begins, 'we are gathered here today to perform a solemn and glorious ceremony.'

This does not sound as if buns are involved, but Mr

McGoldrick is working up to something very big, to judge by the way he pauses and raises his arms and eyes to heaven.

'The Apostle Paul,' he roars, making us all jump, 'speaks to us of those who changed the truth of God into a lie, and worshipped and served the Creature more than the Creator, who is blessed for ever.'

Another pause. 'Saint John the Divine,' he shouts, 'speaks in his Revelations of that same Creature, and how all nations have drunk of the wine of the wrath of her fornication, and the Kings of the earth are waxed rich through the abundance of her delicacies.'

Another pause. 'That creature, dear Brethren, is Antichrist, the Beast, the Whore of Babylon … the Church of Rome!'

I am just thinking of how much my granny would enjoy this, when he steps down from his rostrum and places his hands on the heads of some people in the front row, out of our view. He lifts his head again.

'We have with us today, dear Brethren, three who have been slaves of that Creature, but have received the gift of sight; three who have heard that voice that Saint John heard from Heaven, saying – "Come out of her, my people, that ye be not partakers of her sins, and that ye partake not of her plagues." Yes, Brethren, they have come to God with contrite hearts, asking to be raised out of the pit, and I humbly thank God that He has chosen me to be his instrument.'

'Amen,' say the Brethren, quite loudly. I throw in a Hallelujah and Tommy hits me a dig with his elbow. Meanwhile Mr Mc-Goldrick walks back to his rostrum and stretches out his arms.

'Come hither,' he says.

And, from the front row, a woman and a man and a little girl go and stand before him, looking up. There is something familiar about them, but I have not seen their faces.

'Rosanna Fusco, Gianni Fusco, Angelica Fusco. Do you—'

Charlie and I break into high-pitched whispers, and angry heads turn towards us. We fall silent, but the excitement remains. Our neighbours, the Fuscos, the Papishes! They're turning, joining the Brethren! What a blow for the Pope!

I edge out into the side aisle to see the face of Leaky, who is not yet six years old, gazing up in fright as Mr McGoldrick thunders over her head.

'Do you abjure and reject the blasphemous heresies and the idolatrous practices of the Church of Rome...?'

There is a lot more of the same. He keeps pausing for breath, and in each of these pauses Mrs Fusco, Gianni and Leaky mutter a quiet 'I do.' Then he opens the enormous Bible at a place near the end and begins to trace the words with his finger.

'Come hither,' he thunders. 'I will show unto thee the judgement of the great whore that sitteth upon many waters.... With whom the Kings of the earth have committed fornication, and the inhabitants of the earth have been made drunk with the wine of her fornication....'

Leaky is picking her nose.

'So he carried me away in the spirit into the wilderness: and I saw a woman sit upon a scarlet-coloured beast, full of names of blasphemy, having seven heads and ten horns. And the woman was arrayed in purple and scarlet colour, and decked with gold and precious stones and pearls, having a golden cup in her hand full of the abominations and filthiness of her fornication....'

Leaky has started to cry.

'And the seven heads are seven mountains, on which the woman sitteth. And the woman whom thou sawest is that great city, which reigneth over the Kings of the earth.' He closes the book with a bang.

'Do you, Rosanna, and you, Gianni, and you, Angelica, solemnly accept Christ, now and for all eternity, as your personal Saviour, rejecting all other intercession by priest or martyr or saint?'

'I do,' from three voices.

'Do you, Rosanna, and you, Gianni, and you, Angelica....'

But I have given up listening. I am looking at Gianni and Leaky, the backs of their heads, wishing I could see their eyes, wondering what has happened to make them do this, wondering if they have felt alone all the time they have lived here, if they believe that what they are doing now will make them less alone, or if maybe, maybe, they have really had a vision of God. And if they have, hoping it's not the same vision as Mr McGoldrick's.

'Do you, Angelica...?'

Imagine, I am thinking. Wee Leaky a Prod. I look at Tommy in the seat beside me and wonder what he is thinking, but his face tells me nothing.

CHAPTER 13

Friday, 30 June 1972

I shifted carefully in the seat of the car, searching for a position in which the various aching parts of my body would feel easier. Beside me, Angela drove carefully, concentrating on the road ahead. Now and then her eyes flickered sideways and I did a small performance, uttering small stifled groans, stiffening suddenly and relaxing with deep exhalations. She produced two cigarettes, lit them expertly from the car lighter on the dashboard and handed me one. What was the last movie I'd seen that in?

'Are you sore?'

I tried to do a bitter laugh, but it became a cough and awoke the sick pain in my crotch.

'I never knew,' she said. 'I swear.'

'Never knew what?'

'They said they wouldn't hurt you. I wouldn't have done it if I'd known.'

'Done what?'

I wasn't helping the conversation much, but I wanted to hear her version, to make her spell out the role she had played. It was the only way I knew to punish her. She had been cast in a role in which women could become heroines, legendary women, leading enemies of the state to their downfall. Risking their all for their country. But I still felt that whatever part she had played, she took no pride in it.

'I know what you think of me,' she said, and I nodded.

'Was the whole thing planned? From the time I arrived?'

'Before you arrived.' There was nothing guarded in the way she spoke. 'I told them you were coming, naturally.'

'And you were to keep an eye on me?'

'No.' But she could see I didn't believe that. 'Not at first,' she went on. 'Not until you'd spoken to Ernie. They asked me to watch you then … not to let you out of my sight.'

'And what did you tell them? That Ernie was right? That I was a danger to the cause?'

'No! I never thought that….'

Her voice was raised, her head shaking. 'When I talked to you about Johnny, it all seemed to be news to you. You didn't seem interested; your mind was on other things. And I told them there was no cause for alarm. I said I thought you were telling the truth.'

I wondered why they had allowed her to drive me back to the hotel. Was there something more she had to find out? Or had she asked Tommy if she could talk to me just once more, to say she was sorry? No, that was grasping at straws. I shook my head vehemently, angry at myself for even imagining —

Her voice broke through. 'I did! You have to believe that!'

She had seen me shaking my head and misread it. I let her go on.

'But then you talked to Ernie and he didn't agree. He said you knew more than you should, that you were pumping him for more … and that you'd have to be dealt with.'

I could see that. I had been foolish with Ernie, deliberately provoking him, playing Dares like a schoolboy.

'And you went along with that?' I said to her.

'No!' She sounded confused and angry. 'I told Tommy you were no danger. You see, Tommy doesn't like Ernie, but he can't take risks. There are men's lives … he has to take everything into account ….'

She broke off, collecting her thoughts. 'Anyway, he had to do

121

something. He asked if I would … look after you this evening.'

'That's a neat way to put it.'

'Just to stay close. I told him I wouldn't spy on you; I wouldn't be any good at it.'

'And Johnny was to be around, just in case.'

'No. At least I don't know. Maybe. I wasn't told.'

'Oh for God's sake, Angela – you mean it was just a chance that we went to that place? Just a coincidence that Johnny happened to show up?'

'Well, all right. I told Tommy I was taking you there, maybe Johnny was told – what does it matter?'

'What does it matter! I've just been practically crucified by a young sadist, a friend of yours, and you ask what does it matter?'

'I didn't mean that. I'm sorry; you're confusing me. I didn't *think* it mattered. It wasn't surprising that Johnny was there, he goes often—'

'But he came over, he talked to you—'

'Yes! I'm his sister!'

We were both shouting each other down. I leaned back, telling myself to ease off, that I would learn nothing this way. We had left the lough shore and we were driving along Riverside. In a moment we would be back in the Square, going into the hotel. She would become her official self, put on her manager's armour. I needed to hear more.

'Pull in here,' I said.

She surprised me by obeying without question. The lights of the Square were visible in the distance, but here it was dark. I turned towards her, tried to cross my legs and wished I hadn't.

'All right, Angela,' I said. 'Suppose I believe you…. There's something else that doesn't tie in. You brought me down there. They were expecting me.'

'Yes.' She seemed for a moment not to know how to go on. 'It was all those questions about Mikey. I couldn't cope. When you went out of the bar, Johnny came over and I told him I didn't know what way to answer you. He said I was to bring you down there. He said it was Tommy's orders. That if you asked questions, I was to bring you to him.' She turned to face me. 'As true as God, Billy, he said nothing would happen. He said Tommy would clear it all up.'

She looked away, embarrassed at showing emotion. 'I thought there would be a bit of a chat – I mean you were kids together – and then we'd go off again. There's a late-night place in Templepatrick; they have dancing. I was going to take you there. I thought you'd enjoy it.'

She sounded less upset by all the violence than by the way her plans for the evening had been spoiled. But that bit about dancing in Templepatrick – it was so naïve, I believed it.

'Tell me, Angela. Am I in the clear now?'

'There's no good asking me; they don't tell me. Maybe, now that you've had a warning.'

'They can't really think I'm that dangerous.'

'Why do you think that?'

'They've left me alone with you.'

She shook her head, glancing in the rear-view mirror. I twisted painfully in the seat and saw the parking lights of another car twenty yards behind.

'Johnny?' I asked.

She nodded. 'He's been behind us all the time. But I don't think Tommy told him to. I think he's just anxious about me.'

And about himself, I thought. Could he be wondering if I was coming closer to the truth?

Ahead, where Riverside joined the Square, a group of teenagers crossed, half-embracing and singing. There was a distant shout or two, the sound of music, the Bacchanalia of a small-town Friday night. It must be quite early, around ten, the pubs emptying, the clubs opening. It was disconcerting to see so much normality. On the lough shore it had seemed like deep night. From far off I hear a dull throbbing sound, like distant thunder, but more constant. I took a few moments to recognize it.

'The Lambegs?'

'Yes.'

'A long time since I heard them.'

'They're not in the town. They'll be here tomorrow night.'

'That should be very fitting.'

She didn't seem to follow. 'They're here every Saturday,' she explained, 'leading up to the Twelfth.'

I shook my head. 'I meant it would be fitting in particular tomorrow night. Isn't it proper to have a roll of drums at an execution?'

'Stop it, Billy.' She reached for the ignition key, but I stopped her. 'You knew about it then?'

'Billy – for your own sake, don't ask any more.'

'And what about *you*? If you know about it, you're in more trouble than I am. Can't you see that?'

'Who told you all this, Billy?'

'Tommy.'

'I don't believe you. He wouldn't.'

'He didn't tell me the vital part. He didn't say who was to get it, but that doesn't matter. Whoever it is, it's murder. Tommy's planning a murder and you know it.'

'No!' She was angry now. 'Not murder. There'll be a fair trial.'

I stared at her in disbelief. I was surprised at her vehemence in defending Tommy. She knew about his activities, far more than I did, but she would not allow herself to believe they could include murder. She accepted all that I might say about the others, but against Tommy, their leader, she would hear nothing. I knew that I had discovered something vital, that I should go on.

'He's a murderer, Angela. Maybe he won't pull the trigger, but he'll give the order, the way he ordered me to be beaten tonight.'

'No! He hates violence.'

'All that makes him a coward. He lets others do it for him; he thinks he can wash his hands—'

'He knows that sometimes there's no other way. He has so much to think of: discipline, danger to his men, the people who depend on him….' She trailed off, knowing what she believed, unable to put it in words, then went on. 'He's just as hard on himself as he is on the others.'

'I know what you mean.' I leaned forward and held my back. 'This hurt him more than it hurt me. He did it for my own good.'

'Yes,' she said unexpectedly. 'I think maybe he did.'

I looked again through the back window. The parking lights were still there, but I could see nothing of the car or of Johnny inside. When I turned back, her face was close to me.

'I'm sorry, Billy. Truly.'

'It was turning out so good,' I said, touching her face.

'But you thought I was acting, softening you up. I wasn't.'

I kissed her, pulling her down to me more roughly than I needed. Some confused idea of paying her in kind. I moved away from her then, trying to give the impression that I was not one to take advantage of her sympathy. In fact I was excited by her, and the new movement between my legs had reawakened the pain. She looked a little surprised as I leaned back, but any attempt at explanation would have sounded ridiculous, so I left it, just went on talking.

'I know you're different from the rest, or I think you are.' I wasn't sure if I believed what I was saying, but I went on saying it. 'You have your loyalties, but I think they're leading you astray. You can plead your finer feelings till you're blue in the face, but you'll be as guilty as the rest when it comes to the murders.'

She was looking through her window, away from me, but I knew she was listening. I kept going.

'Johnny now – I can understand you want to be loyal to your brother. To protect him. But you have to stand to one side and see him for what he is. I'm an outsider of course – it's easier for me.'

She turned to face me. 'How do *you* see Johnny?'

'A bigot. Violent, maybe a bit crazy. Someone who'll take his revenge wherever he finds it.'

'Johnny?' She seemed puzzled, as if I must be confusing her brother with someone else.

'All of them,' I said. 'They've murdered a man for his religion.'

'No.'

'And you know it. Whatever you feel about it, you know it happened and you've kept quiet. You're an accessory.'

'Stop, Billy, you don't know....'

'Now they're planning another one, tomorrow, and you're part of that too. One murder leads to another; there's no end. Any one of you could end up like Mikey.'

'No, you don't understand.' She was shaking her head violently, losing control. I couldn't stop now.

'Killed in the most cowardly way of all, shot in his sleep—'

'He wasn't asleep. He wasn't!' She was shouting, beating her knees with her fists.

'How do you know?'

'Because I was there.'

She looked at me for a long moment, frightened. Then, abruptly, she turned the key in the ignition and the car, left in gear, jolted forward. For a few moments my mind would not react, just kept repeating: she was there!

'You saw him killed?'

'No!' She lowered her voice then, trying to keep control. 'We were in the room behind the shop. Mikey and I. And we heard a noise from the shop, breaking glass. Mikey took his gun....'

I stared at her. I had never held a gun, but the way she said it, it was something quite normal, like taking his umbrella.

'Mikey took his gun, and he told me to get out the back. So I went. And as I was opening the back door, Mikey was opening the door to the shop. I looked around, just for a second – and I got a sight of him.'

'You recognized him?'

'Yes. And when I was running down the back entry, I heard the shot. I was too frightened to go back.'

'Who was it?' But she said nothing.

The car drew up outside the hotel.

'Get out,' she said. 'I'm saying nothing more.'

'I think you're forgetting something.'

'I've told you. I've nothing more to say.'

'I'm only trying to remind you that it's my car.' There was no real pleasure in scoring off her.

'Yes,' she said. 'I'm sorry.' She started to open her door, but I leaned across her and held it.

'Wait. We'll go in together.'

'No. You'd better let me go. If I sound the horn....' She glanced at the mirror. I looked round and saw Johnny, squeezed into the little Renault, parked a little way behind.

'All right,' I said. 'Just one more thing. If all you say is true, you know who killed Mikey.' She looked at me, her lips clamped together.

'Whoever dies tomorrow night,' I went on, 'will die because you saw him. If you're not a murderer already, you very soon will be.'

I turned away from her because, although she was still looking at me steadily, her eyes were filling, and I didn't want to start feeling sorry for her. 'And you could stop it all.' I looked straight ahead as I spoke, and heard her whisper.

'No. It's too late.'

The door was wrenched open and Johnny stood there, his huge hips level with my eyes.

'Get out, you bastard.'

I looked at Angela. Her face was wet with tears.

'It's all right,' she said to Johnny. 'He didn't do anything. I just … don't feel well.'

I took the keys and climbed out. Johnny stuck out his chest and stood there in my path, in a way of a twelve-year-old looking for a fight. I walked around him.

'If you think Dessie was rough….' he called after me.

But I was inside the hotel before he could finish. I moved stiff-kneed across the lobby and Geordie was there with my key, concentrating his gaze on a point on the wall beyond my left shoulder, a man of the strictest neutrality. From the window on the first-floor landing, I watched Johnny and Angela standing by the little car. She seemed to be pleading with him, but he was not responding. Then, standing on tip-toe, she kissed his cheek and went into the hotel.

CHAPTER 14

I was lying again, sore all over, on the green candlewick, and found myself, beyond all reason, singing.

You and me, we sweat and strain,
Body all achin' and racked with pain....

I ripped open my trousers and allowed some breathing space to the bruised equipment, wincing as I touched them. Balloons. 'Don't rub them, count them.' The advice of our old, but ever youthful sports master, fighting his wars on one playing field or another, training us in manliness. He would have disqualified Dessie and reported him to the head prefect for bullying. Ten laps of the hockey field, sweat it out of him, kill or cure.

Tote that barge, lift that bale,
You git a little drunk and you land in jail....

Better a jail than a romper room, I thought. I had of course heard of the romper rooms, the jocular name for punishment cells. Good notion for a feature. 'Tales from the Romper Room.' With reconstructions by out-of-work actors. Might even offer shots of my injuries, anonymously. Or maybe not. Let them do their own research.

Folks git weary and sick of tryin'
And tired of livin' and scared of dyin'....

I had begun to shake and breathe heavily. It was as if I had just finished running a marathon, aided by some drug whose effects were now wearing off. The fears that had been suspended during the time of real danger now came rushing back. They wanted rid of me and I wanted to be gone, so the decision was simple enough.

I would go home the next day and everybody would be happy.

But I would use the time I still had to discover the truth. And as long as they knew I was leaving, I would be running no risk by delaying a little longer. Looking back on it now, I can't say why, after all that had happened, I could still think that way. There was no logic in it, no reason, beyond sheer curiosity, a wish to get even. Middle-class outrage.

So I would leave the next evening and, in the meantime, I would try to find out why an army, even such a makeshift corps as Tommy's, should be so worried by one clearly harmless visitor from a distant and innocent past. There were echoes of that past all around me, but they were the echoes heard by every man who looks back into childhood. Regret for the long summers, nothing more.

Suppose I put myself in the place of Tommy McGoldrick, imagine what he was thinking. He would think in the form of a communiqué, in the terminology of officialdom:

> A volunteer, a soldier under my command, has killed an enemy, an act of war. In the course of his mission, he has committed a serious breach of discipline, a crime for personal gain, so he is to be tried by court martial and, if found guilty, executed. During the interval between these two events, William Burgess has arrived in town after an absence of 31 years. He is a man of known republican sympathies, ostensibly researching a television programme, the medium in which he is employed and in which he has gained some notoriety. Having lived here for some time as a child, he knows me and several of my volunteers by name.
>
> To maintain discipline, I must allow the court martial arranged for tomorrow to proceed as planned. At the

same time, I must take all steps to ensure that the events of the past week remain classified, and that no names are revealed to police or media. I have had Burgess kept under observation. He has been pumping Volunteers for information concerning the execution of Michael Doran. He has gone on to ask similar questions of myself. He has refused to heed warnings that he must leave the area by tomorrow. In order to demonstrate to him that he is placing himself in danger by his conduct, I have been compelled to subject him to personal discipline. It is to be hoped that he will interpret this as an indication of the seriousness of our intentions, but I have ordered that full surveillance be maintained tomorrow. If he persists in the course he has been adopting, I shall be forced to assume that his continued presence constitutes a threat to the security of the Battalion, and deal with him accordingly.

I was beginning to feel as I thought an actor must feel, growing into a role, picturing myself in a field-tent on the eve of battle, writing the solemn phrases with a goose quill into a padlocked logbook.

But I knew something vital was missing, that there was more to Tommy's behaviour than a fear that he and his volunteers might be exposed. There would be no one in the town who would not know of them already, chapter and verse, names, ranks and serial numbers. Certainly the police would know. Executions were another matter, but who would give evidence against them? Media men of all breeds were thick on the ground in Ulster but, apart from some verbal abuse and the occasional smashed camera, they were tolerated and ignored by the hard men on both sides. For some reason, my presence was a different kind of threat. It was true that I had known Tommy and his friends, but it was all so long ago. How could it explain their anxiety to be rid of me now?

Of one thing I was sure. The key to it all lay in the secret that they were all resolved to keep from me: the identity of the man who had killed Mikey Doran. So I would have to find that key, identify the man, and it would have to be soon. Before eight o'clock tomorrow night, for his sake. Earlier, for my own.

It must, I thought, be someone from the old gang; someone I knew. Otherwise, why was it so important to ship me out? And whoever it was, unless he was being held somewhere under guard, he could not know what would face him the following night, or he would be far and away by now.

The latest discovery, that Angela had been a witness to the murder, had thrown everything into confusion. What did it mean? I had been trying all along to identify a *man*. What if it was Angela?

No. I couldn't begin to think that. So who then? I have to admit I hoped it was Ernie. It was an evil thought, but Ernie was the kind of person who provoked evil thoughts. He had told me that Mikey was shot in his sleep, which I thought was the only situation in which Ernie would find the courage to shoot anybody. But then Angela said he was not asleep. There were all kinds of contradictions, but I knew Ernie could have done it.

And there was Hughie. He was more changed since boyhood than any of the others, old before his time. He looked as if he drank too much. Annie had said that, hadn't she? He had been sober this evening, but there was a pouchy look about him, a smell of burnt-out candles, slept-in clothes. And there was something else that Annie had said…. Yes – that he was the only one still friendly with poor Stevie. He had lost his business and worked now as a driver for the man who had bought him out. Duffy. A Catholic.

I recalled Hughie marching under the banners in the processions long ago, a proud young Orange blade. I knew what he must feel now at what had overtaken him. Taking orders from a Catholic.

And Johnny, the Taig who turned. There was no need to look far for a motive for Johnny. No need either to ask to what lengths Angela would go for her brother's safety. She would never shop him to Tommy. But supposing she knew it was Johnny – would she shop someone else, to protect him? Would she go that far?

It was of course possible that the following night's victim was a stranger to me. There was an entire battalion in the area and it could be any one of them. Someone like Dessie. But I didn't think so. I was certain that the person involved was known to me, someone in whom I would have a personal and unwelcome interest. And that made me a danger to them.

I wished I could clear my mind of everything and get to sleep. I got up from the bed and looked out of the window. My car was still there and I wished I was in it, driving to Dublin. As I was turning away, I spotted another car across the Square, directly opposite. A little Renault. I hoped Johnny was in it, and that he would sit up all night while I slept. It was a comforting thought.

My breathing was easier now and I was ready for sleep. I undressed painfully and thought of the lough shore, not as I had seen it tonight, an image already blurred, but as I had known it thirty years ago, vivid and alive. And the person I was remembering was not Tommy, but his brother Dan. It was the day we came back from the lough and sat in the Meeting with the Brethren of the Elect of God, the day Johnny and Angela Fusco, then Gianni and Angelica, stood up at the front, the day Tommy McGoldrick's father was saving their souls for God.

It was the last day I had seen Dan. The last day I would ever see him.

CHAPTER 15

Saturday, 7 June 1941

'Do you, Angelica…?' Old McGoldrick is still grinding on about the Mark of the Beast and the Rivers of Blood, but I feel, by the way he is slowing up, making his high notes higher and his low notes lower, that we are on the home straight.

'Rosanna, Gianni, Angelica, ye are of the Brethren of the Elect of God, joined with us and with Him in spirit, mind and body. Now hear the warning of God in the Book of Deuteronomy.'

And he reads slow and deep from the big book.

'If thy brother, the son of thy mother, or thy son, or thy daughter, or thy wife of thy bosom, or thy friend which is as thine own soul, entice thee secretly, saying "Let us go and serve other gods", which thou hast not known, thou, nor thy fathers…. Thou shalt not consent unto him, nor hearken unto him; neither shall thine eye pity him, neither shalt thou spare, neither shalt thou conceal him…. But thou shalt surely kill him; thine hand shall be first upon him to put him to death, and afterwards the hand of all the people. And thou shalt stone him with stones, that he die; because he hath sought to thrust thee away from the LORD thy God.'

He closes the book and walks to the little organ. Turning, he raises his hands above his head.

'Praise God, ye that fear Him.' And we all stand and sing.

When the trumpet of the Lord shall sound, and time shall be no more,
And the morning breaks eternal, bright and fair;

When the saved of earth shall gather over on the other shore,
And the roll is called up yonder, I'll be there....

There are ginger nuts, cream cookies, snow tops, iced diamonds and Paris buns laid out on the table in the room behind the Meeting Hall. This is a big spread even for the Brethren, but I suppose it isn't every day they convert Three Micks. The room is crowded with juvenile Brethren in grey suits, but since they are with their parents, we have a strong advantage in the bun stakes. The only danger is the presence of all the leading adult Brethren, who keep moving the plates out of range and will even start talking at you about the Prophet Isaiah if you don't keep moving. Charlie, for example, has been snared by Mrs McGoldrick, but he is giving as good as he gets.

In fact, though I am not close enough to hear, I can see that Charlie is doing all the talking and that Mrs McGoldrick is visibly alarmed. I can understand this, knowing Charlie's attitude to religion. He has embraced several faiths since going to grammar school and claims at the moment to be an Anabaptist. Whatever Anabaptism is, Charlie is now giving Mrs McGoldrick the two ends and the middle of it, which must be a new experience for Mrs McGoldrick.

I am watching this so closely that my own guard slips and Mr McGoldrick traps me between the harmonium and the table, cutting off my retreat and my supply line in one manoeuvre.

'Billy,' he says, doing his smile of heavenly radiance, 'I saw you at the service.'

'Yes, Mr McGoldrick. You were great.'

'I suppose,' he says, still smiling, 'you came here straight from the picture-house.'

'No.' I feel there is no need to tell him why. Might as well take the credit.

'I didn't want to be late for the service, so I didn't go.'

'You missed nothing, Billy.' I wonder for a moment if he has been there himself. 'It's a pit of sin, Billy. A Slough of Despond.'

I can put up an argument against this, but with the buns running out behind him, it is not the time to start a big discussion. So I nod gravely and let him go on.

'You'll not be saved in the picture-house,' he says. Which I suppose is true enough. 'And you're getting to the age, Billy, when you'll soon have to decide the path you'll take. My own boys, Thomas and Daniel, have made their choice and accepted the Lord. I don't think it's done them any harm, has it?'

I agree that it hasn't, though maybe I see it from a different point of view. I can't believe that Mr McGoldrick has seen Tommy with his arse in the air farting a verse of 'Oh Johnny, how you can love.'

'I gave my testimony, Mr McGoldrick.'

'You did, Billy. To tell you the truth, we weren't too sure what to make of that. Some of us had the feeling you weren't being altogether sincere. It was even said you might be mocking us, but I hope that wasn't so, Billy.'

I deny it with great force.

'God is not mocked,' he goes on. 'For whatsoever a man soweth, that also shall he reap. Do you know who said that, Billy?'

'St Paul. Epistle to the Galatians.' A real piece of luck. I had to learn that verse off for mitching from Sunday School.

'Very good, Billy. And maybe you know the fate of the children who mocked the Prophet Elisha?'

I think a bit, then shake the head and he tells me, still smiling.

'It happened when Elisha was going up the road to Bethel,' he says, as if Bethal was a place out the Randalstown Road. 'And the little children came out and mocked him and said, "Go up, thou bald head." And Elisha turned back and looked at them and cursed them in the name of the Lord. And there came forth two she-bears out of the wood, and devoured forty two children.'

Personally, I consider this a bit harsh, but I nod, as if I think it served them right. He changes his tack.

'The Fuscos would be neighbours of yours?'

I confirm this and, to my great annoyance, he waves Gianni and Leaky over to join us. He puts one on each side of him and places a hand on the head of each. Since Gianni is about a head taller than Mr McGoldrick, and Leaky two feet shorter, it makes him look like one of those Chinese statues you see in the Charlie Chan pictures.

'I suppose you and Gianni here are great friends?'

He cocks his head up at Gianni, who says nothing. I can understand Gianni's silence because he doesn't want to start telling lies so soon after being saved. Having no worries of this kind, I speak up.

'Great mates.'

'Well,' says old McGoldrick, rubbing Gianni's hair and getting Brylcreem all over his hand. 'I'm giving you the job, Gianni, of talking to this young man and his brother about the step you and the little Angel have taken today.'

Leaky is looking the other way, not aware that she is being spoken of. And old McGoldrick goes on and on – mouth like a bucket my granny says – how Gianni, from being a lost sheep, may now follow in the steps of the Good Shepherd and lead other lost sheep, like us, along the paths of righteousness and into the shelter of the fold, and I am worried that any moment now he is going to burst into song.

I think Gianni feels that these extra duties were no part of the deal, but he says nothing. Old McGoldrick then asks after my granny and Uncle Stevie, though the look on his face tells me that he thinks I would be better off in the hands of Jezebel and Barabbas.

His attention wanders now, around the room. Most of the Brethren have left, to get a quick wash and brush up before tonight's Meeting, but Dan and Tommy are standing at the fireplace looking at photographs being shown to them by a very old bow-shaped lady. They are pictures of her son, who is a missionary in New Guinea, and she has been showing them to everybody for years. Mrs McGoldrick is still backing away from Charlie. Mr McGoldrick is looking the other way and I am just slipping round his blind side towards the buns when he gives a great shout and makes us all jump.

'There is a thief among us!'

Everyone stops talking and looks in the direction of his pointing finger. And he is pointing at Ernie, who stands rigid at the other side of the table, his face going first red, then white. Old McGoldrick goes to the table, opposite Ernie.

'Turn out your pockets, boy!' he shouts.

'Who'll make me?' But Ernie is fooling nobody. He is like a trapped mouse.

'Empty them,' thunders Mr McGoldrick.

'Do it, Ernie.' It is Dan's voice.

'Why should I?'

Ernie looks around the room for support, but gets none. He hesitates, then dives his hand into a coat pocket and lays on the table a filthy handkerchief and a stone marble. The rest of us know what a prized possession the marble is and Ernie puts it quickly back in his pocket.

'The other one!'

Ernie looks at us all again, then pulls from the other pocket three ginger nuts and a cream cookie. The cream is squashed and messy, and stuck on the thickest part is a one-inch cigarette butt. As we all look at the booty and hold our breaths, the butt shifts, loses its grip and falls slowly off, landing on a blob of cream on the table, pointing at him like a sword.

Ernie's eyes start to dart about and I recognize the danger signal. He is not brave, but he can reach a point of panic when he will do or say anything, almost without knowing it. At this moment he needs just a small push to go over the edge, and Mr McGoldrick supplies it.

'Do you not know that you're in the House of God?'

By now, Ernie is at the bottom of the table, ready to move either way as old McGoldrick stalks him. He is shaking with rage and fright.

'It's a house of bloody mad eejits and Holy Willies,' he shouts.

And though I don't usually agree with Ernie, I think that this time he has summed it up fairly well.

'Cut it out, Ernie.' Tommy speaks for the first time. The rest of us are struck dumb.

'You stay away from me,' Ernie shouts, as Tommy makes a flanking movement. Tommy keeps coming and Ernie picks up the big copper teapot.

'Stop, Thomas,' says Mr McGoldrick, an order that, in the ordinary way, would cause great hilarity among us. Tommy stops and his father turns his attention back to Ernie.

'You're evil, Ernie Swindle,' he says. 'An evil blasphemer, like your father. And the Lord thy God visiteth the iniquity of the fathers upon the children.'

'You say nothin' about my father.' Ernie's voice is high and trembling. 'He's told me about *you*. The way you can't keep a maid in the house because all you do is ride the arse off them. And *him*!'

Ernie points at Tommy. 'You think *he's* a Holy Willie, but you should see what he's doing when you're not looking.'

We are all holding our breath, waiting for Ernie to reveal that Tommy is in the habit of performing hymns out of his wrong end, but, as Ernie stands breathing heavily, something about Tommy's expression causes him to stop there and to turn his rage on someone less dangerous. He points at Dan.

'And do you know what *he* does? He drinks!'

Everyone turns to look at Dan. 'He drinks cider,' says Ernie. 'He was drinking it this afternoon so he was.'

Old McGoldrick turns to look at Dan, and I chip in.

'He wasn't, Mr McGoldrick. I was with him, and—'

'Silence!'

He gives Dan one of his looks, a promise that the matter of the cider will not be forgotten, then turns back to Ernie.

'This is what happens,' he says, lowering his voice, more in sorrow than in anger, 'when I open the doors of God's House to all those who would enter.'

Then he is off again, roaring. 'The sons of God came to present themselves before the Lord, and Satan came also among them!'

Mrs McGoldrick, who has been standing with her mouth open, now starts to cry and Leaky joins in. I still have not recovered from Ernie's statement about Mr McGoldrick's behaviour with the maids, which has come as a bombshell, not only to us, but maybe also to Mrs McGoldrick. We all know that old man McGoldrick is very hard on sin in general, and fornication in particular, so there is probably no truth in it, but we shall spread it around anyway.

By now, Mr McGoldrick is pretty fed up with all of us and I get the feeling that, if God is listening to him, two she-bears are probably making tracks out of Massereene woods at this very moment, on their way to devour us all. He glares at Leaky, who is yelling her head off, and in that moment of distraction Ernie does something very dramatic. He leaps up on the table and runs along it, over plates and cups and saucers, buns and sugar and milk. In a moment he is off the other end, through the door and away. Errol Flynn has never made a better exit.

This sets Mrs McGoldrick and Leaky off worse than ever. Mrs Fusco hustles Leaky and Gianni away and the rest of us try to sneak out, but old McGoldrick turns from comforting his wife and calls 'Daniel!'

We are just outside the room and I whisper to Dan that he should come on and pretend he never heard, but he just shakes his head and goes back in.

'What'll happen to him?' I ask Tommy, when we are back out on the street.

'He'll get bate.'

'But if he says he didn't do it.'

'Won't matter. He'll get bate anyway. Sure he gets bate all the time; it won't worry him.'

'But it's not fair. It's Ernie should get the batin'.'

'Leave Ernie to me,' says Tommy, in that offhand way he has, and we know we can leave it to him. In fact, at this moment, I would rather be in Dan's shoes than Ernie's.

'Were you really drinking cider?' asks Charlie.

'Bloody sure. We had a bottle each,' I tell him.

'I drink a bottle a day,' says Hughie, with a careless yawn.

The story is growing more every minute and I am not happy that Dan is to get a beating over the head of it, though not as unhappy as I would be if I was getting the beating myself.

'Suppose I went round and talked to your da?' I ask Tommy.

'Wouldn't do any good. He wouldn't believe you.'

'Sure I can try.'

I turn and run back in the direction of McGoldrick's house, which is beside the Gospel Hall, a little way back from the road. Tommy and Charlie shout at me to come back, but I keep going and I slow up only when I come in sight of their gate and see Dan walking like a condemned man between his parents up to his front door. I hang back till they are safely inside, then tiptoe round the side of the house and crouch below the windowsill of the room that old McGoldrick uses as a study. I listen, against the noises of the street, and I hear old McGoldrick's voice as a buzz, uninterrupted. Then there's a new sound, like someone sucking in breath, then clucking his teeth, sucking and clucking, in a set rhythm. I push my head up to the level of the sill and with a deep breath I see what I can through the lace curtains.

Dan is lying face down on a sofa, motionless. His father stands over him, holding a leather strap, the kind you see hanging from basins in barbers' shops. He is talking as he swings it up and away and then down on the bare thighs of Dan, who lies motionless, his shirt tail pulled over the small of his back, bare to the heels, where a pair of socks, waxy on the soles, hang half-off. I strain to hear what old McGoldrick is saying, but the beating is rhythmic and I have to think in the tempo of the blows.

'Chasten thy son while there is hope, and let not thy rod spare for his crying....'

But Dan is not crying, not even moving.

'Withhold not correction from thy child; for if you beatest him with the rod, he shall not die. Thou shalt beat him with the rod, and shalt deliver his soul from hell....'

Or maybe old McGoldrick is saying none of these things. Maybe he is talking of the darkness in which Dan will have his dwelling, the valley of the shadow of death where one day he will lie and dream of the eternal sunshine that he can never share with Mr and Mrs McGoldrick and God and the other Brethren and Gianni and Leaky.

Suddenly, from a little way off, there is a noise like a thunder-clap, but more constant and sustained. It is six o'clock and the drums have started.

CHAPTER 16

Saturday, 1 July 1972

I half-awoke and wondered for a moment where I was. Then, seeing the green candlewick, I was in no hurry to remember. I let my mind float, allowing it to register the warmth of the covers, the high hot sun, keeping out the thoughts of danger, the pain of my body, the hangover.

The First of July, a Saturday. Outside, factory doors were closed for the first day of the annual holiday. Convoys of special trains would already be forming up in the day-trip conveyor belt to Bangor and Newcastle and Ballycastle and Portrush. In Dublin the crowds would be converging on the Curragh for the Irish Derby, and if I had any sense I would be with them.

I leaned over to the radio by the bedside, not the usual thing like a ventilator embedded in the wall, but a large old-fashioned cabinet, with a speaker fretted out of the wood front in the shape of a fleur-de-lys. I fiddled about, looking, from old habit, for the Radio Eireann wavelength. It was surprisingly loud and clear and I found myself turning it low and lying with my ear close to it, keeping an eye on the door, like a member of the French Resistance listening to the BBC. A woman and child discussed Weetabix and then the pips sounded. Nine o'clock. I had thought it was much later.

'... Protestant barricades went up in Belfast last night after a further wave of vehicle hijackings. At least fourteen buses and cars were seized, and bus services in the city were later suspended. The first barricade went up in Willowfield in East Belfast, and UDA men were on the street in force, some of them wearing badges describing them as police. The UDA has said their barricades will not block main roads, but some will remain until security forces act against the Catholic no-go areas....'

I composed a mental picture of Baronets and retired Colonels sitting at breakfast in their Dublin hotels, over from 'the mainland' to watch their horses running at the Curragh, clucking their teeth and muttering darkly. And brightening up at the next bit.

'... Sir Francis Chichester told a French weather ship to go away today when it approached his yacht with an offer of help. He is on his way back to Britain after giving up his attempt to cross the Atlantic single-handed. Sir Francis's son, Giles, is flying out in a British navy helicopter tonight, in an attempt to contact his father. Sir Francis, who is seventy, had been warned not to go to sea because of bad health....'

Not much wrong with the old country after all.

'... In London today, three men were committed for trial on charges of making seditious speeches in relation to Northern Ireland, and on a further charge of conspiring to depose the Queen....'

But I was tiring of the game. I could not shut out any longer the reality of my own situation. I got up, stretched and winced, like the man in the advertisement for Little Liver Pills. I ran a bath as hot as I could bear and prepared to lie in it a long time.

'... Today's Loyalist march in Coalisland, County Tyrone, has been banned. It had been arranged by the Ulster Protestant Volunteers to mark the anniversary of the Battle of the Somme....'

It was eleven by the time I arrived in the lobby, almost a whole man again, and hungry. I gave my key to Lily Blunt and in return she handed me a folded piece of paper. It was my bill.

'I'm not leaving, Lily.'

She shrugged. 'I was told to make it up. You want the room tonight then?'

'Maybe. I'm not sure yet.'

'Fair enough. But if you're not out before two,' – surely Lily was not about to threaten me too – 'you'll have to pay for another day. That's the rule.'

'I'll risk it,' I said, looking at her approvingly. 'I suppose breakfast is out of the question?'

'Not a hope. And you're too early for lunch.'

'Where could I get something?'

She looked at her watch. 'You'll get a sandwich in any of the pubs.'

I walked towards the front door and heard my name called from the door of the dining-room. It was Angela. 'You're leaving?' she said. Hopefully, I thought.

I shook my head and she came over. 'You should heed them,' she said quietly.

I nodded and made for the door, but she called after me. 'Billy, please.'

She was looking at me, as if she wanted me to stay, but couldn't find a reason. I had no inclination to help her.

'Come in the bar; we'll be alone there.'

I had the same mixture of feelings as before, half-wary, half-tempted. She seemed to understand.

'There'll be just the two of us.'

She was like a child crossing her heart. I followed her into the bar and she sat opposite me as she had sat before, fingering the cross on her neck, holding her legs close together under the long black skirt, slanted at an angle, like the posed portrait of some noble young widow in *The Tatler*. But in her face the pretence of poise was gone. She was vulnerable, unsure.

'First of all, I'm really sorry for what happened last night.'

I said nothing. For one thing, there was nothing to say. For another, I had the moral advantage and wanted to keep it.

'And there was something else….' I waited. 'You said last night that … if someone was killed tonight, I'd be as guilty as the others.'

'More guilty. You gave them the name.'

She looked haunted. 'Will you tell me what Tommy said?'

I thought it was an odd question, but I told her. 'He said that if the man's identified, he'll be tried. And if he's found guilty, he'll be executed.'

She nodded.

'But you must have known that?' I said impatiently.

'Yes.' It was no more than a whisper.

Something suddenly struck me, something obvious, though it hadn't occurred to me before. Ernie had hinted it. So had Annie.

'You and Tommy,' I said. 'Are you a couple?'

She sat quietly for a moment, composing an answer.

'Not any more.' There was a silence before she went on. 'We were together … we were going to be married. Then, when the Troubles started, we broke up.'

I didn't ask why, knowing she would tell me.

'Anyone in Tommy's position has enemies. And anyone who's close to him would be in constant danger. Tommy wouldn't have that. He thought that maybe some day, when it was all over….'

She broke off, anxious not to make a big story of it.

'About tonight,' I said. 'Will you do it?'

'Do what?'

'Come forward. You're the only one who can identify him. It's in your hands.'

'You think I don't know that?' She was whispering. 'I've thought of nothing else.'

147

'And still you'll do it?'

She hesitated. Then a barely visible shake of the head. 'I don't think I can.'

I took her hand. 'It's the right decision, Angela – don't be ashamed of it. You'll be saving a life.'

'Yes,' she said. 'I'll be saving a life.'

I had the feeling, without knowing why, that, although she seemed to be just repeating what I had said, she did not mean it in the same way. In her mind she would be saving herself. It was as if I had helped her to a discovery. She was more at ease now, and, I thought, if there was ever a time to get the answer I wanted, it was now.

'Who was it?

She was on her guard again. 'You know I can't tell you, Billy. And you're better not knowing.'

'Why?'

'Well, don't you see?' There was a note of exasperation. 'At this moment you can walk away from here. But if they thought you knew who it was, they wouldn't be able to let you go.'

I felt a little spasm in the throat as this sank in. Strangely, it hadn't occurred to me.

'Fair enough,' I said, with all the nonchalance I could muster. 'Maybe I'd rather not know. But tell me one thing.'

She sighed, as if asking herself if I would ever learn.

'Why *were* you there?' She looked blank. 'With Mikey.'

'Oh.' She shrugged. 'He was my friend. We grew up together.'

'But just how friendly *were* you? If he was shot in his bed, and you were with him—'

'No, I wasn't! How could you think….' She was smiling, wide-eyed. Such an idea! 'There was never anything like that.' She said it easily, without embarrassment, and it was plainly true. But I remembered what Annie had said about Mikey.

'I heard it said that he was a terrible wee man for his nuts,' I told her.

She laughed again. 'He had that name all right … the stories he told me.' She shook her head, remembering. 'I was so fond of him, but there was nothing like that. I was like his sister. He told me everything.'

I said nothing, feeling she hadn't finished.

'I was worried about him,' she went on. 'You see, after the bomb in Johnny's place, there was a lot of anger about. People wanted to hit back. There was no reason to suspect Mikey – I mean he had no form. But he was a Catholic. I just wanted to tell him to mind himself.'

She asked if I wanted something from the bar. More to change the subject than anything else, I thought. I ordered a coffee, and, as an afterthought, made it an Irish Coffee. The hair of the dog. It was not wise, before breakfast, but my head and body were still aching from the night before. The whiskey could hardly make it worse. Angela brought it to me and we said nothing for a moment beyond 'Cheers'. Then, when she must have thought we had left all that behind, I spoke.

'Do you think, if you refuse to testify, that he'll go free?'

'How can I tell?' she said. And I could sense her wondering if I would ever give it a rest.

'But if he does,' she went on, 'there'll be nothing to keep you here.'

It was true. It was my way out. I should have turned, drained the cup, gone upstairs, packed my travel bag and gone home, stopping for breakfast in Dundalk. But I did none of these things, because I knew, whatever Angela believed, that if this man, whoever he was, had broken the law of the Volunteers, he would answer for it, if not tonight, then next week or next year. Tommy McGoldrick would not allow him to escape. And I could at least try to stop that happening.

'So you'll be checking out,' said Angela.

'Give me a chance, will you? I haven't had breakfast yet.'

'After breakfast then? It'll be better for you, Billy.'

'Angela, you can tell me you need the room, or you can throw me out for drunken behaviour, but don't be telling me to leave for my own good. Because every time people here get concerned about me, I wind up with sore balls.'

She smiled. 'All right,' she said. 'It's your choice.' At least she didn't say 'your funeral'.

The Square was hot and dusty as I came out of the hotel, blinking against the light. Across the Square, Johnny's pub was open, though the hoarding remained in place. On either side of his door stood two stalls filled with the traditional festive delicacies: Dulse, Peggy's Leg and Yellow Man. I thought for a moment of going there, but only for a moment, then turned right and walked towards Furey's pub on the corner of Riverside. Approaching the pub, I heard a shout of laughter from a group of men standing around in a semi-circle. I stopped in surprise. It was exactly as I remembered it, thirty-one years ago, when Jimmy Lamont had held his morning sessions.

I came closer and looked over the shoulders of the men to see who the new entertainer might be. The man's head was turned away from me. His hands were in his trouser pockets, pushing back the sides of his long shabby overcoat. A ragged newspaper, folded at the racing page, hung half out of his pocket. The man was talking, but I could not make out what he was saying. But I knew, even before he turned his head to acknowledge the laughter of his audience, that it was my Uncle Stevie.

I turned quickly and walked back the way I had come, certain that Stevie's glassy eyes had not recognized me. I would have known the lines to feed Jimmy Lamont, but not Stevie. Back at the hotel, I looked across at Johnny's pub and wondered again if I should try it. Once more I had the sense of being watched and I moved on, with some vague idea of confusing the watchers. Before I knew it, I had reached the Gospel Hall of the Brethren of the Elect of God, where, presumably, the Brethren still met. It had not changed at all. Even the Wayside Pulpit, on the narrow strip of grass between the railing and the front door still bore its message of advice for all, within the fold and without:

KEEP SHORT ACCOUNTS WITH GOD

I remembered that old Mr McGoldrick had owned a shoe shop and had strong views, not only on sin, but on proper accounting practice. There had been a notice displayed on the counter of the shop, a white card with wee flowers in the corners, and the warning words 'Please do not ask for credit, because a refusal often offends.' And hadn't Ernie said that Tommy had carried on the business? I wondered how he found the time.

An elderly man was snipping with hedge clippers at the tufty grass around the bottom of the Wayside Pulpit. When he straightened up, I saw that it was Geordie, from the hotel.

'Brave mornin',' he said, in the hearty tone of a man with nothing to hide. I agreed with him and asked if he was a member of the Elect of God himself.

'Are you jokin' me?' he asked with some scorn. 'Jasus, I've more to be doin'.'

He pointed with the clippers at the noticeboard listing the

services on Lord's Day. 'Breaking of Bread' was at 10.00 a.m.

'I wouldn't break wind with that crowd, let alone bread.'

He laughed at his own wit, though I suspected he had used the line before. He looked at me nervously, as if wondering if I might be a member of some other coven of the Brethren, sent to check the moral credentials of the maintenance staff. I laughed back to reassure him and he went on. 'Crowd of bloody whitewashed sepulchres – that's my honest opinion.'

He looked defiant now, an honest toiler who would say what he thought straight out and damn the consequences.

'I was in that hall thirty years ago,' I said, knowing that old men often judge the importance of things by their antiquity.

'Is that a fact?'

'Old McGoldrick was preaching that day. Tommy's father. I suppose you knew him.'

'Bejaze, I knew him all right. A wicked old bastard.'

He looked quickly over each shoulder, not because he feared being overhead, but as an indication that he was about to share a secret.

'That man,' he said, 'would be savin' souls all day and ridin' women all night, God forgive me for speakin' ill of the dead.'

'You're not telling me anything I don't know.' We grinned at each other, men of the world.

'How long is he dead?' I asked him.

He screwed his eyes up, peering into the past. 'Must be the guts of thirty years. He had a bit of a tragedy in nineteen and forty-one – that was the year of the Blitz.'

I knew the story, but I let him go on.

'It's a terrible thing to lose a child that way.' He shook his head. 'He went into himself after that, although he didn't give up the preachin'. But he died within a year.'

'And Mrs McGoldrick?'

'She lived another twenty years.' He lowered his voice. 'They had a maid you know, years before. Daisy. Old McGoldrick put her in the family way and she left. But after he died, Mrs McGoldrick brought Daisy back to the house, herself and the child, and they all lived there together. She wasn't the worst.'

I thought back to that day in the Meeting Hall, the day Johnny and Angela were saved for God. And the tea and buns. It seemed Ernie had been right after all. And Tommy must have known.

'Does Tommy still go to the Meetings?'

'He's never set foot in the place since the father died.'

'And the Fuscos?'

'None of them,' said Geordie. 'They go no place. They're all heathens, like meself.' He laughed again, more sure of his ground now.

'If you're nearly finished there,' I offered, 'come on and I'll buy you a pint.'

This was obviously the right note to strike. He had a thirst you could photograph. But he shook the head virtuously.

'I'd have to finish up here first,' he said. 'I do this job every Saturday, the grass and the bushes and changin' the boards. It isn't worth it for all they pay me, but if I do somethin', I like to do it right.'

I nodded, in appreciation of his high principles.

'Then I'm back on duty in the hotel after dinner.'

'I tell you what,' I said. 'I'll go over to Johnny's and you can join me as soon as you're finished.'

'Johnny's?' He was suddenly on his guard.

'I'm an old friend of Johnny's.' I smiled at him, as openly as I could, and walked back across the Square.

153

CHAPTER 17

Johnny's bar was high and narrow and all the rooms in the building were of the same proportions. The public bar on the ground floor was long and high like a corridor and the space behind the counter was as narrow as that before it. With a row of customers along the bar, there was barely room to make it to the loos at the other end.

There was no trace of bomb damage to the bar itself, or, it seemed, to the stock and equipment behind the bar, but there were sheets of plywood where the front window had been. These prevented any natural light from entering and, despite the electric light, the bar was still dim in a way that seemed to force the drinkers to talk in subdued tones. Where the high ceiling should have been, long sheets of heavy canvas were loosely stretched, but the original ceiling had been so high that the sag of the cloth was not oppressive. Along the wall faced by the barmen was a mirror stretching the length of the bar, presumably to lend extra width to the room, and giving the barmen a three-dimensional view of the drinkers. There were no ladies present and I presumed that, before the bomb attack, they would have been confined to the select lounge bar upstairs, now with a great hole in its floor.

I stood at the end of the bar, close to the door, where I could see down the length of the room, but I recognized none of the half-dozen drinkers. The barman was young and energetic. I ordered a pint and selected a pork pie from the dismal collection in the misty chrome and glass dispenser.

'Johnny not here today?'

'He's up in Belfast for the rally.'

The barman pronounced Belfast in the local way, with the stress on '-fast', something I'd forgotten. I would have liked to ask what rally, but it would have marked me as a stranger.

'Will he be back tonight?'

'I'd say he will, but not in here. Not on a Saturday.'

He moved away from me, had a second thought and came back.

'Are you a friend of Johnny's?'

'An old friend.'

'If you want to leave your name, I'll tell him—'

'No, it's not important.'

He moved away again, but he had looked more carefully this time, making sure that he would be able to describe me later.

'God, I've a desperate drouth.'

I turned to see Geordie climbing on the stool next to mine, wiping his mouth with a khaki handkerchief and shaking his head in a wide sweep of a gesture that implied he could say more, but no one would believe him. I ordered a pint for him and we took our drinks to a narrow bench below what had once been the front window.

'First today,' he said, and swallowed half his pint.

I knew, judging from Geordie's reports on old McGoldrick, that he had tales to tell, but old McGoldrick was safely dead. And I had the feeling that he would be less forthcoming about the living, especially such as Johnny, men with secret lives. Still, I could try.

'I knew Johnny of course,' I said. 'And Angela. They were Gianni and Angelica then.'

Geordie nodded, non-committal. I tried again. 'I remember they day they turned....' I glanced at him and the mask slipped for a moment, but it was only a moment. 'But I never knew Mikey Doran,' I added.

'Whisht will you?' said Geordie.

I was getting somewhere, so I kept going. 'Of course Gianni lived next door, but the Dorans were just up the street.... Funny I don't remember them.'

I had deliberately raised my voice when I said the Dorans' name and Geordie was becoming agitated.

'Will you for Jasus sake keep your voice down.'

'Why? They're all the one kind in here.'

'There's a lot of hard men about. Mention the wrong name here and it could cost you a kneecap.'

'Sorry. I'm a long time out of here. I think of them all as kids I used to know.'

I paused and took a drink, hoping to see him relax. When I spoke again, I kept my voice low.

'I suppose Johnny and Mikey would have been friends at school, before Johnny turned?'

Geordie still looked worried, but he answered readily enough.

'I never knew them that well when they were young lads,' he said. 'I knew Johnny's da, and Mikey's da as well – they were great pals. But that was before the war. Johnny's da never came back from the war.' He was still talking low, but more easily. 'Of course Johnny got a bad time from all the young Catholic lads, the time he turned. And young Mikey Doran was the cheekiest of them all. Used to shout names after him, "Oul Johnny Turn-the-Coat". But then, you see, Johnny was an easy man to torment, the size of him.' He chuckled to himself. 'Oh, he was an impudent wee hoor, Mikey. Of course he was a Catholic.' Geordie said this as if in mitigation. Like, what could you expect? 'But there was no real harm in him. He just liked tormentin' people.'

I wondered if Johnny would have been able to excuse him in that way. I doubted if his sense of humour would be up to it. I wondered, too, if it meant anything that Johnny was away today, at his rally. Was he staying away because he had something to fear? Because he had been tipped off? Despite what I knew he thought of me, I would have liked an opportunity to talk to him. I would have to wait.

I somehow managed to finish the fly-blown pork pie. It was warm and soft on the outer crust, hard and cold in the core.

I bought Geordie another pint and left him with it. Outside, the prospect of going back to the dismal hotel didn't appeal to me and I decided to take a walk up Church Street. I passed by the Roma Grill, which had once been Fusco's Ice Cream Parlour, and looked for a moment at the Ideal Furniture Emporium, once Burgess's. It meant nothing to me.

I walked slowly up the long hill, towards the Manse. That at least would not have changed. As I walked, I looked at the shops and houses to see if anything struck a chord. 'Tricia's Fashions' – that was new. Used to be a house, I thought. And an estate agents, where the Maypole Dairy had been. Then a shop that seemed to be closed, with Venetian blinds pulled down. I glanced up at the fascia board and saw the name: Dorans. In blue print, flaking a little. I stood and stared, reliving my last visit, thirty-one years earlier. A woman with a pram steered around me and hurried on nervously. The door, with a 'Closed' sign hanging inside, was a few inches open. I pushed it and looked inside. No one was there, but I could hear the sound of a vacuum cleaner. I looked around the shop, which I had seen only once before. Nothing appeared to have changed. I looked into the cabinet with the ice-lollies, then up at the shelves with the sweet-jars, all well-filled.

A voice startled me. 'We're closed.'

I turned quickly and saw a tall woman in the doorway to the back room of the shop, the hose of a vacuum cleaner in her hand.

'Did you not see the sign?'

'I'm sorry,' I said, searching for something to say that would make sense. 'I just came to offer my condolences.'

She stared at me. I had seen her for no more than five minutes, all that time ago, but the only difference I could see now was that her hair was white. She was just as tall, just as straight and her nails just as red as I remembered.

'Are you from the newspapers?' she said. The voice too was the same. 'Because if you are, you can just go out the way you came in.'

'No,' I said. 'I met you once, a long time ago. You won't remember.'

She stood still, said nothing, trusting no one.

'I came in one day – it was a Saturday – and I bought forty gobstoppers.' She waited for me to go on. 'Well, that's it really. I mean it's unusual for a kid ten years old. I thought maybe you'd remember….'

'Look,' she said. 'I've sold forty thousand gobstoppers since I came here. Now I've things to do, so—'

'But there was something else. While I was here, that day, your son Mikey came in from the back and tried to nick a choc-ice from the cabinet … at least I *suppose* it was Mikey.'

'It had to be,' she said flatly. 'I only had the one.'

'I'm really sorry,' I said, knowing how inadequate it must sound.

'Go on now,' she said, pulling on the hose of the vacuum cleaner. 'I want to clear up and get home.'

'You don't live here then?'

'No. We had a lot of break-ins. So Mikey put a bed in the back and started sleeping here.'

She shook her head, looking up and around at the sweet-jars, and asked herself 'For what?'

She started the vacuum cleaner with her foot and I left.

CHAPTER 18

Back in the hotel, I swallowed as much lunch as I could, bearing in mind the great wedge of pork pie lodged in my stomach. Angela was not there and I told Lily Blunt that I wanted to keep the room. She made a note in the book and closed it over.

'You had a visitor,' she said. 'Hughie Brown. He said to remind you about the cricket match. And if you'd like to take a wee race over.'

Strange, I thought. He warned me off yesterday. Still, it would help to pass a long afternoon.

I climbed into the car and drove through the town to the cricket ground. The match had already started and the home team were batting as I parked the car and walked to a green-painted bench close to the pavilion. It was a very opulent building compared to the wooden shack I remembered from my own time there.

As children, Charlie and Hughie Brown and I had spent most of our summer there, playing on the boys' team or practising with a cork ball against the pavilion rails, a special kind of game in which you got three chances before you were out.

As I sat down, I saw Hughie standing at the top of the pavilion steps, giving a pat on the shoulder to a thin, red-headed boy going out to bat. He gave no sign that he had seen me, but he walked slowly down the steps and came to sit beside me as if we were cricketing companions of long standing who sat here every Saturday.

'I was looking out for you,' he said. The voice was lower now, but the vowels were the same.

'I didn't think you'd be inviting me, Hughie. You said I wouldn't see the match, one way or the other.'

'I did,' he said, but he offered no further comment.

'How have things been for you?' I asked.

'What way do you mean?'

Hughie was not a man to say more than he needed.

'Well, it's been a long time,' I said. 'Something must have happened you…. Like, did you ever get married?'

'I did. She ran away ten years ago, with a man from Ballyclare.'

'Rotten.'

'She was,' said Hughie, misunderstanding me. 'So I moved back in to look after the mother. And I'm still there.'

'In the house on Riverside?'

He nodded. 'The very same.'

'With the lav over the river?'

'Still there,' he said. 'Mind you, we put flush toilets in twelve years ago.'

I nodded approvingly.

'But I still use the old one,' he said. 'You can aim at the ducks.'

I smiled, remembering.

'Shot,' he shouted, as the red-headed boy steered a ball through the gully for four.

'Do you still play yourself, Billy?' he asked.

'Not for years.'

'I was thinking of giving it up myself,' he said, and sighed, 'but they asked me to stay on and captain the Seconds. They're a young crowd. I played on the First team for years of course. Vice-Captain.'

He had been Vice-Captain of the boys' team too, and it occurred to me that all these jobs were right for Hughie. He was a natural born second-in-command. He sat in silence for a moment, watching the game.

'What happened to the gang, Hughie?'

'Well, there wasn't much left of it after yourself and Charlie left. Tommy joined in with us. In fact he took us over. He was a tough boyo even then.'

'Does he ever come down here? To the cricket?'

'Ah no, not Tommy. He has more on his mind....'

A shout went up from the pavilion and I turned to see the boy with the red hair walking back from the wicket, his head hanging and his off stump knocked back.

'He didn't get in line you see,' said Hughie. He stood up. 'Will we take a walk around the boundary, Billy?'

He walked towards the pavilion gate and I followed. The new batsman was already on his way to the crease and, as we reached the gate the red-haired batsman came through, not daring to look up for fear that someone might applaud and embarrass him further.

'Well done, lawd,' said Hughie. 'Tell the next mawn to get on the pawds.'

I remembered, when we were boys, how the traditional walk around the boundary was something that only the old ones did, men watching their figures. The young long-haired men lounging on the pavilion benches were likely thinking the same of Hughie and me. When we had walked out of their range, Hughie spoke again.

'You stayed on then?' He paused, not really expecting a reply, and went on. 'You're a desperate eejit, Billy. It's not you they're after.'

'Just the Fenians?' If he suspected any mockery on my part, he showed no sign of it.

'That's right,' he said. 'There'll be no peace till we're shut of them.'

'That's a lot of people to get shut of.'

'There's more of *us*.'

Despite the harshness of Hughie's words, there was no venom

at all in the way he said them. He gave them not as opinions, but as first principles, beyond doubt.

'You're not used to fighting, Billy. You should go home and leave us to it.'

'But I *am* home, Hughie.'

'Not any more you're not.'

'I suppose that's where we differ, you and I. This is Ireland. I'm an Irishman, so this is home.'

'For Jaze sake, Billy, wake up. Just look around you – what do you see?'

'A lot of Irishmen trying very hard to be British.'

'And you think we're not?'

I shrugged. He stared at me a moment and then looked away.

'You might be right too,' he said wearily. 'We're neither one thing nor the other, Billy. But that doesn't mean we're nothing … though if you were to read the papers, not just the southern papers, the English ones too, that's what you'd think.'

I thought I'd said enough, too much maybe, so I let him go on.

'I hear you have a good job, Billy.'

'It pays the rent.'

'And so had your da. And so had *my* da. Jobs were scarce in them days. You had to look after them.' I knew where this was leading. 'And if there wasn't enough jobs to go round,' he continued, 'then you kept them for your own. You gave them to the people who wanted to build Ulster up, not the fuckers who wanted to tear her down and make a United Ireland. Lord Brookeborough himself said he wouldn't have a Catholic about the place, because if they got power, they'd destroy us.'

It came back to me that Hughie had lost his business to a Catholic.

'And he was right,' he said. 'He told us that if de Valera couldn't take us over one way, he'd do it the other. Breed families of ten or fifteen wee Fenians and one day they'd have all the votes and all the jobs. Peaceful infiltration they called it.'

'Ah, but it didn't work out that way,' I said, trying to sound reasonable. 'People like Brookeborough made sure there'd be no jobs *for* them. Packed them off across the water to Liverpool and Glasgow.'

'And wasn't he right?' said Hughie. 'I wish to God we had somebody like him today. The whole world talks about fifty years of Unionist misrule. For Jaze sake, we were only doing what the English *taught* us to do, standing up for the Crown. But then when the Civil Rights crowd came along and the world started calling us names, the English were the first to join in. And when the blood started flowing, they disowned us. Threw us to the dogs. I wouldn't mind, but they made enough Papish blood to flow in their time, when it suited them.'

He seemed to be talking less to convince me than to reassure *himself*, and yet there was a certain sad honesty about all he said.

We heard shouts as the new batsman hit the ball hard and high over our heads for six. Hughie shuffled over to field it and threw it back with a jerky underarm action, the kind of throw we used to associate with the elders of the team. There was good-humoured applause from the pavilion and shouts of 'Good man, Hughie!' He went on talking as if he had not been interrupted.

'Civil Rights Be Christ!' He spat. 'The right to work – did you ever hear that one? Crowd of wasters, holding up the wall of the Labour. They wouldn't know what work was if they found it in their soup. And then there was the People's Democracy – wee Bernie! Jasus, if you threw a bar of soap in among that crowd, it would be like an atomic bomb. And they were the heroes! The reporters came across the water in droves and they built wee Bernie

Devlin into Joan of Arc. Said the Loyalists were lettin' down the British way of life. Your crowd in Dublin loved it, Billy. It was up your barrel.'

And it was, though I didn't say so. I shared none of Hughie's ideas, but I wondered if I wouldn't have felt as he did if I had stayed on in the North.

'Of course,' he said, 'they were happy enough to call us British for fifty years, when we were fightin' for them and buildin' their ships and their aeroplanes. But as soon as we started to fight to keep what they had given us, we weren't British any more. We were Irish. Did you ever see an English paper calling a UDA man a Britisher? By Christ you didn't! Bloody Northern Ireland, they say, pity we can't just tow it out into the Atlantic and scuttle it.' He laughed briefly. 'Jasus, Billy, you wouldn't know who to hate.'

He groaned and I looked around sharply, wondering if he had been affected by his own depression. But he was looking out at the cricket pitch, where one of the batsmen was sitting on the crease holding his midriff while the fielders gathered round in sympathy. The bowler stood a little apart, hands on hips, chewing.

'He's pretty fast,' I said.

Hughie agreed. 'Sends them down like fuckin' reindeers,' he said. 'But he has a bad action. He'll rupture himself before he's thirty.'

It seemed odd to me that Hughie could talk with such feeling about the things that mattered to him and still have room for thoughts of young men's games. The boy was on his feet again. A little crackle of applause came from the fielders as they went back to their places, and Hughie and I continued our walk.

'Your old man was at the Somme wasn't he?' he said.

'Not for long,' I said. 'He got shrapnel in the knee on the first day and they sent him home. Eighteen he was.'

'I heard that. My da was there too. Ulster Division. He went through it all. Came back in 1916 with a lungful of gas. And all the time that was going on, the Fenians were keepin' the home fires burning, stabbin' us in the back.'

'That was over fifty years ago, Hughie. You weren't born, or thought of.'

He went on as if he hadn't heard me. 'It was the first of July, the start of the battle of the Somme. My da lived through the war, but the gas killed him in the end.' He stopped and turned to face me. 'But you're right, Billy: it was over fifty years ago. And today, all over England, people are marchin' in memory of the men that died. For King and fuckin' Country. But not in Ulster. They won't let *us* march, for fear we'll annoy the Fenians.' He spat again and walked ahead of me, his head turned towards the game.

'Good-looking bat, the little dark fellow,' I said, trying to leave Hughie's thoughts behind.

'That's me own wee lawd,' said Hughie, without any show of pride. 'Sixteen. He got seventy last Saturday. Keeps his head down.'

'He looks set for another good score,' I said.

As I spoke, I found myself wishing I was out there again, playing cricket, worrying only about the next ball, watching the ball skim over the boundary, adrift from the harsher realities.

'I've to be away at half-seven, finished or not,' he said. It was the first time he had referred to himself.

'Army Council?' I made a poor job of sounding flippant.

Hughie turned and looked at me, shaking his head, not answering. Letting me know that it was none of my business.

'I have a wee message for you, Billy,' he said at last.

I thought of asking if this was what he had risen to, after all the years. A messenger boy. But I didn't. It would have been too close to the truth. He had never had much of a life. Why remind him?

'You're to go home,' he said. 'Now. And you're not to come back.'

'Who says?'

'Your old mate Tommy. He thought you'd have been away by this time – that's what we all thought.'

I said nothing and he went on. 'Have you your suitcase in the car?'

'Why do you want to know?'

'I thought maybe you'd be callin' here on your way home. But I haven't noticed you saying good-bye.'

He looked expectantly at me, but I let him go on.

'Anyway, I was told to tell you that somebody would be calling to the hotel about eight tonight, in case you'd still be there.'

'Is that the whole message, Hughie?'

He seemed to weigh this up and, when he spoke, there was a sense that this part was between ourselves, off the record.

'I have to tell you, Billy, that Tommy's not the same as the rest of us. The way we see it, we're here to do what the name says. Defend Ulster. If they kill one of ours, we kill one of theirs. An eye for an eye.'

'And Tommy doesn't agree?'

'Oh God, he agrees all right. As far as Tommy's concerned, Fenians are all enemies of the state. They're all targets.'

'You can't say that, Hughie. You can't say that all Catholics are Provos.'

'No, but if they're not Provos, they want the same thing as the Provos. To take us over. So they're all targets. Tommy believes it. I believe it too, but with Tommy it goes further.'

I could find nothing to say. There was silence for a moment, as Hughie searched for words.

'You remember the father,' he said. 'Goin' on against fornication and wickedness, God forgive the oul hypocrite.' He smiled at me and intoned softly. 'I am Jesus' little lamb, Yes by Jesus Christ I am....'

I smiled back, remembering. 'You're not saying Tommy took after the father?'

'No. He hated him, after what happened to Dan, but he has the same kind of madness in him. Just like the father lived for the Brethren, Tommy lives for the Cause. Anything that lets down the Cause lets us *all* down. So it's not just Fenians you see. It's *anybody* who lets us down.'

I knew what he was trying to tell me, and that the warning was a serious one. He shook his head now, as if giving up on me. He seemed to feel that he had said enough, done all he could.

'I'll say good-bye to you now, Billy.' He offered his hand. 'Of course, if you were still in the hotel at eight, I'd probably see you later, but I hope that won't happen. I hope you'll get sense, Billy.'

We had completed the circuit of the boundary line and he went back into the pavilion, to talk to the lawds. I stayed for a while and saw his son reach fifty, but I was no longer thinking of the game. I had liked Hughie as a boy, even though, technically, his gang and ours had been at war. I liked him still, but I could hardly believe that, in the years between, such a good-natured person could have become so bitter. If he had told me little about himself, he had at least given me one insight into the drama that had begun a week before and which would end that night. Driving into town, I felt relief in knowing that I would soon be going home, but there was also some satisfaction that, without any great risk to myself, I would see Tommy once more before I left, to make a last attempt to stop the killing planned for tonight.

I would ask no more questions. Indeed, I no longer wanted to hear the answers. I felt sure now that Angela was as anxious as I was, probably far more anxious, that there should be no further bloodshed. If Tommy was the one who would call to the hotel tonight, I would have my chance and, if Angela was there as well, we might between us dissuade him. But I would need to take care. I would have to convince him that I was no longer curious, that I was just pleading a case before leaving.

As I walked into the hotel, a clock struck six, and the drums began.

CHAPTER 19

The Lambeg Drums are not beaten, they are chapped. To produce more noise than a normal buff-headed stick would generate, they are chapped with long whippy canes, and the result is deafening. Another effect of the use of canes is that every chap is distinguishable from the chap it follows, no matter how dizzily fast the chapping may be. Both these effects were lessened as I closed the double glass doors of the hotel behind me. The noise became bearable, staccato became legato, though a stranger in the hotel would still conclude that something had gone badly wrong with the plumbing. I walked over to Lily at the reception desk and, with her usual prescience, she handed over my key without looking up.

'Is Angela about?' I tried to sound casual.

'She's not far away. Go on into the bar and I'll send her in when I see her.'

'No, I'm going for a lie-down. Could you ask her to drop up and see me?'

'You can't drop up,' Lily said. 'You can drop down, or you can speely up.'

'Tell her to speely up then,' I said, refusing to smile. And an afterthought. 'You could tell her I'll be going off tonight.'

'You went off years ago,' said Lily. 'Do you want your bill now?' She produced it from a drawer, like magic.

'You must think I'm going to do a runner,' I said, taking it. 'And, by the way, I'm expecting someone later. If he comes asking for me, just send him up, will you?'

169

'I go off at nine. What time will he come?'

'About eight.'

I went upstairs, pleased that the first part of the operation had gone so smoothly. Lily had not even been curious. And Angela, relieved to hear that I was leaving, would come up willingly enough. To reassure her further, I pulled out the little travel case, threw it on the bed, packed it quickly and left the lid up. Then I took out my chequebook and left it with the bill, conspicuously, on the dressing table. There was nothing to do now but wait and I lay on the bed, drifting on the tide of the drums.

It was hard to tell, just by listening, if they were drumming for pleasure or if it was a match. Stevie, or any of my uncles, would have known. My granny would have known best of all, for no one was as knowledgeable as she was in the art of the Lambeg drums. In an exhibition, the two drummers would be aiming at unison, and perfection would be reached if the two drums sounded like one. But in a match, each drummer would try his best to confuse the other and put him off his rhythm. They would miss a chap here and there, or they would suddenly quicken the speed of a roll, or they would without warning increase the volume of the chapping. They would do all this, not only to prove who was the better drummer, but to show who had the better drum. I had listened to many a drumming match as a boy, but I had no ear for the techniques. It was just the noise that excited me, and the sight sometimes of blood oozing through the fingers of the drummers after a long match.

But my granny could talk with the best of them about the technicalities, the rolls and doublechaps, and about the quality of the drum, its tone and ring. Like all the experts, she called a drum a 'bell' and she could tell by its ring if the tightening of the skin on the drumhead had been carried out with the proper skill and devotion. Every drum had a name and she knew all the famous ones. I could remember the names of some of the best that came to our town and the crowds that gathered to admire them. Names like 'The Terror of Tandragee', 'The Tullyhue Queen' and 'Cromwell Our Defender'. And the granny would tell us of the great fabulous drums like 'The Chiming Bells of Laurel Vale', or 'Roaring Meg', named after the famous cannon that defended the Walls of Derry, two hundred and fifty years earlier. I remembered her singing about it.

When James and all his rebel band came up to Bishop's Gate,
With heart and hand and sword and shield
We forced them to retreat....

It was as if she had been there.

The noise of the drums was enough to deaden the thought of what the night might bring, but now they were coming closer, bringing with them their own special menace. I got up, closed the windows tight and came back to the bed. It was half-past six, just forty-eight hours since the idea of coming here had first entered my head. I switched on the radio to hear the news from Dublin.

'... the Pope is in excellent health, it was officially stated in the Vatican today....' In some haste, I turned down the sound. '... and is not to retire at the age of seventy-five. The statement was made by the Papal Deputy Secretary of State, Monsignor Benelli, in an interview on Vatican Radio. Speaking of what he called persistent rumours about the Pope's retirement, Monsignor Benelli said that these rumours had never had any foundation and even less so now, after the Pope has spoken....'

At this moment, I wondered, was someone not far from here writing FTP on a wall?

'... In Belfast this afternoon, a man was taken to hospital, after being hit by a ricochet, during an exchange of shots on the edge of the Catholic Ardoyne district....'

'... The hooded and gagged body of a man, found shot dead in the Protestant Woodvale district, has not been identified....'

I had heard announcements like these a hundred times and listened with half an ear, but with the smell of last night's musty sack still in my nostrils and the sound of the breech of Dessie's rifle still in my ears, it was suddenly more real. The announcer went on with his litany: a man shot from a passing car near the Shankill–Falls peace-line; a girl with her head shaved and tied to a lamp-post in Ballymacarrett. I listened for news of the shooting and bombing here, outside my window, but there was no mention. That was yesterday's news. The story was dead, but tomorrow it could be revived. Or tonight.

'... The UDA has put up about a hundred barricades in the city. Permanent structures are going up in the Shankill district at Wilton Street. A UDA spokesman has said there would be many more if the Catholic No-Go areas were not opened within the next fourteen days. Behind the barricades, Police and UDA patrols were seen on the streets practising riot duties with shields commandeered from the British Army....'

The UDA, it seemed, had taken over. Young men in their thousands had come forward in their hoods and combat jackets to the defence of the only Ulster they knew or understood. As the Catholics, with the Provos spurring them on, were setting up Independent Republican enclaves behind the barricades of their own No-Go areas, the UDA's leader, Harding Smith, lay in jail in London, charged with an arms plot. Without a leader, without a Parliament and with their traditional enemies thumbing their noses at the Queen's Writ, their anger had fused them into a moving mass of destructive energy. And I had chosen this weekend, from all the weekends of the last thirty years, to revisit the scenes of my childhood.

'... The winner of the Irish Sweeps Derby at the Curragh this afternoon was Steel Pulse, at ten to one. Scottish Rifle was second at ten to one, with the Irish-trained Ballymore third at three to one....'

That was a consolation. My shirt would have been on Ballymore.

'... In Armagh tonight, more than twenty masked UDA men, along with a colour party carrying the Ulster flag and the Union Jack, defied the ban on processions when they came out from behind their barricades, to pay their own tribute to the men of the Ulster Division who died at the battle of the Somme. About two hundred Orangemen with five bands paraded through the city, for the traditional wreath-laying ceremony at the War Memorial....'

A week ago, even a day, this news would have done nothing for me, but now I almost cheered. Not for the glorious victory of the Somme. I could see no glory in taking six months of killing to capture seven miles of mud at a cost of twenty thousand lives. Not even for my father, who had been wounded there. But simply for Hughie, who, for so little return, had kept the faith. And in cheering for Hughie, I must have been cheering that small sentimental defiance on the part of all the other Ulstermen who felt as Hughie did. I thought about that and I wondered if, in this small symbolic way, I was showing some trace of tribal instinct, long buried. I had been back among my tribe for just twenty-four hours and during that time there had been very little of the joy of homecoming. But I was glad that on this occasion at least they had been able to declare themselves.

If I were to stay a week, I wondered, would I begin to feel as they felt? And if I had not left here at all, if I had stayed and grown up with the old gang ... would I be doing as they did?

The phone rang. 'She's on her way up,' said Lily, and hung up before I could speak.

I switched off the radio and looked at my watch. It was after seven. Then I stood, picked up a shirt and stood holding it poised over the open travel bag, like a conjuror in mid-trick. I had to stand like that for some time, feeling more and more foolish, until the door was knocked. She came in looking tired, in need of sleep. I smiled at her, threw the shirt in the bag and zipped it.

'You're really going then?' She was trying to seem regretful, but the relief was plain.

I lifted the case from the bed and invited her to sit down, which she did, with her usual voluptuous modesty. As I talked to her, I walked back and forth from the bathroom, the way they do in films to inject movement into a dull scene. 'Can I get you a drink?' I called from the bathroom.

'No ... thank you.'

She was wearing a white high-necked woollen dress which had hung loosely on her when she came in, but which, as she lay back, settled on her like a snowfall. The dress almost entirely covered her, but every part of her body seemed to be trying to escape. And though I am usually cynical about these things, I felt sure that she was completely unaware of the effect.

I wondered what my chances were. The night before, at the Roadhouse, she hadn't exactly closed the door. She had allowed me to kiss her. And before Johnny got his oar in, there had been plans to go on to – where was it? Templepatrick, that was it. Tempestuous Templepatrick. Who knows what seeds might have been planted there? And later, back at the hotel?

All right, she was Tommy's girl, but that had ended now. She must have needs. But I mustn't rush things. It was just after seven. I had more than an hour.

It must seem strange that, in such a moment of danger, I could have such carnal notions.

'I wish you'd go, Billy,' she said, derailing my train of thought.

'What a thing to say.'

'I mean it.' I sat on the bed beside her and did the old trick of running my fingers through her hair.

'Looking at you now, going is about the last thing on my mind....'

She giggled. 'Stop that now,' she said, but made no move to stop me. 'I'm serious, Billy. You know what they did to you last night. If you go now, that's an end of it. If not....'

I put a finger on her lips and leaned over her. 'You're starting to make a habit of this, aren't you?'

'Of what?'

'Issuing warnings to boyfriends. First Mikey, now—'

'No!' She looked angry.

'I'm sorry,' I said. 'Forget I said it.'

But of course she couldn't. I had put him back into her mind.

'You must have been very fond of him,' I said.

She nodded. 'I didn't have many friends. Not when I was really young. There weren't many Catholic kids about and then we changed over – you remember?'

I remembered.

'It was my mother's idea, I think, after my dad went missing in the war.'

I hadn't known that, though I recalled someone saying – old Geordie was it? – that her father had not come back. But that he was missing on that day they came to the Meeting House, I hadn't known that.

'I don't know why she did it; I think she was just frightened of being alone. And lonely. Everyone keeping their distance. And she

175

hadn't ever been much of a Catholic anyway, not like my father. Anyway, it didn't change things. Johnny and I started going to the Protestant school and the other kids either ignored us or made fun of us, called us dirty names.'

Little bastards I thought. But then I thought again of what would have happened if I had stayed and I knew that I would have been one of the worst little bastards of all. She went on, reliving it all.

'Johnny wasn't very bright at school. There was an American song came out at that time, "Johnny Zero", you remember? About a stupid kid at school – "Johnny got a zero, Johnny got a zero…." Well you can imagine. They used to get round him in a circle and sing it at him and he would go wild; he wouldn't know who to go for. Then the kid – in the song I mean – joined the Air Force and became a fighter pilot. And all the other kids changed their tune and sang 'Johnny Zero is a Hero today'. So that's what Johnny did. He joined the Air Force. Maybe the song gave him the idea. That was the way he was, very simple. Anyway, school wasn't much fun for either of us. I tried to stay friends with the Catholic kids, but they were just as bad. They called me Turncoat and a Souper. I didn't know what that last word meant; they probably didn't know either, just repeating what they heard at home. But none of them wanted to know me. Except Mikey Doran.'

I was sitting on the bed now, close to her waist, one arm resting on her other side, touching her shoulder. But she hardly seemed to notice me. 'Mikey was delicate you see,' she went on, 'so he hadn't many friends either. We got used to playing together because there was nobody else we could play with. Even Johnny didn't like Mikey because Mikey used to shout things at him – "Hey Tarzan, where's your ape?" And then he would run away. I remember the first time Johnny told me not to be playing with that wee Papish Mikey Doran. I just didn't understand. But I stayed friends with

Mikey all along, even after Tommy and I….' Her voice trailed off for a moment.

'… so you see, there was nothing wrong that night. I know it looks as if I went to him behind Tommy's back. And I suppose I did, but it wasn't for that, it was to warn him. After what happened in Johnny's, I knew somebody would be targeted. I just didn't want it to be Mikey.'

She looked up at me, as if pleading to be believed, but there was no need. I leaned over, as if to whisper, my face touching her cheek. 'I believe you,' I said.

She stayed quite still, and, taking this as a signal, I moved my lips over to hers. Suddenly I was pushed back and she sat up.

'No!' She shook her head violently and her black hair tumbled about her face.

'Why not? You want it too—'

'No, I don't!'

'Angela, you're a free woman—'

'No! I love Tommy, no one else! I thought you understood that.'

I stood and moved away. 'It's not the impression you gave last night.'

'It was my job. I had to stay close to you.'

'Ah yes,' I said, aiming at irony and not quite making it. 'You were protecting me.'

'That would be incidental,' she said. She was as cold as I had ever seen her. 'My priority – my *only* priority – was to protect Tommy.'

'I would have thought Tommy had enough muscle around him for that.'

'That's not what I mean!'

Her eyes were blazing now, angry with me for not understanding.

'Up to now, Tommy hasn't killed anybody. I want to keep him from that.'

As I looked at her, I felt that same hopeless certainty. She was telling the truth. She was calmer now.

'You must go,' she said. 'Before it's too late.'

There was a loud knock on the door. I looked at my watch, which showed a little after seven-thirty. Before I could look up, two men stepped into the room. One wore a combat jacket, the other a kind of cape, though the day outside was fine and hot. The man in the cape went to the window and pulled the curtains closed. His face was unknown to me, but the other man was Ernie Swindle.

Angela was still on the bed, but sitting up now. Ernie looked at her, then at me, and leered.

'I hope we're not disturbing anything,' he said.

The man in the cape, younger than Ernie, was grinning, enjoying it all. He probably knew little of what was going on, but would enjoy telling the lads in the pub about it, much later. This guy in the hotel, havin' it off with the manageress, caught them at it. As he kicked the door closed, the barrel of a gun, pointing down, showed beneath the cape.

Ernie, standing at the end of the bed, wiped the leer from his face, as if telling us that the time for small talk was over.

'You're to come with us,' he said.

'Are you not a bit early?' I asked him.

'You were told to get out of here, Billy, and you've had all day to do it. We're not waiting any longer.'

'It's all right by *me*, Ernie. I stayed because I wanted to be there tonight. I wanted to have my say.'

'Well, you're going to get your wish, aren't you? You might even get a bit more than that. Come on now, the two of you.' He walked around the bed and nudged Angela in the ribs.

'Don't dare touch me!' Her eyes were full of anger.

'Oh I'm sorry, love. I didn't think you were that fussy. Come on now.'

The man in the cape, still grinning, had raised his gun to point at us. As I picked up my chequebook from the dressing-table and put a hand in my inside pocket, the gun was swung in my direction.

'It's all right, no panic,' I said, and began to write the cheque. But I was shaking inside, not for fear of what Ernie might do, but of what he might say. He was plainly intent on telling Tommy some highly coloured version of what he had seen tonight in the hotel room. And if Tommy had any doubts at all about what Angela had been doing with Mikey that night, what would he believe now?

I finished writing and put the cheque in my pocket. 'All right then,' I said. 'When you're ready.'

As Angela stood up from the bed, Ernie tried to take her arm, but she shook it free and walked to the door. The man in the cape followed her out. Ernie turned to me, the leer back on his face.

'Tell us, Billy – is she a good ride?'

I hit him as hard as I could with my fist, on his teeth. I had never done such a thing before and it was nothing like in the movies. He simply swayed back a bit and looked surprised and the only blood I saw was on my middle knuckle, which really hurt.

Then the man in the cape ran back through the open door and rammed his gun painfully into my stomach. I couldn't help feeling, as I followed him from the room, that I was out of my league.

There was no one in the lobby except Lily Blunt, who did not even look up from her post behind the reception desk. I stopped at the desk, ignoring a nudge in the kidneys from the man in the cape, close behind. 'Have to pay my bill,' I explained, as I handed the bill and cheque to Lily and went on walking.

'Do you want a receipt?' she called after me.

'No,' I said. 'No need.'

CHAPTER 20

As we came out of the Square, the thunder of drums pounded my ears. I was directed to take my own car, with the man in the cape in the back seat. Ernie drove ahead of us, with Angela. We drove to the lough shore and stopped close to the hut where I had been the night before.

From outside it looked peaceful, even picturesque, with the late sun whitening the lough behind and throwing the hut into silhouette. But inside, it was as we had left it, starkly familiar. Angela and I were escorted by the man in the cape while Ernie went off to another hut nearby, Company Headquarters I supposed, to make his report. In my quarters, a piece of oilcloth was tacked over the small window, leaving the room dim and damp. On the bench running along the wall, where we were told to sit, lay the sack they had used as a hood the night before. It was folded neatly, and I remember thinking of the houseproud nature of Ulster folk, in love and war, 'Still to be neat....'

The man in the cape stood by the door, chewing silently, his mouth politely closed. In fact, in all the time he was with us, he said not a word. Angela did not speak either, but I could understand that. She would be imagining, not without pain, what was passing at that moment between Ernie and Tommy.

We waited no more than five minutes before Tommy came in. The man in the cape left without having to be told. Tommy took a small oil-lamp from the top of a press, placed it on the table and lit it carefully. Replacing the globe, he looked up but not at either of us. I knew from his expression that Ernie had told his tale, omitting nothing and adding much. The silence seemed endless and I decided to begin.

'Tommy, I came here yesterday on an impulse. Nothing else. No hidden agenda.'

He looked at me without expression.

'I could hardly have picked a worse time to visit, could I?'

More silence. I was on my own, more confused by the minute, but I ploughed on.

'Things have happened here in recent times…. I only vaguely know about them, from the outside. And I've no wish to know any more. But tonight, somebody – I don't know who – is going to lose his life. And if there's anything at all I can do to stop that happening – not just for his life, for yours too, for all our sakes, well … that's it really….'

'Listen to him, Tommy' said Angela, with a plea in her voice. I was surprised to hear her speak for me.

'I'd just like you to hear me out,' I went on. 'And then I'll be on the road for home.'

He spoke, for the first time.

'I don't think you'll be on any road tonight, Billy.'

I stared at him and I saw, suddenly and clearly, what he was saying. I thought all along that if I showed a clear indication of going home, and that I just wanted to have my say before leaving, they would let me go and good riddance. I thought I had taken every precaution. They had all seen me – Ernie, Angela, the one in the cape – packing my bags, checking out, paying my bill. Now I realized that none of this counted. For some reason I couldn't make out, it was too late.

'I don't think you'll be on any road tonight, Billy.'

That's what he had said, and he went on now.

'You had your chance to go—'

I cut across him. 'And I'm going. The car's outside—'

Tommy shook his head, slowly, almost regretfully. He had taken on a role now and he was playing it to the hilt. Calm, quiet menace. Robert Mitchum.

'How do we know?' he asked, holding his palms upwards, a reasonable man. 'You said before you were going and look at you, still here. How can we believe you?'

'What in God's name would I stay for?'

'You see, Billy, you know too much now. If we were to let you go, how do we know that you wouldn't just head for the nearest barracks and bring them here?'

'I've told you—'

Again he talked me down.

'Oh you've told us plenty, Billy. But, you see, we don't believe you. We don't trust you. And you have to have trust.'

'Oh you do surely,' I said. I was angry now, doing myself no favours. 'Do you mind telling us your plans, Colonel?'

I had used the title to goad him but he seemed not to notice. He still did not look at me, and when he replied, there was no anger.

'You know well, Billy. You had enough warnings.'

He even sounded regretful.

'There'll be two trials then? Or will you do us both together, like a double wedding?'

'The court martial takes precedence,' he said flatly. 'You're not a Volunteer, so you're not entitled to that.'

'You talk as if a court martial is some kind of honour.'

'It is, in a way.'

'I hope you can make *him* see that, the poor devil you're going to murder.'

For the first time, Angela spoke.

'Don't, Billy, it's no use.'

I turned on her.

'You think the man's going to die because he stole? You really believe that? You don't think it's a bit drastic?'

'No trial has taken place,' said Tommy. 'But when it does, the charge won't be theft; it'll be murder.'

'Now just a minute,' I said, confused. 'He was a legitimate target, you said so yourself.'

Tommy spoke as if he was reading from a manual.

'If a Volunteer goes out on a mission to take out a legitimate target, he's doing his duty. If he goes out to steal, and kills in the course of the theft, he's a murderer.'

For a moment, I was struck dumb. The terrible self-righteousness. Killers are heroes. Thieves are shot. I thought I could see more clearly the true reason for what Tommy was planning. But if I was to have any chance of preventing it, I must stay calm.

'Listen, Angela,' I said – and I was aware of the danger of even saying her name in Tommy's presence – 'this man who's going to die, I don't know who he is; I don't suppose it matters. But I *do* know that he won't die because he's a thief, or because he's a murderer, or to keep the cause pure and undefiled.' I turned on Tommy. 'He's dying to save this man's vanity.'

'No,' said Angela, shaking her head. 'You don't understand....'

'Oh but I think I do,' I said. 'It wasn't just because you were alone with Mikey, it was because someone *saw* you with him—'

'No. Tommy *knew* we were friends. He knew there was nothing more than that—'

'That's enough,' said Tommy.

But I was not to be stopped now. A dog at a bone.

'Of course he knew. But he couldn't have it thought, not by anyone, that his girl was having a bit on the side, making a fool of him.'

'No one thought that,' said Angela. 'No one *could* think that.'
The tears had begun to flow. No sound, just tears.

'None of this is relevant,' said Tommy.

He spoke like a magistrate, someone anxious to dispose of a tiresome case, one in which he had no personal stake. But Angela had not finished. She took his hand and talked into his eyes, as if I wasn't there.

'I went that night,' she said, 'because I knew Mikey was in danger. I wanted to tell him to get away. I didn't have time to sit down, I didn't even take my coat off and all of a sudden he was dead. And I came and told you because I didn't understand why Mikey should die. He never harmed anybody....'

She released his hand and sat back, the tears still flowing.

'Ah but you see' – I was off again – 'that's of no importance. As he would say himself, it's not relevant. The relevant fact is that Tommy here is an important man, aren't you, Tommy? Even at school, you were the leader of the gang. And now you're the Colonel. Play your cards right and you'll be the Brigadier. So nobody's going to make a fool out of *you*, are they? And if anybody tries, or even looks as if they're trying, then they have to be punished. They don't have to have *done* anything, it just has to look that way. And if anybody sees it, or even *thinks* he sees it, that's enough. He can't be allowed to walk away and talk about it; in fact, it's better if he doesn't walk away at all. Better for *you* I mean. Better for the cause. But then that's the same thing, isn't it?'

I stopped for breath and turned to look at Angela. She had not lifted her head since I'd begun. Tommy had not moved a muscle. He looked up at me with no expression, except maybe a kind of curiosity, wondering if I had finished. I knelt by Angela's chair, forcing her to look down at me.

'Angela, you remember what I said to you last night? That a

man was going to die because you saw him at Mikey's house?'

She said nothing, never even raised her eyes.

'Well maybe I was wrong. Maybe he's going to die because *he* saw *you.*'

I turned back to Tommy, to see how he was taking it. There was a faint contemptuous smile, but I knew he was listening. I had no choice but to go on, in the hope that something would get through.

'All that stuff you gave me about the cause,' I told him. 'It was rubbish, wasn't it? All balls and bang-me-arse, isn't that what they say in the army? I'm not saying you don't believe in the cause, but it doesn't apply to this little episode. Not relevant. You say that anything a man does for the cause can't be a crime. And anyone who commits a crime for personal gain and uses the cause as a cover is a criminal and must be punished accordingly.'

He nodded. He was watching me closely now.

'But isn't this exactly what *you're* doing? You're ready to kill this man, not for what he did, but for what he saw – or what you *think* he saw. And maybe you'll kill me too, for the same reason, some suspicions about me and your girl. You know they're not true – they exist only in Ernie's dirty little mind. But that's not relevant. If anybody believes it's true, you have to take action. Because you're the Colonel, the Head Man. Whatever you do, Tommy, it'll be personal. But you'll do it in the name of the cause.'

He was still looking at me, but there was a vagueness in his eyes, as if he had lost interest.

'You said she was my girl.'

'Isn't it true?'

He shook his head, stood and turned his back.

'Tommy,' Angela whispered.

'Not my *girl*,' he said quietly. 'My wife.'

For a moment I could think of nothing to say.

'I'm sorry,' I said eventually, foolishly.

'No one else knows,' he said, turning to face me. 'And no one will.'

It was the most chilling thing he had said. No one, he was saying, would hear anything from me. I wouldn't be around.

There was a knock on the door and he opened it. A voice spoke, a stranger's.

'The court's convened.'

Tommy went out and closed the door.

I was as wise as I had ever been about the identity of the man to be tried, the man now sitting not more than a dozen yards away, in the next hut. I pictured him standing between two armed men before a table where Tommy, just about now, would be taking his place. The table would be draped with the Ulster flag and there would be a gun and a Bible. Tommy would sit opposite the prisoner, flanked by two lower-ranking officers, because he would have seen it done that way in the pictures. The trial would not take long. And I was next.

Angela stood, looking straight ahead. She had made no attempt to mend her face, still streaked with tears. Eventually I spoke.

'Why didn't you tell me you were married?'

'Tommy wanted it like that. For my safety. We told nobody.'

I tried to think what might be proper to say. But there was no need. Angela went on, remembering.

'We were married in a Register Office in Belfast, with two witnesses in off the street. One of them was a bus conductor. The honeymoon was one night in the Grand Central Hotel on Royal Avenue. After that we came home, Tommy to his house, me to my hotel.'

'Not the ideal basis for a marriage.'

'It will be,' she said. 'We'll be a family, like any other.'

I looked at her, wondering what she was telling me. And she smiled timidly, like a child.

'We're expecting,' she said. 'About Christmas.'

'Well, congratulations.'

It was all suddenly incongruous, each of us remembering our manners.

I thought it was time for a change of subject.

'I see you're not giving evidence.'

'No.'

'You were right to say no.'

'I didn't have to. It was Tommy's decision. He said they'd get a confession.'

Yes, I'd say they will, I thought. 'Strange though,' I said aloud, 'when he had *you*, an eyewitness. It would simplify matters.'

'Of course it would. The others wanted to call me but Tommy said no.' She looked at me and shook her head. 'You still don't see do you? If he had called me, and something had gone wrong, it would have made me an accessory. Tommy wouldn't have that.'

'No. It must be wonderful to have that power. Life and death.'

She should have been angry at that, but she spoke quietly enough.

'You think you're qualified to judge, don't you? It isn't easy to live normal lives here, to stay human. But you can't know that; you haven't suffered. You sit and watch from a safe distance. You drink a bit and play around with women and you buy your wife a dress to make it right—'

'I don't have a—'

She went on, talking over me. 'You never had to fight in your life, but you think you have the right to come here and lecture us about the way we are.'

She shook her head – what was the use of talking? But she went on.

'I tried to warn Mikey and I tried to warn *you*, but it wasn't because I cared about you, not in that way. I cared about Tommy, no one else, do you understand? You couldn't imagine what Tommy means to this town, how people look up to him. I would do anything to stop him killing. Anything.'

She walked over to the tap on the wall and began bathing her face. For once I had the sense not to argue. Whatever about Tommy, his wife was speaking the truth. She had not being trying to save me, or Mikey. Just Tommy. And not only had she failed to save him. She had lost him.

The door was pushed open. Ernie came over and looked down on me.

'You ready?' he said.

I stood, taking a quick glance at my watch. Eight-forty.

Ernie stood aside. I went out and he followed. Angela stood watching us go, her chin high. The Colonel's Lady.

It was not dark yet. The sun had split on the horizon and the air was still luminous. The sound of the drums, like effects on an old Tarzan film, rolled towards us over the housetops. As we reached the next hut, one of the two young men standing guard pushed the door open, but Ernie shook his head in irritation and motioned me on towards the third hut, the one closest to the lough shore. There was just time for a glimpse of the interior, lit by oil lamps. It seemed crowded, but there was no clearer impression than that.

The third hut, the biggest of the three, was the one in which fishermen kept boats and tackle. As we approached it, two Volunteers were dragging a light skiff from the open doors to a slipway that led directly down to the lough. We watched them a moment as they half-ran with it down the little stone pier. They were in their early twenties and grinned and abused each other as they worked, ignoring us, because we were not of their generation. Our problems were not theirs.

Ernie nudged my back and we went inside. There was a table and a chair and a bench, as in the other hut, but down one wall lay another small boat with an outboard engine.

'I have to tie you,' he said.

He was clumsier than Dessie had been, but less rough. He sat me in the chair and tied my wrists behind my back. Then he tied my ankles and sat on the table looking at me.

'Now tell us, Billy,' he said. 'What was she like? Was she worth it?'

So I could strike Ernie from the list of suspects. He had never been a likely candidate anyway. I thought of something I had seen written about another underling: *Judas loved no one but himself. His bitterness was that he was so little worth loving.*

'I never laid a finger on her,' I told him.

'Oh I believe you, Billy. Thousands wouldn't.'

'She was trying to get me to go home while I still could.'

'And wasn't she right? Didn't I tell you the same? If you'd listened to me, you'd be home now, safe in your bed.'

It was a bit rich, I thought, to be looking for credit, but that was Ernie. I started to kick my feet, which had gone to sleep, and he backed nervously away.

'It's all right,' I told him. 'I'm not trying anything.'

I was thinking. There was a faint hope, but I would have to take it carefully.

'I think you made a mistake, Ernie.'

He gave a monosyllabic laugh, like a hiccup.

'That's a good one coming from *you.*'

'Yes. I've made a few bloomers all right. But I'm new here. *You* should have known better.'

'All right, Billy,' he said, humouring me. 'Tell me where I went wrong.'

'You told Tommy what you saw. Or what you thought you saw.'

He laughed. 'Bejasus, I'd have been in more trouble if I hadn't.'

'The man who's being tried next door – do you know what the charge is?'

'I do of course. And don't try and get anything out of me, Billy, because you'll be wasting your breath.'

'Don't worry, Ernie, I'm in the picture. It's robbery and murder. They'll shoot him in the kneecap for the robbery and in the back of the head for the murder. But that's not why he's on trial. It's because he had the misfortune to see the Colonel's lady in a wee Fenian's bedroom.'

Ernie laughed again but there was a note of caution. I pressed on.

'Tommy didn't like anyone to see that sort of thing. Especially an ordinary Volunteer like yourself, Ernie. A buck private.'

'All right, Billy, you've had your say. Now do us a favour and shut up.'

'Why should I? I'm in there next. What have I to lose?'

I watched for some sign of unease, a realization that his reports back to Tommy might have done him less good that he had thought.

'Of course you don't know what goes on at these trials, do you, Ernie? You're not allowed in, are you? It's only officers.'

He was doing his trick of stretching back his lips, trying to show how little he cared, but I felt I was getting to him.

'I don't believe you even know who's in there.'

I was guessing now.

'Oh I do, Billy. I don't envy *him* and I don't envy *you*.'

'Did you see him arriving?'

'They had a hood on him.'

'Who are *they*?'

'What's it matter?'

'You don't even get to see the prisoners, Ernie. Even when they came for *me*, it was the other one who had the gun.'

'I don't like guns.'

'What age was he? Nineteen? Twenty? Your superior officer. And the other ones in there, all about the same age, but they're on the inside and you're out in the cold. How does that feel, Ernie?'

'You know nothin' about it,' he said. 'I could carry a gun if I wanted. There's more ways to serve than that.'

'Well I'm glad you feel that way. Because no one's going to do anything for you, certainly not Tommy. I don't think he ever forgave you over Dan.'

He looked up sharply. 'It was nobody's fault what happened to Dan. Tommy never blamed me for it. He never said the name to me in thirty years.'

'And you think, because he said nothing, that he's forgotten? Tommy doesn't forget anything, Ernie. He's a man who bides his time.'

'You're not doing yourself any good talking this way,' said Ernie. 'I've been in this town all my life. I see Tommy every day. He trusts me.'

'Is that why you're still at the bottom of the pile? The oldest buck private in the Army?'

'I'm telling you for the last time to shut your face!'

There was bitterness in his voice, but it was not all aimed at me. I leaned forward as far as the cords would allow.

'Listen, Ernie. I'm going to be the next in there, so whoever's getting the treatment at the moment doesn't really concern me. It's just somebody who's got in Tommy's way. But I'm not a fool, Ernie. I know enough not to take chances with Tommy without a bit of insurance. I'm telling you this now to give you a chance to save *yourself*. You can take it or not; it's up to you.'

He was listening closely, and pretending not to. 'When you came to the hotel tonight, you asked for me at Reception?'

He nodded.

'And the girl at the desk said you were to go straight up, that I had left that message?'

Again he nodded, and I felt a wave of relief that Lily Blunt had told him that he was expected. I would send her flowers if I got out of this. Diamonds.

'Didn't you think that that was strange? That I should set myself up, leave my door open, allow myself to be brought down here and be shot? I'm not that tired of living, Ernie.'

He was yawning, but it was just theatre. I knew he was listening.

'You see, I left another message at the hotel. If I'm not back at the hotel by nine, they're to ring the police and send them here.'

'You expect me to believe that?' he said. But I had a feeling that he did.

I stood up and shrugged. 'It's up to yourself. They'll be here in ten minutes. And there's no way out, it's a dead end. Funny place to pick really. You and everyone else here will be arrested and charged with murder. Maybe two murders.'

There was a long silence before he spoke.

'I can't,' he said. But he was arguing with himself, not with me.

There was a murmur of voices outside, a rhythmic sound of feet on gravel, then the single sharp crack of a rifle. Neither of us spoke as the brief echo faded. I had never been more afraid. Things were happening far more quickly than I had expected. I knew I had to use the moment.

'How would you like to go that way, Ernie?'

'There's no chance.'

'You think you're important to them, Ernie? You're not you know. You're shit.'

He threw himself on me and pulled my hair back with one hand while he punched wildly at my eyes with the other. I pushed myself back and the chair fell to the floor. Ernie fell on top of me and the shock of the fall seemed to sober him up. He yanked the chair upright and walked away. I watched him from the floor.

'It wasn't me who said that, Ernie.'

'Who was it then?'

'Hughie. Wee Hughie Brown, your superior officer. And Johnny Fusco said you were only a messenger boy. He said you'd never be anything else.'

'Fuckin' moron,' said Ernie, in a whisper.

'Tommy never said anything about you though. I mentioned your name and he laughed.'

I wondered if I was going too far. But there was no going back. There was one down and one to go.

'That's not a Provo who's being shot out there,' I told him. 'It's a Volunteer, probably a friend of yours. Tommy wanted him shot and that's enough. None of you are safe now.'

The sound of the shot affected him more than anything I could have said, but I kept going.

'Once he's started to kill, he won't stop. Life will only get cheaper....And what's cheaper than a buck private?'

He went to the door, opened it a few inches and peered out. He stood there a moment, not moving, then closed it and came back to me.

'What'll I do?' he asked.

He was no longer thinking of Tommy or me or anyone else. Just himself.

'You can stay here till the police come,' I told him. 'That means prison. You'll be out in five years, but I believe that things can happen in prison. Or you can go to the police. Tell them where to find us. Tell them that there's one dead, and if they want to keep it to that, they'd want to hurry….'

'And what'll my life be worth if I do that?'

'A lot more than if you stay here and wait for them to come,' I said. 'But it's up to yourself.'

'There's a man outside,' he said.

'You're going for a pee,' I suggested. 'You'll be back in a minute.'

He opened the door and stood, it seemed like for ever, while I willed him to go. At last he pushed the door wider, went outside and kicked it closed. Left alone, I had another thought: that if he believed me about the police, he might just as easily head for home. He would be safe in bed when the cops came and out of danger. And he would not be an informer. He was not too clever and I could only hope that such a simple answer would not come to him.

The window of the boathouse was uncovered, but it was so grimed that this hut was as dim as the other, and the light was fading. I tried to concentrate. What were my chances? My watch said a quarter to nine. If the police got the call by nine, it would be twenty minutes, maybe half an hour, before they got here. If Ernie went to them, ten to fifteen. We had heard the shot outside five minutes ago and the first hearing had begun ten minutes before that. Whatever else might be said about Tommy, no one could accuse him of hanging about.

I was expecting any moment to be called. After that, I could expect no more than ten minutes' worth of citizens' rights before the considered judgement of the court would be pronounced. There be no taking to a place of execution. It was convenient to the courthouse, two minutes from the lough. Maybe I could stretch the proceedings by conducting an elegant defence, objecting to the inadmissibility of evidence, by asking for the court to be cleared so that points of law could be discussed in camera, and, if all else failed, by a long oration in the great Irish tradition of speeches from the dock.

A new sound came from outside. Since I had been brought to the hut, the drums had become a natural background and any new noise could be distinguished. What I heard now were the faint footfalls of more than one person walking on the grass outside. And a sound of rustling, but harsher, reminding me of the dry rattle of canvas, putting up a tent in a high wind, pulling the covers from a cricket pitch after rain. All sounds of childhood, that I could not have heard or thought of in thirty years. I thought of the scenes of a lifetime that were said to flash by the eyes and ears of a dying man, and I pushed the thought aside.

Now something new and different was added: the thud of something falling on wood, then the liquid creaking of a boat rocking on water. The realization of what it was crept up on me and I moved involuntarily, as if to check that it was not *my* body that would be weighted down and dumped on the streets of the city under the lough. Not yet.

The creak of oars came next, loudly at first, then fading as the boat drew farther out on the lough. The first case was disposed of. It would be a matter of minutes before they came for me. Straining my ears to listen for footsteps, or better, for the engines of cars, cars with sirens, I leaned far back in the chair and looked around at the gear in the hut: lines, nets, gaffs, cans of fuel. I began to think of acts of sabotage.

If I could get hold of a gaff, plunge it into a fuel line, set the place blazing. I had no clear idea how I could do that, or what good it would do, but it was what Rockfist Rogan would have done, carrying on his normal daily work of foiling spies and smugglers and international criminals, thinking nothing of it. Where were the old heroes when you needed them?

The boat was coming back now. I listened as the men jumped out and dragged it up across the shingle. Then the footsteps and the low voices as their boots moved, out of time, past the hut. A door opened and closed and there was nothing to do now but listen and wait. It was just minutes before I heard them again, the footsteps, muffled on grass, approaching the hut. Just that, and farther away, the drums.

As I watched the door and waited, it seemed to me that it had all happened before. And suddenly, as if it were yesterday, it all came back.

CHAPTER 21

Saturday, 7 June 1941

It sounds like Niagara Falls, but it is only the drums. We are all standing outside the shop in Church Street, holding our ears. But it is no good, because there are four drums going and, as old McGoldrick would put it, the gates of hell shall not prevail against them. It is about nine o'clock, near dark. My granny sits in her chair outside the shop and mouths the words of a song as she listens and bangs her stick on the pavement. Watching her lips, I work out which song it is. Her favourite.

And when we came to that great hill, they were ranked on every side,
All offering up their pagan prayers, but we wouldn't be denied,
For we ris' our pikes against them and we quickly won the day,
And we kicked five hundred Papishes right over Dolly's Brae –
And we kicked five hundred Papishes right over Dolly's Brae.

She must have been singing this over the beat of the drums, for her song has a march rhythm and I know that the drums are chapped to the rhythm of a dance they're playing now. And the fife player, capering about on the fringe, is no help. His tune is inaudible to the listeners, but they say the drummers can hear enough of his tune to keep them in the right tempo.

Willie is the eldest of the drummers and the other three seem to follow his lead. He sweats, smiles and nods in a fatherly way, leading them through all the secret passes of the music, like Geronimo leading the Apaches through the Chiricahua Mountains.

I look around the crowd and see that they are all wearing fixed foolish grins and tapping their feet. All except Tommy McGoldrick, who never smiles much. At the other side of the circle, looking nervously in Tommy's direction, is Ernie. Earlier in the day, since he publicly called Tommy's father a Holy Willie and accused him of riding the arse off the maid, and he must be hoping that Tommy will not hold it against him.

Charlie and Hughie are beside me, shouting the odd crude word, safe in the knowledge that no one will hear them. Outside Fusco's shop next door, Gianni stands, with Leaky on his shoulders, claiming his new-found right to take part in a Protestant celebration. The fact that the drummers are here shows that the news of Fusco's conversion has not spread as fast as it might. The drummers usually choose a venue close to a Catholic home and the Fusco house has always been a favourite spot. Or maybe the news is known after all. Maybe conversion will take a little longer than the Fuscos think.

Somewhere in the crowd, on the side nearest the Square, there is a disturbance. Someone is trying to pick his way through and the crowd is pushing him back and laughing. I am not tall enough to look over the heads of the crowd and see who it is, but I can see people looking round and grinning. It seems that whoever it is must be moving round the back, trying to find someone to let him through. Then I hear them calling.

'Will you go on home to hell, Jimmy, and take your boxes with you!' Then I catch sight of Jimmy Lamont's thin anxious face, bobbing over the heads, boxes in both arms and more tied round his shoulders. And what's worse he's calling my name.

'Billy Burgess, come here I want you.'

This is not good for my reputation and I turn away, pretending not to see him. But he goes on calling my name and they all start looking at me, telling me my mate wants me. I'm not very happy about this but they have made a path for me through the crowd and I have to go to him.

'What are you shouting about, Jimmy?'

'You're to come down to the lough.'

'Who says?'

'I was told to tell you. You're to come down to the lough.'

He is leaning over me, his thin lips wet and his red tongue darting in and out like the little hot thing in the pickle bottles, flicking spit right and left. I am angry, because the other fellas will jeer at me for ever about the way loonies stick together, and because spit is landing on my face. I can't show my annoyance by shouting at Jimmy, because we have to shout anyway, to be heard among the drums.

'I was told for to tell you,' he says.

And I know he will go on saying it all night if I don't do something, so I get hold of his arm and shake it and two Tyler's shoe boxes fall to the ground. He scrambles down to collect them and someone who thinks he's funny kicks his behind. The two of us are left sprawling on the footpath, covered in boxes and shame. Jimmy starts to gather them up, muttering to himself about the distance between Duncairn and Ballymena. I see my chance and, as I am starting to push my way back through the crowd, I hear him calling after me.

'It was wee Dan McGoldrick told me. You're to come down to the lough.'

At this I stop and go back. 'Is Dan down there?'

Jimmy nods frantically, like Harpo Marx.

'Was he let out?'

'He told me for to tell you. He has Sammy Laird's boat and he says you're to go out with him.'

'You mean you're going down to the lough tonight? He wasn't codding?'

'You're to come down,' he says.

This is a big surprise. Only an hour ago, I watched through the window of his house and saw the hiding Dan had taken from his father. When this happens, he is always sent to bed. Or worse, to the Evening Meeting. If he is really down at the lough, it means he has juked out of the house against his father's orders, and will be in terrible trouble. I know that Dan's trouble is partly my fault. The main one to blame is Ernie, but I know that Tommy will settle up with Ernie. And it was my stupid yarn about the cider that started it all. So I ought to go and see Dan, and try to persuade him to go back home before his old man knows he's gone. But I know what Dan is like, and if he is determined to go out on the lough tonight, he will do it and expect me to go with him. It's almost dark now. And the lough at night frightens me.

There is a sudden shout and movement in the crowd. Three or four men have arrived from the direction of Furey's pub on the corner of Riverside and are pushing their way noisily through the gathering. Before I see them, I know who the leader is, by his voice, and sure enough, I hear other voices calling his name.

'The hard Stevie. Are you giving us a stick-in, Stevie?'

'Give that man a drum.'

The drums break off, and the voices, which have been raised in competition, sound loud and harsh against the silence. I know that they are strapping Davy Doak's drum to Stevie's chest and, from the new excitement, I can guess that the crack is going to be good. I start to push my way back to my place at the front. Jimmy shouts after me that I'm to come down to the lough but I pay him no heed. When I arrive in the middle, Stevie is standing with his shoulders back and his chest stretched out to support the great drum. I can't see its name, only the name of the maker: *William Johnston, Moore Place, Sandy Row, Belfast.*

Stevie totters back, not from the weight of the drum I'd say, and catches sight of me.

'Come here, wee Billy,' he roars. 'Come here to your Uncle Stevie!'

I go over to him, pleased at being picked out, and he takes a coin from his pocket and slaps it into my palm, making sure the crowd sees.

'Buy yourself a Cailey Sucker,' he shouts, pushes me away and takes the canes from one of his cronies. Back with Tommy, Charlie and Hughie, I open my fist and they crowd round to look. Half a crown! Jesus!

'Half a that's mine,' says Charlie.

There are four brief chaps from Willie and the storm of the drums breaks over us again. But it is different now. Stevie has none of the restraint or the discipline of wee Davy, the man he has replaced. He batters away on his own, ignoring the others, standing out like bagpipes in a brass band.

The crowd seem to enjoy it and shout their support but some of them are looking nervously over at my granny. She is still sitting in her chair but she is not banging her stick or singing. She is working her lips over her gums in a way I recognize as the overture to a sudden rage. Then, when she can bear it no longer, she jumps up from her chair and claws her way from one shoulder to another, into the arena.

'Stop it, you drunken scut,' she shouts. 'You're wreckin' it!'

The drummers' heads are thrown back and it takes them a moment to notice her and to trail off, one by one. Stevie is the last to stop, and he stops only because she is poking him with her stick, careful, even in her rage, not to touch the skin of the drum.

'In the name of Jasus what's up with you?' asks Stevie. He knows the crowd is nudging and grinning and that his reputation as a hard man is in danger.

'It's his mammy,' they are saying. 'He won't stand up against her.'

'You're not on your own, you know,' she tells him. 'There's three drums along with you.'

'They can catch up with me,' says Stevie and there is a small cheer.

'You're doing the double-time and they're doing the single-time. Sure any eejit knows it's the single time for four drums.'

'Away home,' says Stevie.

'Bejaze if I do, I'll bring you with me. And I'll get a better tune from your arse than you'll ever get from that yon drum.'

The crowd laughs and claps. They're on the granny's side now.

'Listen to Willie,' she says. 'He was born with a drum on his belly. Follow the light and the heavy – that's the Antrim way.'

'I'll do it my way,' roars Stevie. 'Now get out of my road!'

He attacks the drums once more and she raises her stick and brings it down on his shoulders, again and again, until he has no choice but to stop. The other drummers stand watching.

'Will you sit in your chair and stop annoying me?' says Stevie.

He turns to face her. Then, pushing his stomach forward, he butts her with the drum. She clutches the shell with her hands to keep from falling, but the impetus carries her backwards towards the shop. Wee Davy, anxious for his drum, runs forward and rescues it. Together, Stevie and the granny totter through the shop door, and the crowd, by now cheering both of them, make a passage for them. They disappear through the shop door and terrible noises are wafted out to the street.

The drummers and their supporters grin and shake their heads as they move off up the street. They are heading for the Catholic Church on the Hillfoot Road, where they will stop for another performance. It's Saturday night, so all the Micks will be at Confession, to make them right for tomorrow. And the lads will deafen them with the drums and will shout abuse.

Holy Mary Mother of God, you're a Mick and I'm a Prod....
Brrra-ta-ta-ta-ta-ta-tata! Brrra-ta-ta-ta-ta-ta-taa!

I feel a tug at my elbow.
'Come on,' says Charlie.
'Where?'
'Any place. She'll be raging. If we stay here, she'll make us come in.' Charlie is right, as always. Whenever there's a fight between my granny and Stevie, the only sure losers are Charlie and me. We collect Tommy and move off towards the Square.

It is dark now, and with the blackout still on, there are no street lights and no lights in the shops. Ernie, still anxious, follows a little way behind. We go as far as the Albert Fish and Chip shop in the Square where we spend one and six out of the half-crown on a bag of chips and a Crunchie bar, which we eat on the premises.

'What'll we do now?' asks Hughie, which is a bit forward, since he's not in our gang at all.

'We could go to Frazer's orchard,' says Tommy, but this is turned down. The apples are still small and hard, not worth the risk.

'We could go to the Guide hut and meet them coming out,' says Ernie, but there's no support for that either. We like talking *about* girls but not *to* them.

'We could go down to the lough,' I suggest, but they all look at me as if I'm mad.

'At night?'

It is Tommy who says this and I wonder for a moment if I

should tell him what old Jimmy had said – that Dan is down there already. But in the end I don't.

'Are you mental?' asks Ernie.

Up to now, I haven't been keen on going, but this, from Ernie, has decided me.

'Are you scared?' I ask him.

'No, I'm not scared. But I'm not mental either.'

'You're eggy,' I tell him. 'Eggy' is the greatest insult of all.

'Who's eggy?'

'*You're* eggy.'

Having just bought them all chips, I feel fairly safe, and no one seems to mind me calling Ernie eggy. But no one offers to come with me to the lough. As so often happens, I have talked my way into a corner. I screw my chip bag into a ball, drop it on the table and search for a parting shot.

'You're *all* eggy,' I tell them, and walk out of the chip shop.

All the way down Riverside, in the dark, and down the stony path to the lough shore, I get more frightened by the minute. In the distance, from the Hillfoot Road, the drums have started again, and all I can think of is Bela Lugosi in *Voodoo Man*. The reeds, with just light enough to cast shadow and just wind enough to sway, look alive and dangerous. I run along the overhanging gables, whistling. There are three slipways and a hut at the top of each.

At the end of the third slipway, like something growing out of the water, sits a skinny figure, with square shapes sticking out of his back and shoulders. I am ready to turn and run when the figure straightens, rising like a salmon, and I can see that it is old Jimmy Lamont, boxes all round him. I come close to him and I can see that he is as frightened as I am. We sit together, staying quiet at first; then I look about me and see that Sammy Laird's boat is missing from its mooring on the first slipway.

'Is Dan away?'

'He said he'd bring me and he didn't. He went on his own.'

'Is he gone long?'

'He said he'd bring me and he never did.'

'Is he gone long?'

'Went on his own so he did.'

The moon is up now, pale like water biscuit. I peer out but there is nothing from here to Maghery.

'He wouldn't bring me with him.'

'Which way did he go?'

But Jimmy is still full of his old complaint and repeats it, over and over. I grab his bony arm and raise him to his feet.

'We have to look for him,' I say, shaking him. 'Which way did he go?'

'Yonder,' says Jimmy , pointing to the south, where a rock juts out into the lough and where the reeds are thickest.

'We can't see from here,' I tell him. 'Come over to the point.'

And we start, half-running, to the west, where the path peters out and the ground rises steeply to a high rock where you can stand and look out over the whole lough. Jimmy runs ahead of me like a goat and, when I catch up with him, he is already pointing towards the reeds.

'Yonder.'

I follow where he is pointing and see the boat at the end of the reeds, where the lough shore shelves away steeply. The boat is empty.

'He's away,' shouts Jimmy. 'He's away below.'

'Get help, Jimmy,' I tell him, scared to death. 'Up the town. Get Stevie!'

In a moment Jimmy is gone and I am left alone on the point, staring down at an empty boat and the reeds and whatever lies below.

CHAPTER 22

Saturday, 1 July 1972

The door of the hut was kicked open and the sound of the drums flooded in. Tommy stood there with two of his young guards, one carrying an automatic rifle. The light was almost gone and their faces were in shadow. Tommy looked at them and stood aside. The man came in, opened a clasp-knife and cut through the cords on my wrists and ankles. Tommy looked sharply round the hut.

'Where's Ernie?' he asked.

'Why ask *me*? I'm not in your battalion.'

'When did he go?'

'Hard to say. I had other things to think about. He's probably round the back, having a pee.'

Tommy gave me a look of distaste, as if telling me that Volunteers don't pee.

'Go and find him,' he said, over his shoulder.

The unarmed man went off at a trot, calling on someone unseen to give him a hand.

'All right, Billy. Up.'

I had always thought that if I found myself in this position, if someone wanted to kill me and asked for my co-operation, I would not give it, on the grounds that with death so near, I would have nothing to lose by being awkward. I have never understood those people in books and movies who walk obligingly to the edge of a cliff or the ledge of a high building, or even the real-life prisoners of war who walked in an orderly procession into the gas chambers. And yet, when Tommy asked me to stand, I stood, and when he

206

asked me to walk out of the hut, I obeyed. Several Volunteers stood by the other hut, smoking and watching, all strangers.

There was no sign of Angela. I looked out to the lough, but the boat I had heard leaving and returning, and whose cargo I believed I had guessed, was nowhere to be seen. I was careful not to look at the road in the direction of Riverside, for fear of rousing Tommy's suspicions. And there was no need to look. If the cavalry appeared on time, I would hear the bugles. But for now, there were only the drums.

Someone pushed my back and I started to walk towards the other hut. There was another push, harder, on my shoulder. I turned, and the young Volunteer who had untied me jerked his head in the direction of the slipway. Again, I did as I was told and walked down within a yard of the water's edge before turning.

'When's the trial?'

'What trial, Billy?'

It was Tommy who spoke. For a moment, a rarity for Tommy, he seemed to be smiling.

'I'm entitled to a hearing,' I said, and discovered I was trembling.

Tommy shook his head. 'I can try anyone under my command. You said yourself you weren't in my battalion. I have no jurisdiction.'

I had a wild moment that he was going to let me go. He had frightened me. He had tried and executed his thief. I had found out nothing. He must be satisfied. He would let me go because I was no further danger to him. I was not worth a bullet.

But the hope lasted only a few seconds. Tommy nodded to the young Volunteer and the boy raised his rifle to his shoulder.

'Turn your back,' the boy said. His voice was high-pitched, not quite a man's.

I shook my head. It was late for defiance, but I found it impossible to make a movement that was designed to be my last.

'You're going to get it one way or the other, Billy,' said Tommy. 'Turn around.'

For the first time, I knew what it meant to be petrified. Turned to stone. I would not turn, but it wasn't courage that stopped me, anything but. My body just refused to go along with the idea that in a moment it would have no purpose. A discontinued line. No light. Turned off at the mains. And then, just as all my body's functions were suspended, I heard my own voice.

'You know you won't do it.'

It was as if someone else had spoken. I had some notion that if I kept talking. I would be safe, that he wouldn't shoot me in the middle of a sentence.

'Of course *you* won't be doing it, that's what you're telling yourself, isn't it? It's someone else. *You're* not a murderer.'

The rifle swayed, pointed at one eye then the other. The boy waited for a sign and Tommy's face never moved a muscle. But somewhere in it I could make out the man who was loved and respected, the Colonel. I had not believed all that I had said to Ernie. It's just too simple to believe that a man's character can change so totally; that Mr Hyde should take over so easily. It must be possible to make a man like Tommy see that he is not being true to himself. My voice went on, and I listened.

'Why don't you take the gun yourself, Tommy?'

I pointed to the boy holding the gun.

'What age is he? Eighteen? Nineteen? You'll let him do it and you'll walk away and say you never killed anyone.'

Another thought came to me, though there was a risk it would anger him more.

'Think of it this way, Tommy. Would you have let Dan do the job you're asking this boy to do?'

His expression never altered, but he still gave no order.

'What's your name, son?' I said to the boy.

He said nothing, just glanced at Tommy, but Tommy would not respond. He still looked in my direction and he seemed to be listening too – not to *me,* but to some other voices that called on him down the years. I went on talking, trying to join my words to the voices already in his ears.

At a sound of creaking from behind, I began to turn my head, realized quickly what I was doing and jerked it forward. Whatever else, I musn't turn my head. The boat came alongside the jetty and I swivelled my eyes towards it, recognizing the boat I had seen dragged down the slipway earlier, the same two young men at the oars. They sat looking at Tommy but he gave no signal and they shipped their oars and sat there rocking, incurious.

'Why, Tommy? I have a right to know.'

He gave a gentle shake of the head. Not only had I no right to live, I had no right to be told why not.

'Not that I have to ask,' I went on. 'You don't have to pretend any more about security, military necessity. We both know now, don't we? It's personal now, isn't it? But you'd like to pretend it's official. Standing orders. It makes it easier.'

The boy looked at him and steadied his rifle but Tommy still would not look at him. I told myself now that he would not let the boy do it. If anyone killed me, it would be Tommy himself. There was some belief left in him, God knows from where; certainly not from his father. But it would not allow him to do something he knew to be wrong. I felt he was searching for some justification and not finding it, and that the longer I could prevent him from finding it, the longer I would live.

From behind the hut came a sound of running footsteps. Tommy and the boy looked sharply around and I could maybe have taken them off guard, but the moment passed too quickly and the chance was gone. In any case, the sight of the person who now joined us was a shock I could not have recovered from. It was Ernie.

Without looking away from me, Tommy was asking him questions – where he had been, why he had left his post – but I hardly heard. The hope of help from Ernie had gone. If there was one remaining hope of rescue, it would be too late now. Things had happened too quickly. I had miscalculated the time that events would take, just as I had miscalculated Ernie, Tommy, Angela, everyone and everything. I would be dead in minutes, unless I could make a run for it, and what were the chances of that? In front of me stood Tommy, Ernie and the boy with the gun. In the boat at the jetty sat two more Volunteers. Behind Tommy, watching from the huts, were five Volunteers and there were more inside. Behind me was the lough.

'He was trying to make me go,' Ernie was saying. 'But I was having none of it. He said he had called the police; they were to come at nine.'

Tommy glanced at his watch, peering in the darkness.

'He said that did he?' He was smiling, and I wondered why.

'But I think he was bluffing,' said Ernie. 'He told me to go to the police and save my own skin.'

'And you went, Ernie?' said Tommy. Ernie denied it loudly, blustering, but Tommy kept talking. 'Billy's not such a bad judge after all. He knew his man.'

'I never went near the police,' said Ernie sullenly. 'We have a man posted at the entrances to the Riverside. I went to warn him to be on the lookout.'

'We won't be needing him,' said Tommy, with a certainty that worried me. Ernie was red with humiliation. I knew that he had started out to betray Tommy, but he had allowed himself to think. He had calculated that he would better off taking his chances with his comrades than to become an informer and mark himself down for something worse at some time in the future.

'Move back,' said Tommy to the boy with the gun. 'Down the jetty. Keep your gun on him.'

The boy moved awkwardly backwards, and Ernie with him.

'You too,' said Tommy to the men in the boat. 'I want to talk to him.'

They pushed the boat away from the jetty with their oars and rowed a little way off, the bottom of the boat scraping the shingle. When he judged they were well out of earshot, Tommy spoke quietly.

'Now, Billy,' he said. 'You've talked enough. You always used to talk your way out of anything and it usually worked for you. Great one for taking chances … cocky wee bastard. But you were only risking a good hiding in those days. And you never grew up. It's a pity you never grew up, Billy.'

For someone normally so taciturn, it was all strangely rambling. But that suited me. It must be close to nine o'clock. There was still a chance. The longer he talked….

'I never answered you, Billy, because I don't think you'd have understood. They say that when a man reaches this point in his life, near the end, when it's too late, he gets a clearer sight of things. So maybe you'll understand now. You haven't taken me seriously, you see. I kept telling you we meant what we said and you never tried to understand that. When I say I'll do anything I have to do to preserve our way of life and all that we hold dear, I mean just that. You believe I started that way and then lost sight of it, got to like the killing, the buzz. You think my priority now is just to stay on top, to set standards of my own and make the rest of the world live by them. But you see, Billy, they're not *my* standards. They're *ours*. I'm talking for all of us…. You're from the

Free State, so I don't have to tell you what de Valera said. "When I want to know what the people of Ireland are thinking, I look into my own heart."'

He smiled. 'Well I'm sure you know what we think of Mr de Valera, but I know what he meant now. Because the people of Ulster are all I care about. And an enemy of Ulster is an enemy of mine.'

He was holding his head high and looking down at me. As his eyes caught the reflections of light from the moon on the water, he had a luminous, fanatical look.

'No man can serve two masters. No thief, no whoremaster can serve *me*!'

I could have been listening to his father. But even his father had not wrapped the cloak of a Redeemer so closely round himself as Tommy was doing now. He was no longer talking about a cause, he had *become the cause*.

'You knew Dan,' he said.

He was in another time now.

'You know what my father did to Dan. And I hated him for it. Maybe you heard the stories about my father, about the women he slept with, and I used to think it was just spite. But it was true you see. My mother knew it was and she was frightened to say it. I hated him and I was glad when he died.'

He paused for breath. 'We had a maid – Daisy.'

Daisy. I remembered the name and I half-remembered something about her. Someone had mentioned her recently, but there was something else, far further back…. Tommy was still talking.

'Daisy got pregnant. I was only a child at the time. She went away in disgrace. Then, after my father died, my mother brought Daisy back, herself and the child, and she helped to bring us up.'

I remembered now. I remembered Daisy's other name and

the thought closed in on me and blotted out all other thoughts. Daisy Blunt.

'So you see, Billy – Lily Blunt was brought up with me. She was Daisy's daughter. She's my half-sister. My father was her father.'

He put his hand in his inside pocket and took out a piece of paper.

'Your cheque, Billy. I'm afraid it's bounced.'

He called over his shoulder to Ernie. 'He wasn't bluffing, Ernie. He left a message at the hotel all right, and he did it under your nose.'

He looked at the cheque, turned it over and read from it.

'To Lily Blunt. Urgent. If I do not return by 9 p.m., send Police to lough shore.' He crumpled it up and threw it on the ground before me.

'You were always too smart, Billy. You just picked the wrong woman.'

With all hope gone, I was suddenly very tired. If he had asked me at that moment to turn my back, I would have obeyed, and I hoped it would be quick.

But he gave no such order. There was a new strident sound. Everyone turned and looked towards the town. Incredibly, two police cars, followed by two dark-coloured Land Rovers, were turning off Riverside and coming at high speed along the narrow road to the lough shore, sirens blaring, louder and more urgent than the ones I remembered from the Blitz. Tommy was the first to recover.

'Scatter,' he called. 'Over the gardens – anywhere! Bring all weapons!'

Then to the boy behind him with the gun, he shouted 'The gun! Here!'

The boy hesitated, wondering if Tommy meant he was to shoot.

'Give it here – quickly.'

The boy started to hand it to him, but his hesitation had given me time to react. I was sure now that Tommy intended to finish me off himself. Before he could take the rifle, I had dived between them, trying to knock it from their hands. I was off balance and they both struck at me as I fell. I could feel the cold barrel of the rifle under my body. Rolling away, I managed somehow to get hold of it and send it flying across the jetty into the lough. Tommy reached for my throat but I rolled clear, ran off down the jetty and, with no other available choice, jumped in the water. I was a fair swimmer, but dressed as I was, my body stiff with tension, I could not stay under for more than seconds. I came up, heard confused shouting and Tommy's voice above the rest. Deafening rattles sounded around me and I went down again, twisting my body in the direction of the reeds. I don't know why I headed that way. Perhaps some long-buried memory of Johnny Weissmuller lying for hours on the bed of a jungle river, breathing through the long hollow canes that were always close at hand. I reached the reeds and came up gulping and choking, unable to tell the thudding of bullets all around from the thudding inside my chest.

The police cars had parked and others had joined them. Search-lights swept over the shore and the water and I saw a confused hither-and-thithering of people, in uniform and out. Tommy stood by the jetty, staring around wildly, rifle in hand. The boat by the jetty, its engine already roaring, had filled with Volunteers. Two of them were doing their best to drag Tommy towards the boat but he was resisting. A dozen uniformed police were running towards the shore. I saw all this in a few moments and ducked below again. When I resurfaced, I heard the sound of a second engine and watched as another boat, newly painted and more modern than the others, approached the shore, flashing its lights.

Standing in its bows were two uniformed men, one speaking into a loud-hailer.

What words were said I can only guess, but the operation was over in minutes. Tommy called an order and the Volunteers, caught between land and lough, gave in without a struggle. All of them, police and prisoners, knew one another by name. They had grown up together.

I kept my head above the surface now and saw Tommy stepping unaided into the first of the Land Rovers. Behind him came Angela, but she was told to stand aside. She would be taken separately. Regulations.

More Volunteers, no longer armed, were being loaded like sheep into the wagons. A man in a raincoat shouted at them to keep coming and cuffed them now and then with an open hand as they passed by, but the uniformed men just watched. I stood up in the chest-high water, raised my hand above my head and called out. Two policemen stationed at the water's edge swung around and aimed something at me, something I couldn't make out, but it was enough to send me diving again. As I dived I found myself falling. My hand caught on something thicker than a reed and I gripped it in panic, my lungs bursting. Coming again to the surface, calling at them not to shoot, half-staggering, half-swimming towards them, I realized that I was still holding something. It was a rope.

Then they caught hold of me, splashing around in the shallower water, twisting my arms, gripping my neck tightly from behind. And I was explaining, coughing and retching, telling them that I had almost been shot, uttering a few misplaced thanks to God, telling them about the rope, that there was a body in the reeds – for God's sake bring out the body. Then I passed out.

I awoke, lying on a bank, shivering, a policeman's coat over me.

In the distance, I heard the sound of engines, receding. Close by, people running. Leaning up on one elbow, I saw that a large group of people were running towards me.

I looked towards the road and saw more people running from the backs of the houses on Riverside. All around was a taste of nervous excitement, of curiosity overcoming fear. I heard voices on loud-hailers; I saw broad ribbons of light from the headlights of cars, streaming out over the lough. Another sound came from behind me. Looking around, I saw that the people who had gathered to watch were converging on me.

I started to slither away, but I saw that they were looking and pointing at something on the lough, behind me. I looked and saw a boat coming towards the shore, the man in a raincoat standing in the bow. The people around me broke into a semi-circle, none of them wishing to come too close. It was odd, after all the fears I had gone through, to think that anyone could be afraid of me. But they were not interested in me; they were looking at the boat, as it drew up by the jetty. They simply stepped around me, as they would to avoid a dog's mess on the footpath.

Lit by the headlights of the cars, the boat came closer. The man in the raincoat stood facing us, the moonlight shining on his bald dome. Ulysses was bald too, I remembered. I stood up with the others, peering out through the darkness, not at the man standing in the boat, or at the dark-uniformed men who were rowing, but at the crumpled covered body that lay at their feet. And in the sudden silence I became aware of something in the background, the muffled counterpoint of drums.

CHAPTER 23

Saturday, 7 June 1941

There is no sign anywhere of Dan. They are all down at the lough shore now, people who have no right. They are excited to be there, where it has all happened, and later they can tell their families that they were there, right to the end. So there is no going home.

There are men in small boats searching the lough where Sammy Laird's boat has been found drifting, the part where the bottom shelves steeply away, close to the reeds. One of those out on the lough is Tommy. He has been out there for hours, alone, but he is safe enough. We are all watching and the lough is calm, like a pond.

At the beginning, the searchers have been calling Dan's name as they row back and forth, but they have stopped that now. They just look. All our friends are there, Ernie, Hughie, Charlie, even the Fuscos. No one has ordered us home to bed. Old Jimmy Lamont has told the searchers where to look, and although in the ordinary way no one would pay any attention to Jimmy, they heed him now, since no one else was here. And if Jimmy knows nothing else, he knows the lough.

But they will not let him into the boats and he sits by himself, talking, arranging his boxes, glancing up fearfully now and then at Mr and Mrs McGoldrick, who are standing close together, alone, exclusive into death.

It is very dark and people are beginning to say that they will call off the search until morning. They cannot use lights because of the blackout. I can just make out my Uncle Stevie, lying full length in one of the boats, peering over the side into the water.

A sudden shout goes up from another boat and they all converge. At the same time the rest of us, on the shore, move in a mass towards them. Which is stupid, because we can go only a few yards to the water's edge.

Stevie is there first and a small dim shape is pulled out of the water into his boat. They seemed to be rowing in slow motion, but eventually they reached us and Stevie lifts the body and lays in on the shore. He has to get help, for although Dan is light, there is a heavy stone tied to his body.

People all around are crying. Mrs McGoldrick is trying to keep her tears in and the result is a strange high-pitched sound, like a night cat. Not until the McGoldricks and their dead son are taken away does anyone speak of what they have seen. They tell one another what a terrible thing it is and ask each other why he did it. Some are saying that he had no life at all in that house, and old Jimmy has become excited and keeps telling anyone who will listen that he didn't kill himself at all, that he just went down to see the roundy towers and the pointy spires at the bottom of the lough.

And everyone tells Jimmy to shut up and go home to his mother, and they revert to asking one another, again and again, why did he do it? I say nothing because Dan had wanted me to come to the lough and I didn't, and maybe if I had, I could have saved him. If he had wanted me to.

CHAPTER 24

Saturday, 1 July 1972

The man in the raincoat jumped from the stern of the boat as it struck the shingle, and no one went to help him to pull it on the shore. My eyes, and the eyes of the other watchers, were on the sodden bundle that lay in the bottom of the boat.

The two uniformed men put their hands under the armpits of the dead man and drew him carefully out of the boat. They hesitated, then pulled him farther until they reached the grass, for they felt he would be more comfortable there. The body was hooded, and around the hood was the short end of a rope that had been cut through. In the boat lay the other end of the rope, fixed to a breeze block.

The uniformed men looked up from the bundle on the grass to the man in the raincoat, waiting for orders. He gave a nod and the watchers shuffled urgently forward, like ants.

'Stand out of the light,' said the man in the raincoat.

A space was made and a narrow light from the open door of the hut streamed through, lighting the body. One of the men knelt, took the two top corners of the hood between thumb and forefinger and began to pull it away. When it was almost free, it seemed to stick on something. He jerked it away and moved his hands quickly back, in a way that he would take the cap off a boiling radiator.

The action pulled the dead man's head back, thrusting his chin forward and giving his thin waxy features an arrogance they had never worn in life.

It was Stevie. There was an intake of breath from the bystanders, a chorus, whispering his name.

'Oul Stevie Burgess,' said one policeman.

'Jasus, what did *he* ever do?' said another.

They raised him gently and the cry was more audible now as people turned away. The back of his head was gone, and with the light on the wet grey mess, it had the appearance of being eaten away. The policeman at his shoulders lowered him to the ground and turned away, white. The man in the raincoat said nothing, but draped the hood around Stevie's head and lifted him. They brought him quickly to the police ambulance and it drove away. I went to the man in the raincoat and told him I was Stevie's nephew, that I had come to try to intervene, that I had almost ended up as Stevie had – but he cut me off. He told me to call at the Station the next morning, then climbed into the last of the police cars. The crowd began to move away now, holding each other close, shaking heads.

One woman stayed, watching the cortege move off to Riverside. She waited there until the last car had disappeared, then turned and saw me. It was Annie. I went over and put an arm around her shoulder. 'God you're soakin' wet,' she said.

I was saying things to her, meaningless conventional things. When she spoke, she was calmer than I was.

'Wee Hughie Brown came for him,' she said. 'I thought nothing of it at first, like they were friendly enough, him and Hughie. I thought they'd be going to Furey's. And then I thought, why would he come here? Like, they're in Furey's every night, the two of them. And Hughie never called for him before…. So I thought something was wrong. I rang Furey's and Stevie wasn't there. They asked was he sick or what?… And that's what made me afraid…. So I rang the police.'

'But how did they—'

She went on as if I wasn't there. 'When I mentioned wee Hughie, they knew. Like, he was one of them. And it was down here they always met....'

'Do you know why?'

'It was over wee Mikey Doran, wasn't it?'

I said nothing and she went on. 'I knew Stevie had done something wrong that night,' she said. 'I had seen him earlier on in the town and he was well squiffed, but he wouldn't come home. He would spend every penny he had when he was like that and it wouldn't worry him, nothin' would worry him. Except if he had to come home without sweets for the childer....'

From the moment I saw the body of Stevie, I had begun at last to piece together the whole sad charade. It was clear to me now why I, more than anyone else, had seemed a threat to them and there could have been no simpler reason. It was my Uncle Stevie they were planning to kill, and suddenly here I was, out of the blue. Blood was thicker than water, they would say. I knew that later, when I had time to think it all out, the other things that had puzzled me would fall into place just as simply. The only thing I could never have envisaged was what had brought Stevie to do it. And now Annie was telling me. It was sadder and simpler than all the rest. '... He'd done things before you see. He'd have no sweets and no money and he'd be looking in a window and see the sweets and he would just break in and lift them.'

I shook my head unable to find words.

'Poor wee Mikey,' she went on. 'I suppose he was sitting in the bed scared stupid when he heard the noise. He must have come out with his gun and Stevie went for him. Stevie had no gun you see. He used to have one but he sold it for drink. It's easy to sell a gun....'

I would learn later that this was just how it had happened.

A policeman, who had been talking into an intercom, came over and took Annie's arm.

'I'll take you home, Mrs Burgess,' he said.

'Aye,' said Annie. 'It's getting cold.'

She turned to me again.

'I'll tell you a funny thing…. When he came home that night, the childer were waiting up for their sweets, the way they'll be waiting up tonight. And he had them in four wee bags with the name of Doran's shop on them. I thought it was funny because it was a shop he never went into. Do you see what I'm saying? He must have taken the sweets out of the big bottles and put them in bags … and then he weighed them! I can see him doing it, looking at the scales and taking a sweet out of the bag to make the exact quarter.'

She paused.

'That would have been just like him,' she said.

And she went away, back to 'Stevannie', to explain to her children that their daddy had been killed for bringing them sweets. It was not much of a cause to die for, but I knew of causes that meant even less.

I walked to the car, ice cold and dripping. A policeman was waiting for me. He asked if it was my car and I told him it was.

'I've to drive you home,' he said. He held out his hand for the keys.

'It'll be a long drive,' I told him. 'Home's Dublin.'

'Where are you staying?'

'I was at the hotel but I've checked out. It'll be all right—'

I reached for the driver's door.

'You can't drive,' he said. 'Look at the cut of you. Anyway, I have me orders, so give us the keys.'

I handed them over, wondering where he would take me, but too tired to ask. I remembered getting in the car, but some time after that I fell asleep or passed out, a bit of both maybe.

I awoke with something squeezing my arm, and looked around me. I was on a narrow bed, in a narrow room, naked under a sheet and heavy blankets. An unhappy-looking man with a stethoscope sat on the bed pumping up one of those things you take blood pressure with, on my upper arm. I worked it out that he was a doctor. A policeman, one with stripes on his arm, stood by the door and my travel bag was on the floor by the bedside locker.

'Where am I?' I asked, aware that it was not a very original question.

'Police Station,' said the Sergeant.

So it was a cell. I had never seen a cell before, except in the films, and this seemed better than most of those. The doctor removed the thing from my arm and the Sergeant spoke again.

'Which way is he?'

'Could be worse,' said the doctor carefully.

He stood and packed his gear away. 'You have a lot of bruising there,' he told me. 'But other than that....'

And having delivered his diagnosis, he left. My watch, which was miraculously still going, told me it was one-thirty in the morning, which explains why the doctor seemed so unhappy.

'Get some sleep now,' said the Sergeant. 'We'll be asking a few questions in the morning.'

'Right,' I said, trying to sound as if this would be no trouble. 'By the way, where are my clothes?'

'They're in the boiler room, getting dry. They're a bit shook, but unless you've an iron in your bag, there's not much we can do for you.'

I had one clean shirt and one pair of socks in the case. As the doctor had said, it could be worse. He turned out the light and he left. Seconds later, or so it seemed, there was a loud bang on the door and I sat up to see daylight flooding in through the little high window. A policeman, my driver from the night before, came in, carrying my breakfast in one hand and a bundle of rags, which turned out to be my clothes, in the other.

'Morning,' I said cheerfully. I sat up in the bed, then, remembering my naked state, slouched down again and pulled the blankets up. Leaving the clothes on the bed and the breakfast on the bedside locker, he told me I was to be dressed and ready for my interview at nine and then went out.

If the room, in daylight, was a little drab, there was no lack of colour in the breakfast. It was the kind of breakfast you get in holiday resorts, described as Full English, something I never normally eat. But, just to please them, I ate all this one except the black pudding. I looked at my suit, the almost new Donegal tweed, stained in many shades of green and brown, shapeless but dry. I would have liked to use the bathroom but I was unhappy about going out into the main office of the police station wrapped in a sheet, so I decided to dress first.

It was time to rehearse what I would say to them, how little I could get away with, but, as it turned out, I needn't have worried. The interview room was nothing like the scene I knew from television, the bare cell with the bare table and the plainclothes men, one nice, one nasty, trying to goad me into confessing things. There were two of them sure enough. The man in the raincoat, from last night, who turned out to be a Detective-Inspector, and the uniformed Sergeant who sat beside him but never spoke. No recording either, no microphones, no little asides put in 'for the benefit of the tape'.

And, strangely, almost no questions. It was as if the Inspector, who seemed from his appearance to have been up all night, had the answers he needed and was unwilling to give me the opportunity of contradicting them. He knew all about me. Name, family, friends, background, what I did, where I lived. What had brought me here, everyone I'd talked to, my interest in all of it, professional and personal, contained in a thick file that he kept in front of him, thumbing the pages rhythmically. And with each new piece of information read out, he would flick his eyes up at me and I would say yes and he would pass on to the next. Eventually he closed the file and told me he thought that would cover it.

'You've had a hard time,' he said. 'Could have caught your death of cold.'

I could have caught my death in other ways, but I let it pass.

'But would you not say,' he went on, 'that you might have brought a lot of it on yourself?'

'Could be,' I said.

'Though God knows,' he added, 'nobody deserves that class of thing. It's not my job to advise you, but I would hope that you'd think twice before making any more of these excursions.'

'I wouldn't say there's any danger,' I told him.

'Good'. He stood now, an indication that the interview was over.

'Before you go,' he said, 'if you would like to make a voluntary statement about what happened on the lough shore last night, or what brought you here, you're entitled to do that. But there's no obligation.'

'No,' I said. 'I'm happy to leave things in your hands.'

'We have your address, in case we may want to talk to you again, but I don't think it will be necessary. So, unless you want to report anything of a criminal nature, you're free to go.'

There was a short silence. It was evident that they were as anxious to be rid of me as I was anxious to be gone.

'Do you have any such complaint?'

I hesitated, but only a little. 'Not a thing,' I said.

I was on the road by ten, nervous of being watched from upstairs windows as I drove through the Square and up Church Street, looking neither right nor left, but conscious of the landmarks. The hotel, the Gospel Hall, Johnny's Bar, Furey's, Fusco's Roma Grill, the shop door where the granny always sat, the Manse.

There was just one building I could not have passed without a glance: Doran's shop, closed and shuttered, with its jars of caramel cream whirls and jelly babies hidden away for ever.

Then it was Belfast and the M1 to Dublin. Driving through Newry and the border post, my spirits began to rise. Dundalk, Drogheda, Monasterboice, listening to the radio, music only, staying clear of Loyalist feuds and IRA ceasefires, trying to think of work that lay ahead. And of Orla, who would be home tomorrow. We'd stay in, bottle of wine, early to bed…. How would I explain the bruises? Not sure yet but I would think of something.

And of course she'll want to stroke them all and kiss them; she's like that. Balbriggan, Swords, it was almost exhilaration now. Then turning past the airport and seeing the lights of Dublin coming closer, the idea came to me.

What a bloody good cutting-edge television feature I could make out of it all! Or no, not a feature, a drama-documentary. 'Death in a Small Town'. Very real, explicit reconstructions, played by top people. Why waste it? Of course I'd change all the names. Wouldn't want any of the old gang to feel I'd used them. And I would concentrate on the human side; bugger the politics.

I turned the key to the flat at one o'clock, picked up the phone and called in sick. For once it was almost true. Then I phoned for a takeaway, opened a bottle and spent the rest of the day in bed, with a notebook and a Biro, doing a scene breakdown. We could do the lough shore scenes at Lough Dan in County Wicklow. And I already had a great idea about who would play Angela. I'd had my eye on her for some time....

Paul rang, back from his business weekend. He told me he'd been ringing me all day and asked me where I'd been and I told him not to ask. He went on to tell me what a boring weekend he'd spent and how sorry he was to have missed our trip to the West. And he suggested we might try it again at the end of the month, the weekend of the Galway Races. I told him there was someone at the door and hung up.

Over the next two weeks I wrote pages of notes, working and reworking the ideas until I had a draft treatment I felt I could show to the Head of Features. In my introductory notes, I stressed what I thought should be the core image: the three grieving women. One grieving a husband, one grieving a lover, one grieving a son. He loved it.

CHAPTER 25

Monday, 24 July 1972

I had barely completed my draft when the news came in of Bloody Friday. And I have spent the weekend sitting dumbly before the television, watching over and over the pictures from Belfast. Bodies shovelled piece by piece into bin-bags. A head stuck to a wall. Seagulls swooping to feed on flesh and bone.

This morning, two letters arrived by the same post, both hand-written, both postmarked Duncairn, County Antrim. The first from Annie, was written in a thick strong hand, with an old-fashioned fountain pen. She wrote just as she spoke, no airs.

> Dear Billy
>
> Thank you very much for the flowers you sent for Stevie's funeral they must have cost a bomb. I'm sorry you weren't able to come but I know you're a busy man. There wasn't much of a turnout. There was a good crowd out on the street to see it go by, but not many walked behind the hearse. Like they wouldn't want to be seen by the hard men. I was at the inquest on Mikey Doran and you could hardly get into the place it was that full. There was one funny thing that came out about the way poor wee Mikey ended up. This man from the police told all about the smears of blood on the shop floor and the back hall where Stevie dragged Mikey along the floor and put him back in bed.
>
> The police said that he did that to make it look like

Mikey had been shot in bed, but I knew that wasn't right. Because I knew Stevie better than they did, better than anybody. Every night he had to put the children to bed and tuck the clothes in around them. Like, that's just the way he was, he was very tidy.

And I got a letter from Tommy McGoldrick. He's in jail now, waiting for his trial, so I suppose somebody smuggled the letter out for him. And do you know what he says in the letter? He says he's sorry for the grief I've suffered. And he understands why I did what I did, calling the police. And he says he's given orders that, for the sake of the children, no harm should come to me or mine. I wonder if he expects me to write and thank him. The children miss their daddy and so do I. All the best.

Ann Burgess

The other letter, more bulky, was from Angela. It was typewritten, and it had a cautious distant feeling, beginning 'I thought you ought to know....' and going on in the same formal tones to tell me that she was 'enclosing the findings on the inquest on Michael Doran'.

And I have spent half the night reading it, all thirty pages, over and over. Not that they contained anything that I did not already know, but the flat unemotional recital of the facts, in all their trivial detail, was strangely affecting. The Coroner's verdict was that Mikey was shot with his own gun, by Steven Burgess, in the course of a robbery. The evidence was overpowering. Stevie's fingerprints were on the gun, the door, the shop counter, the scales and the two sweet-jars containing caramel cream whirls and jelly babies. Even the paper bags that held the sweets from those same jars were brought, empty now, from Stevie's house.

In the course of the inquest, the matter of Stevie's own violent death was mentioned, and a police witness testified that Thomas McGoldrick had been arrested on a charge of murder and that he was in custody, awaiting trial.

In what the newspapers described as a surprise development, Thomas McGoldrick made a surprise appearance, under police escort, and read a statement in which he took full responsibility for the death of Steven Burgess. When questioned by the Coroner, McGoldrick refused to answer.

I went back now to Angela's letter, to read again what she had to say about her husband:

> I am proud of Tommy. He has acted as I would have expected, and taken all the responsibility on his own shoulders. None of the others had that strength. He is in prison now awaiting trial. He has refused legal aid and will plead guilty.
>
> He will refuse to testify and will get life. Better than death maybe. But only just. I still believe that some time in the future there will be a healing process, some kind of agreement under which paramilitary prisoners on both sides will be released. I can only wait and pray for that day.
>
> Yours sincerely
> Angela McGoldrick

Not Fusco. McGoldrick. It was in the open now, for all the world to see. She would be happy about that, if happy is the word. I put the letters down and looked at my draft lying on the desk.

'Death in a Small Town' (Working Title)

by

William Burgess

Then I took the scissors and cut up the pages carefully into small pieces. I can't say why I did that. Good ideas don't come often in this business. Bit of a waste of time really. But it seemed to me that time was the waste that mattered least. Far worse the waste of lives, waste of love.